PRAISE FOR STOKER & HOLMES

"Gleason has vamped up the familiar world of Holmes and Watson...to paranormally exhilarating effect."

— THE NEW YORK TIMES

"This book has it all...the vivid setting and the finely drawn, compelling heroines make this a fine choice for readers who like their stories with stem punk spice and smart, strong women."

— SCHOOL LIBRARY JOURNAL

"The author's writing exudes energy, romance, and humor, and she gives her heroines strong, vibrate personalities as they puzzle out the expansive mystery unfolding before them."

— PUBLISHERS WEEKLY

"With its fog-shrouded setting, its heart-racing and clever plot and, most of all, its two completely delightful, kick-butt heroines, The Clockwork Scarab is pure, delicious fun from beginning to end."

— RACHEL HAWKINS, NEW YORK TIMES BESTSELLING AUTHOR OF THE HEX HALL SERIES

"Charming, addicting, and oh-so-much-fun! I absolutely couldn't put it down!"

"Colleen Gleason manages to twine together steampunk, Holmesian mystery, Egyptian mythology, and even time travel into a seamless and fun read."

"Thank you, Colleen Gleason, for giving the world the teenage female equivalent of Sherlock Holmes! Where has she been all these years?"

"The mishmash of popular tropes (steampunk! vampires! Sherlock Holmes!) will bring readers in, but it's the friendship between the two girls that will keep them."

"Two strong, intelligent heroines who establish themselves as worthy of the legends that surround each of their families, come together to solve a most dangerous mystery. Gleason's writing is witty, humorous, tense, and beautifully Victorian."

"Victorian-inspired girl-power at its finest. Daring young ladies born of famed literary legacies are beautifully written and artfully woven into a historical past with fascinating futuristic elements."

THE CARNELIAN CROW

A Stoker & Holmes Book

COLLEEN GLEASON

Avid Press

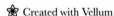

Miss Holmes

~ *In Which Miss Holmes Is Outsmarted by a Corvus* ~

THERE WAS A SOFT TAPPING AT MY WINDOW.

Normally it wouldn't have disturbed me, as I am blessed with the ability to slumber deeply, but tonight I was wide awake. Unfortunately, that had been the case for many weeks now. The dark circles beneath my eyes had become large and puffy enough that even Mrs. Raskill had seen fit to make comment.

Declining to rise unless I ascertained that someone or something needed entrance to my bedchamber—the most likely candidate being Miss Stoker, of course, considering the mode of entrance—I peered at the window from the warm comfort of my bed.

The tapping had ceased, and all I could see through the glass was a shaft of moonlight, just touching the edge, and a row of snow-covered roofs across the mews. Thick smoke chugged from a nearby chimney, dark against a charcoal-gray sky, and stars blanketed the heavens.

In the distance, I could hear the constant hum of the mechanized world in which I reside: the dull click of cogs and wheels, a rhythmic clunk of clockworks and pulleys, and the hiss of steam emitting from every corner of London.

Tap, tap, tap.

I sat up. It was a raven—or perhaps a crow; I couldn't see the shape of its tail, and the difference between the two jet-black specimens in the Corvus genus are hardly discernible otherwise.

And this particular raven (or crow) was using its beak to tap at my window.

How extraordinary.

"Go away," I suggested flatly, certain the creature could not only hear me, but comprehend. They are amazingly intelligent birds. "I'm sleeping."

Or, more accurately, trying to sleep.

The sad truth was, ever since the events related to the Theophanine chess queen and the great checkmate that had been carried out by the Ankh, I'd been nothing short of miserable.

My career as a member of the secret league of females working for Princess Alexandra was effectively over. I had nothing to do: no investigations to be carried out, no crimes to solve, no riddles or puzzles or enigmas on which to focus my agile and active mind.

Since late September—over two months—I had not been summoned to the British Museum, where my probably former mentor Irene Adler was employed. In fact, I'd received no communication whatsoever from Miss Adler.

Even the haven of my laboratory had so lost its allure that I'd even agreed to allow Mrs. Raskill to clean up the shambles of my most recent study—which I had neglected ever since that mortifying moment at the British Museum when I realized the master villainess known as the Ankh had outsmarted me.

And on top of that shameful event, the person I considered my closest friend—the one person who truly seemed to appreciate me for who I was, blade-like proboscis and clumsiness and all—had left London.

Dylan Eckhert had not only left London, but he'd left 1889 as well, and returned to his own time: the futuristic year of 2016.

Tap, tap, **tap.**

I glowered at the window. What on earth was wrong with that addled creature? I knew crows (and ravens) liked shiny objects, but there was nothing about my window that should attract the bird.

Muttering a few unladylike syllables (if Miss Stoker could utter them, I supposed I could as well—particularly since no one was in the vicinity to hear), I flung the heavy bedclothes from my person and slid my feet onto the floor.

Wincing at the harsh chill that somehow managed to seep

through the rug next to my bed, I went to the window, intent on shooing away the irritating creature. He could find some other window at which to rap.

Though it was dark, I managed to avoid stubbing my toe on anything other than the Milford's Gentlelady's Easy-UnLacer, which I'd forgotten to put away in the wardrobe. Muttering still more unladylike sounds, I raised my foot in order to rub the digit that had connected quite forcefully with the corner of the device's stand, and would have unbalanced had I not put my hand out and caught the edge of my dressing table.

By now I was fuming: at being awakened (the crow couldn't know I hadn't actually been sleeping), at being required to leave my toasty-warm bed, at the pain in my toe (it was still throbbing), and at the indignity of nearly falling onto my cluttered dressing table. Therefore, one can understand the violence with which I accosted the feathered menace.

"Go! Away!" I said, flapping my hands at it. The creature stopped tapping, but instead of flying away, he (surely it must be a male; his persistence even in the face of my annoyance reminded me of a certain Scottish Scotland Yard investigator) cocked his head and looked at me.

Yes, he was definitely looking at me: even in the drassy light of predawn, the moon glow cast him in an eerie sort of spotlight that enabled me to see how his beady eye was transfixed on my person.

In fact, the weight of his eyes was so sharp and intense, I couldn't help but drop my own gaze to ensure that I was properly covered by my night frock.

I tried again. "Be off, you!" I flapped my hand.

All to no avail. The crow (by now I'd ascertained the shape of his tail and made that determination), seemingly unmoved by my antics, merely tilted his head, shuffled on his feet, and, fluttering his wings, said, "*Caw.*"

"I have neither the time nor the inclination to engage in

conversation with you," I informed the beast. "Now, leave off tapping and be gone!"

He merely ruffled his wings again, shifting, and then fixed me with his other eye.

Drat it. I couldn't even frighten a blasted *crow* from my windowsill; how on earth could I ever expect Princess Alix or Miss Adler to engage me again?

To my shock, tears stung my dry, sleep-deprived eyes. I blinked them back bravely, and then I did a very foolish thing.

I opened the blasted window.

(Evaline, who is currently reading over my shoulder as I write these words some years after the fact, has interjected her opinion that opening the window wasn't, in retrospect, a foolish decision at all. But I rest my case that in the moments immediately following, it most certainly seemed to be.)

When I opened the window, a gust of chill winter air sent goose pimples erupting everywhere on my person, and, even worse, when I flapped my hands vigorously at the crow, instead of flying off, *he glided into my bedchamber on a flutter of wings.*

"What on earth—no! You are not invited," I informed him in my most no-nonsense voice. "Remove yourself at once!"

He not only ignored my command, he perched himself on the top of my mirror as if he had every right to be there. For a moment, I had a strong sense of sympathy for the unnamed storyteller in Mr. Poe's "The Raven." Who would have thought a crow—or raven, as was the case in that tale—could be such a stubborn creature?

It was then that the indignity became too much, for the winged beast opened his mouth and *dropped something on my dressing table.*

I didn't know whether, like bovines and felines, crows often regurgitated their food, but I was incensed. I spun around and yanked up the pillow from my bed—made of feathers from one of his distant cousins; perhaps I should threaten to do the same to him!—and flapped it toward him.

He responded with an emphatic "*Caw!*" and commenced with making a full observation of my chamber with his beady black eyes.

"Get...out!" I cried, and that was my second mistake of the night. (Evaline, still looking over my shoulder, is in full agreement with this statement.)

I was so agitated that I forgot myself and swung the pillow like a cricket bat. I missed the crow, but unfortunately, on its descent from my wild strike, the pillow swept over my dressing table and sent the bulk of its contents flying and tumbling. Some of the glass bottles shattered, and their contents spilled and oozed onto the rug.

By now my toes were numb from the cold air pouring through the open window, and every part of my body was prickling and shivering.

I hadn't slept in what seemed like weeks.

My bedchamber was now the scene of a calamity of broad proportions.

I no longer had a job or any worthwhile activity.

I had been outsmarted by a cunning and dangerous villainess *in public*.

And I had a *crow* in my bedchamber.

For the first time in my recent memory, I began to cry.

(Evaline, still filled with suggestions for this manuscript, is questioning whether at that point I had closed the window.)

(I'm already ruing the fact that I even told her I was writing down the account of this case. I should have done what Uncle Sherlock's biographer does. Dr. Watson never allows him to read the stories until after they are published.)

Perhaps it was my pitiful sobs that instilled pity in my nocturnal visitor, for through my angry and violent laments, I discerned the sharp flap of wings.

I looked up in time to see the beast fly through the open window into the cold December night—leaving in his wake the destruction of my bedchamber and what little was left of my dignity.

～

THE NEXT MORNING, I NEEDED TO SPARE NO MOMENT TO consider whether that event had been an unpleasant dream. As if the destroyed contents of my dressing table were not enough of a reminder of his presence, the crow had had the audacity to leave a single black feather on the sill as he flew out.

I almost flung open the window once more in order to rid myself of the beast's calling card, but the chamber's temperature had finally become bearable again and I was disinclined to submit myself to that freezing air—especially now that I wouldn't be climbing back beneath the covers.

Mrs. Raskill was cooking something in the kitchen (it smelled divine), and I had a mess to clean up.

Not that I had anything else pressing on my schedule for the day, I thought grumpily as I made my bed.

Listlessly, I began to collect the perfume and oil bottles, hair utensils, tray, and other objects I'd sent flying during my nocturnal tirade. Miraculously, only two bottles had broken, and in relatively short order, I had replaced most everything on the table.

And that was when I saw it.

I'd almost forgotten about it (me, a Holmes!—which was testament to exactly how mentally depressed and slow I had become over the last month) when I saw the one item that belonged on neither my dressing table, nor in my bedchamber at all.

It was no larger than two digits of my little finger, and appeared to be a soft, dingy white...something. Although at first I regarded it with distaste as some sort of regurgitation from the crow, once I looked more closely, I saw that it was a tiny cloth-wrapped packet.

Mildly curious (after all, crows are known for stealing

shiny objects, not ones that look like a minuscule laundry package), I picked it up.

As I did so, I realized the crow had not had the object in his mouth when I first noticed him at the window. He couldn't have done, for he responded to my command to "Be off!" with a sassy "*Caw!*" and would have dropped the item then if he'd done so. Aside from that, I would have noticed him holding it in his beak.

I considered for a moment whether I was wrong, and that perhaps the bird had not dropped this package onto my dressing table after all, but quickly rejected the possibility. I had seen it fall from his beak. And the object did not belong in my chamber.

Having assured myself of this, I cleared the recently replaced health and grooming accoutrements to the side of my dressing table and turned up the lamp that hovered above it. With the help of a tiny pair of scissors, I was able to cut the string that bound the packet. Carefully setting it aside for further examination, I carefully unrolled the flimsy cheesecloth to expose the object that had been bundled inside.

It was a charm, and it dangled from a small pin. The whole thing was, as I indicated previously, no larger than the top half of my little finger.

I found it quite fascinating that the tiny pendant itself was in the shape of a bird—even, perhaps, a crow.

How coincidental.

And I knew Uncle Sherlock's opinion about coincidences.

Not to mention this was the most interesting thing to have happened to me in months. I needed to examine the pin and its wrappings more closely, and subject them to a number of chemical and mechanical tests.

I gathered up the wrappings and stood, hardly giving propriety a thought as I padded from my bedchamber still wearing my pink flannel night frock and with my hair in a long braid swaying down my back.

I had no fear of startling my father, the eminent and respected Sir Mycroft Holmes, with the sight of my feminine *dishabille*, for he never slumbered at home when he could sleep at his office or his men's club. Which was to say, never. The last time I had seen my father, in fact, had been during the chess queen debacle. Unfortunately, he had been present when I realized how I'd been duped by the Ankh.

Though there was no chance my father could have been subjected to the shock of my informal garb, I had forgotten about both Mrs. Raskill and her nephew, Ben, who visited occasionally, but always on Tuesdays to take her to the butcher shop.

It was Tuesday.

I was in such a state as I burst from my chamber toward my laboratory that I nearly ran them both over from where they were conversing near the kitchen, clearly readying themselves to go out.

"Mina!" shrieked Mrs. Raskill. "What on earth are you—"

"It's no matter," I called back, hardly sparing a thought for the possible embarrassment I could be feeling at the fact that a young man had glimpsed me in my voluminous night frock. "I'll take my breakfast in here," I added to forestall any further comment from the housekeeper.

Once safely in my laboratory, I turned on the gas lamps— sparing a moment, as I nearly always did, to lament the fact that electric lighting (which was so much clearer and cleaner than gaslight) was illegal in London—and scrabbled through the drawer to pull out my Ocular-Magnifyer.

As I settled the handy device in place over one eye, anchored by an ingenious fitting that settled over my head like a jaunty hat, I could not help but be reminded of Inspector Ambrose Grayling, who had gifted me with the tool after mine had broken during the events related to the clockwork scarab and the Society of Sekhmet. Though Grayling hadn't been at fault, he had taken the blame for the accident, and the replacement he'd sent me was a far finer model than the one I'd owned previously.

Therefore, I was always unusually careful and deliberate when using the eyepiece and affixing it to my head.

Once the magnifyer was in place, I adjusted the focus and magnification and commenced with a closer examination of the pendant. The bird-shaped charm was roughly the size of a large lima bean, and hung from a small bar that was actually a pin. Both the pin-like bar and the charm were flat, and were made from a sort of cloisonné in dark, rich red. The hue was more of a rusty red or mahogany color than a crimson or scarlet.

The back of the tiny crow pendant was smooth, brushed gold, and it had a minuscule marking on the back, stamped into place. It took more fiddling with the focus of my magnifyer before I was able to discern the shape of the marking. It appeared to be two Cs, facing each other. Or perhaps an infinity symbol; it was difficult to tell.

Although I spent many more minutes examining the object, I found no further clues, nor any indication of its origin. The wrappings were simple white string and plain cheesecloth—the sort of which could be found in any household. There was nothing extraordinary about either. Nor did I find any other remnants that might have clung to it.

Either I had passed my prime as a Holmesian investigator, or there was nothing more to see.

I was just pulling the Ocular-Magnifyer from my head when I became aware of a thunderous pounding from beyond. It took me a moment to realize it was someone at the front door, and then another moment to remember that Mrs. Raskill had been on her way out when I saw her—heavens! It had been over thirty minutes since I'd come into the laboratory and become absorbed in my examination of the charm.

I had no idea how long the person had been pummeling the door, but the rattling of the object in its frame had an air of urgency that I decided couldn't be ignored. Thus, I rushed from the laboratory and to the front door, flinging it open before I quite thought the action through.

Perhaps Miss Stoker had begun to rub off on me.

"Inspector...Grayling," I said faintly when I saw who it was standing on the front stoop...now staring at me in my night frock.

(Evaline must not have heard this element of the story previously, for she has forced me to stop and has pressed me for minute details on the night rail I was wearing. For some reason, she appears quite gleeful about this particular part of the tale. In favor of expediency, I shall add those details to the commentary herewith.)

I was, in fact, in no *great* breach of etiquette in regards to the amount of skin and the shape of any limbs exposed, for the night frock was lengthy enough to skim the tops of my feet. It had long sleeves with ruffles at the wrists, and it buttoned up snugly to my throat. It was, of course, made from warm, heavy flannel and was as loose as a flour sack. The fact that it was simply a garment in which I slept is truly the only reason it might have been considered a moment of impropriety; I had been known to wear a ball gown that exposed more skin and shape than my night rail.

(Evaline seems disappointed by this confession, but I must press on with the narration. I do believe I'm going to hide this manuscript and discontinue working on it when she is present.)

"Miss Holmes." Grayling's face seemed particularly ruddy this morning; perhaps it was the wintry air. He held a hat in his bare hands, and a thick woolen muffler was wrapped around his throat. He'd shaved closely, and in good light this morning, I observed, and Angus (his beagle, who was not present) had recently acquired a fondness for shoe lacings.

"It's freezing out there; either step in or not, but I must close the door," I said, refusing to acknowledge the fact that I'd answered the door dressed as I was. Though my bare toes were tiny ice cubes, my face was hot as a furnace. And my insides shivered like jelly.

I also hadn't seen Grayling since the mortifying chess game we'd played as part of the Ankh's master plan.

"Right, then." He hesitated. Then, with a swift intake of breath, he stepped over the threshold, bringing with him a waft of chill air mingled with peppermint, damp wool, and mechanical oil. A quick glance behind him confirmed my suspicion that he'd driven his steamcycle this morning. It sat near a snowbank, gleaming in its copper and bronze glory. A puff of white smoke still trailed from one of its five tailpipes. Though he was holding a proper hat, the protective head covering he wore while riding the cycle dangled from one of the steering handles.

"Er…I apologize if I woke you, Miss Holmes." Grayling glanced pointedly at the clock on the parlor mantel shelf, which read half past eleven o'clock.

"Oh, no, no," I replied blithely, swiftly buttoning up the overcoat I'd snatched from the hall hat rack and struggled into. "I was just in my laboratory and lost track of time."

"Well, that's a relief. I thought perhaps you'd fallen asleep with your Ocular-Magnifyer in place." He gave a rueful smile and made a little circle in front of one of his eyes with a finger, indicating the round impression that was obviously imprinted on my face. "It's a safety hazard, you know—using any sort of tool or mechanism when one is in danger of falling asleep."

"Naturally I wouldn't be so foolish as to operate any sort of machinery or work with any delicate projects in that situation," I informed him.

"Naturally." He seemed to be having difficulty keeping his eyes from straying to the floor, where my icy bare feet were poking out from beneath the ruffle of my night frock.

"Perhaps I should…erm…Would you please excuse me for a moment, Inspector?"

He appeared mightily relieved at this request, and replied, "Of course, Miss Holmes. Take your time. I'll just peruse your library."

As I'd seen his attention flicker toward my father's generally unused study, where the open door revealed shelves upon shelves of books, as well as a number of interesting devices and objects on one of the long tables therein, I was neither surprised nor put off by his comment.

I don't believe I've ever washed up and dressed myself so quickly as I did that day—and yet with as much care to my appearance. For when I caught a look at myself in the dressing table mirror and saw the dark red circle that still hadn't faded around my eye socket, and the state of my loosened braid (frizzed, straggling, and wild were the descriptors that came to mind), I quite literally gasped in horror.

No wonder Grayling had appeared so taken aback by my appearance. It hadn't been the night frock or my bare feet at all.

However, I was efficient and effective at setting myself to rights, and with the help of the Easy UnLacer (which, in spite of its name, was also devised to lace *up*) I was even able to wriggle into one of my undercorsets in record time. When I emerged from my bedchamber, it was with my hair smooth, shiny, and neatly twisted into a figure-eight knot at the back of my head. I was wearing a perfectly average day dress of sky blue with tiny white flowers and dark blue flounces at the wrists and hem. And I had pulled on stockings and buttoned up shoes, to the relief of my half-frozen feet.

"Inspector Grayling?" I called out when I didn't see him in my father's study.

"In here."

He had invaded my laboratory and was holding the delicate crow charm in his long, freckled fingers. Those digits extended from a strong, wide hand, which in turn came from an equally freckled, equally broad wrist and forearm. As usual, he wasn't wearing gloves. In fact, I didn't believe the man owned a pair—except for the white ones he'd worn on two formal occasions.

"Where did you get this, Miss Holmes?" He'd affixed my Ocular-Magnifyer to his face, and when he lifted his head to look at me with a sharp gaze, its effectiveness was marred by the fact that one gray-green eyeball was magnified into an ungainly appearance.

"Inspector Grayling. While I'm pleased to see you've made yourself comfortable during my *toilette*, I am still unclear as to why you are here today. Perhaps you'd care to enlighten me about that, instead of questioning me about my personal activities."

His mouth tightened, and he tore off the eyepiece. To my surprise, his expression had changed to something fierce and very nearly frightening.

To be clear, *I* wasn't frightened of *him*. Not at all. In fact, I couldn't imagine anyone with whom I might feel safer. Not even Uncle Sherlock. But there was an unyielding glint in the inspector's eyes I'd never seen before.

"Mina, *I need to know how you got this.*"

Miss Holmes
~ *A Corvus of a Particular Color* ~

I COULDN'T DECIDE WHETHER TO BE MORE SHOCKED BY THE fact that Inspector Grayling had used my given name, the flat anger in his voice, or the rude demand that accompanied it.

Until that moment, I'd always thought of him as a sort of mild-mannered, stiff and proper, more than adequate homicide detective—likely partly because of the way Uncle Sherlock spoke about Inspector Lestrade and the others at Scotland Yard—despite the fact that Grayling had never been the least bit bumbling like Lestrade. In fact, he'd been quite heroic on a number of occasions, and had usually matched me clue for clue during any investigations we'd conducted together.

But at that moment, I saw him as someone far more frightening and even a little intimidating. Someone with strength and determination that had been previously hidden beneath stilted manners and a cognoggin personality.

In other words, he seemed far more like a serious force to be reckoned with than merely a man a few years older than myself that I regularly attempted (and usually succeeded) to outwit.

(For some reason, Evaline finds this last comment hilarious. I am definitely putting this manuscript away where she can't find it; she is terribly distracting.)

It was only because of this unexpected reaction to Grayling that I actually answered the question (which was not only harshly spoken, but prying—and not at all his business).

"A crow delivered it to me through my window last night," I replied.

A look of incredulity passed over his face that might have been amusing had it not come on the heels of such ferocity —and then was replaced by the same anger as before. I could see that he was struggling with himself; those long fingers were closing and opening into fists as if they were intent upon grabbing me by the shoulders and shaking me. His face turned grim, and his eyes darkened with determination.

"Miss Holmes," he said in a flat, cold voice. "If you don't see fit to respond with a reasonable answer, I'll—"

"You'll what?" I retorted, suddenly aware that something serious must be at the root of this uncharacteristic response. "Drag me off to Scotland Yard and toss me into a cell?"

His fury evaporated instantly, leaving his demeanor like air deflating from a balloon. His eyes widened as if he were in shock, and he exhaled sharply.

"Miss Holmes, please accept my sincere apology for…for overstepping." Now the color of his face was more pink than red. "I was—I simply…" He cleared his throat. "I was utterly out of line. My behavior was completely unacceptable. Please forgive me, Miss Holmes."

What happened to "Mina"? I wanted to ask.

Dylan had always called me Mina.

Dylan.

No, now was *not* the time to think about him. Not on top of everything else.

"Never mind," I said briskly, pushing away a torrent of thoughts related to Dylan Eckhert, my friend who'd returned to his time a hundred years in the future, and my confused thoughts about the man who stood before me, looking more miserable than I'd ever seen him. "Incidentally, that was the truth."

"What?" Grayling responded in a milder tone, but still laced with skepticism. "That a crow delivered this charm to you?"

"Yes." I proceeded to explain, and had the satisfaction of seeing both confusion and wonder fill his expression. "The interesting thing," I added at the end, "is that I heard the crow caw before I opened the window. So he couldn't have had the item in his mouth at that time."

"That means he might have found it on your windowsill while you were deciding whether to let him in your chamber," Grayling replied dryly.

"Well I certainly didn't intend to allow him entrance. But perhaps we could ascertain whether that was the case."

"Certainly. I'd be more than happy to look out the window, or climb onto the roof if necessary to see whether there are indicative marks in the snow on or near your window. It should be quite obvious."

"Of course."

Despite the fact that it was, strictly speaking, wildly improper and completely beyond the bounds of privacy to allow a young man into the depths of one's bedchamber, I put those qualms aside for the sake of investigative procedure. I was confident Uncle Sherlock would have felt the same way.

It took Grayling only a few short moments to draw his conclusions after he stuck his head through the open window and looked around from the gable that made up part of the wall of my chamber. When he withdrew and turned to me, he said, "From the markings in the snow, it appears the crow didn't find the small bundle there, but that he brought it with him—most likely in his talons—and then dropped it for a moment. You can look for yourself," he added, gesturing to the window even as he closed it, "but I'm certain you'll come to the same conclusion."

"I see no need. I trust your observational skills."

His auburn brows rose. "And what would your Uncle Sherlock think if he were witness to a Holmes complimenting a police investigator?"

"In this case, he would likely have no choice but to agree with me," I replied, suddenly overwhelmed by the heat rushing up over my face and a stuttering of my pulse when Grayling looked at me in surprise.

He appeared to want to say something, then thought better of it. "Right, then, Miss Holmes. Perhaps we should—er—return to the laboratory. There's more—er—space in there."

Which was a bald-faced lie, but I wasn't about to call him on the fact that my laboratory was chock full of objects, while my bedchamber was sparse and neat.

The fact was, my bedchamber had seemed to shrink to a smaller size the moment he walked in. And my neatly made bed had seemed to grow to disproportionately dominate the room, even though I knew that was a fanciful thought. I was relieved he hadn't appeared to notice anything about the room—including a pair of silk stockings I'd left hanging over a chair—but went directly to the window in question.

"Apparently you've seen something like this charm before," I said, once back in the laboratory. "And it appears to have caused you some consternation."

He gave me a brief, abashed glance, his cheeks pinkening a little. "Miss Holmes, I was unforgivably rude earlier. I simply... I didn't expect to see something like this in the possession of someone like y—what I mean to say is, as a proper young lady, you have no business— I—er. Ahem."

Grayling must have noticed the stiffening of my spine and the flattening of my lips—not to mention the chill in my eyes —as he stumbled about his explanation, and so decided to cut his losses. So to speak.

"I have no business *what?*" I asked. "As you're well aware, I'm not a typical *proper* young lady."

"One cannot argue with the fact that you seem to attract dead bodies with the same alacrity as the bodies in question lure flies."

"What is the charm?" I demanded, tired of this shilly-shallying. He was clearly attempting to come up with a dull story that would explain his violent reaction as well as appease my certain curiosity, knowing full well that my curiosity had been roused far beyond a mild interest.

He sighed. "It represents a sort of establishment. Not *that* sort of establishment," he added quickly when my eyes bolted wide. "At least, as far as I know. But The Carnelian Crow seems to be a rather…unsavory place dressed in the garb of a well-to-do dinner club."

"The Carnelian Crow," I mused. "It sounds intriguing."

"I was certain you'd have that reaction," he replied with a sigh. "Miss Holmes, believe me when I say this is not a place for a young, well-bred lady like yourself."

I peered at him carefully. "And what do you know about it, Inspector Grayling?"

"It's been in business for quite some time—several years, perhaps more. There have been whispers about a secret red crow for more than five years. From what I have been able to ascertain, the establishment is a place where very seedy activities happen—of a sordid or—erm—vulgar nature. Most likely illegal or criminal efforts, or a place where those who undertake that sort of enterprise might meet each other in private."

I frowned. "That all sounds rather vague, Inspector."

He grimaced. "Gaining access to or information about this particular club has been quite challenging for myself as well as my Scotland Yard colleagues. Until recently, I wasn't even certain it was a place rather than some other entity— such as a criminal sort of person or even an object. We didn't even quite know what we were looking for. But within the last few months, there have been more—shall we say, louder and more discernible—whispers about it, which enabled me to learn even that much."

"Have you ever been to The Carnelian Crow?"

He pursed his lips. "I have not. Only because…well, I don't precisely know where it is. Apparently, the entrance or entrances are well hidden, and they have been known to change as well. The only ones who know how to access the club are those who have gained admittance through some sort of membership process or invitation. And I've yet to find anyone who has—or, at least, who is willing to admit it."

"That makes it even more intriguing," I said, a smile tugging at the corners of my mouth.

He sighed, but he was also fighting a smile. "Again, Miss Holmes…I was certain you'd have that reaction. The more intriguing, inappropriate, and inexplicable a topic, the more fascinated you seem to be."

"How well you've come to know me." I found myself looking up at him for a moment. My gaze connected with his as we shared a brief interlude of amusement. But I couldn't seem to pull my eyes away…and I didn't really want to. I felt as if I were beginning to tumble into some deep, warm, intriguing depth, and—

"Right, then, Miss Holmes," he said quickly, shattering the moment as he looked away, back down at the small carnelian crow he still held.

I recovered myself immediately, furious that my cheeks felt warm and that my palms seemed to have become damp. "Incidentally, Inspector Grayling, you haven't seen fit to advise me of the reason for your call this morning. Surely you had no idea a crow—an ebony one, not one of carnelian stone—had delivered this mysterious pendant to me last night; therefore, you must have had a reason for interrupting your day to come all the way here."

"Yes, of course." He appeared to fidget a bit on his feet. "I did have a purpose for the visit. I was…er… Well, I was curious as to what current case you might be working on. As you're certainly aware, normally our paths tend to cross when you are investigating a matter, and I couldn't help but notice I hadn't—er—encountered you or Miss Stoker for several weeks. More than two months, in fact. Since the—er—disconcerting events related to the Theophanine chess queen. I thought perhaps if you were on a case, we might—I might — Well, I was merely curious."

I blinked. I wasn't certain what to make of this manufactured speech. He claimed he had come to discover what I was working on—which, of course, was a large, empty *nothing*—in order to…offer his assistance?

As if I needed it.

I was, after all, a Holmes.

A disgraced one, but still a Holmes. After all, even Uncle Sherlock had been outsmarted at least once—by Miss Adler, in fact. And he had recently indicated he was being quite challenged by a mathematician named Dr. Moriarty.

"I didn't mean to interrupt your day," Grayling said awkwardly. "I suppose I should let you get on to it. But, please, Miss Holmes…I know how you like to stick your nose into places where it really shouldn't be—"

"Is that a comment on the size of my proboscis?" I retorted sharply.

"No, good gad, not at all, Miss Holmes," he stammered. Then, mouth flat and eyes averted, he shook his head, giving a brief bow. "I'm sorry to have bothered you. However much you might dislike me, Miss Holmes, I do hope you'll heed my warning about The Carnelian Crow. Good day."

Before I could respond, he turned and stalked from the laboratory. I stared after him, stunned by the turn our conversation had taken and the sentiments he had expressed—*dislike* him? Why, that was absurd…wasn't it?—and heard him pause to snatch up his hat from the parlor.

"Inspector," I said, suddenly galvanized into action, starting after him…but it was too late. I heard the front door close behind him, and by the time I reached the entrance, he'd climbed onto his steamcycle and was gunning the (probably illegal) engine. Its roar, along with the fact that he'd pulled on the protective headpiece and was looking away from my front door, made it impossible for me to gain his attention.

As he wheeled the cycle around and blazed off, I stared after him for a moment, wondering what precisely had happened. It had been a very strange conversation, and it unsettled me. I don't like ambiguity, and the reason for his visit was completely confusing.

For some reason, that entire event took over my thoughts —superseding even the intriguing information I'd learned about the tiny red charm—and I realized I wanted to talk to someone who actually might know more about a topic (specifically, the male species) than I did.

I needed to speak with Evaline.

Miss Stoker

~ Wherein Our Heroine's Life is Completely Tossed Up ~

EVERYTHING WAS JUST FINE UNTIL FLORENCE RUINED MY breakfast.

Well, not exactly *fine*.

In fact, things weren't really all that great, to be honest. I'd had yet another sleepless night. Partly because I'd spent most of it skulking around Whitechapel, Smithfield, and Haymarket, hunting the UnDead.

I'd staked a few, too, of course. That was to be expected.

But the real reason I hadn't slept yet again wasn't so much because I'd been out all night. It was because I hadn't seen hide nor hair of that sneaky, kiss-stealing rogue called Pix.

In the past, I'd never had any trouble finding him. In fact, more often than not, he found *me*. Loitering beneath my bedroom window. Showing up in disguise at society balls. Serving in an opium den (the memory of him in that scandalous Far Eastern garb of sleeveless and open vest—with *no shirt*—made me flush every time I thought about it). Skulking in a church at midnight—dressed in priest's robes! Even climbing into my chamber by moonlight.

But it had been almost two months since I'd seen him at all.

Last night I'd finally given in to my irritation—all right, *fear*—and gone to Fenman's End, the dingy, dangerous pub in the scariest part of London that Pix owned and operated. If Pix wouldn't come to me, I'd come to him. And I'd give him a piece of my mind. After all, the man had kissed me more than once. He'd even given me a gift: a unique vampire-hunting weapon. It was a small, gun-sized crossbow with perfect-sized stakes, made specially for me.

And since then…nothing.

As usual, Bilbo was behind the bar. He knew me and glanced over as I sat down. Since I had learned the hard way that his loyalty lay firmly with Pix, I figured if anyone had information, it would be Bilbo.

Yet, even as I sat down on the creaky stool, I was angry with myself. I had no business chasing after a slick pickpocket. Even if his kisses made my knees weak. He was a criminal, after all.

"Wot'll ye 'ave, Molly-Sue?" Bilbo asked as he swept by on the way to get someone else's ale.

Anger and frustration made me brave. "I'll have an ale."

The barkeep squinted at me. "Ye will, will ye?"

"You heard me."

He turned to spit a stream of something long and dark onto the floor, and my stomach lurched. Maybe I'd be better off not having anything to drink here. "What e'er ye say."

Moments later, he set the glass in front of me. It had a thick head of foam that slopped over the side, and there were fingerprints decorating the glass. I decided I wasn't ready to try ale yet. "I need to see Pix."

"You'n 'alf o' London, there, Molly-Sue."

That made my stomach lurch again. "What do you mean?"

"I mean 'e ain't 'ere. Ain't been 'ere neither. And people bin in 'ere arsking questions—jus' like you."

I tried not to show my rising concern. "Do you know where I can find him?"

"No. Ain't seen 'im."

"Do you think he's…is he in trouble?" I asked, ignoring the demands from the other customers waiting for Bilbo.

The barkeep shook his head. "'e's always in trouble."

My heart sank. "If you see him," I said, sliding off the stool, "tell him I need to speak to him."

Bilbo's shoulders drew up. His expression was serious. Even worried. "I'll tell 'im." He didn't sound very certain.

I left Fenman's End then, more shaken than I had been when I arrived. And all without breaking anyone's thumb or being involved in any sort of altercation. That was some sort of record for me, but one I couldn't dwell on.

But why should I worry about Pix? I asked myself as I walked down the filth-strewn block toward Seven Dials. He was perfectly capable of taking care of himself.

But I couldn't help but remember the way the Ankh had spoken to him. She knew things about him. She'd tried to kill him—and, in fact, had succeeded.

What if she'd tracked him down again?

Then I brushed those worries away. Pix was slick and fast and very smart. He'd probably show up in the next day or so, acting as if nothing had happened. And I might even let him kiss me.

Dawn was breaking as I got into bed. Though I should have been tired, I tossed and turned. I couldn't keep from thinking about my last conversation with Pix, in shadowy St. Sequestrian's. Something had changed then. Something between us. He'd been so…intense.

"Would you have done it to me? Tell me, Evaline."

"Done what?"

"What ye did to Dancy."

I'd hesitated, because it *had* been a question on my mind: if Pix had been turned UnDead, as Mr. Dancy had, would I have killed him?

I answered Pix truthfully: *Yes.*

And he'd *thanked* me. But I'll never forget the way his dark eyes looked when he did so: bleak, and yet resolute.

And now he was gone.

I wasn't certain if I should be angry or relieved or worried. So I tried to put him out of my mind.

And then Florence came into the breakfast room and helped by ruining my day.

No, actually, she ruined my entire life.

I was enjoying a warm apple muffin-puff spread with cinnamon-honey butter when she sat down at the table with a gleam of purpose in her eyes—not unlike that of my colleague Mina Holmes.

But in this case, I knew the gleam portended nothing

good for me. Especially when I saw how serious her face was. Dull. Almost sad.

"Evaline," she said, folding her hands primly on the dining room table. "Bram and I had a long discussion last night. I have some things to tell you."

"All right." Her expression made me nervous. I could tell this was going to be unpleasant. I hoped she didn't want me to go shopping with her for a new wardrobe for a round of Christmas balls and fêtes that I had no intention of attending.

She looked down, and her fingers tightened to white. Now I was really nervous.

"The Lyceum hasn't been doing well. There's talk that it could be closed. Attendance is down, and with the new laws that have just gone into effect regarding taxes on steam engine parts, and imports, and some of the changes Parliament has just passed…well, to be blunt: our financial situation has become dire."

I stared at her. I wasn't certain about all of that tax business and what the government was doing—it didn't affect me; I was a vampire hunter—but those last words did hit me. "Dire?"

"Very dire." Her mouth was white at the corners, it was so tight.

Now, suddenly, many things began to make sense to me. The whispered, hissing conversations I'd heard between Florence and my brother Bram. The extra amount of mail that had been piling up on the salver in the front hall—letters that Florence snatched up before I could see what they were. Bills, many of them unpaid?

"All right," I said, unclear as to how this would affect me. "Well, I have no need for any new frocks, Flo. We don't have to give any dinner parties over the holiday," I added, trying not to sound relieved. "And I don't mind missing—"

"Evaline," she began in a hard, impersonal voice. "It's… it's more than that. We… Well, Bram has been spending so much extra time working on his novel that he's neglected our finances. Even worse, some of his investments weren't very smart, and with the change in laws and taxes and tariffs… well, things are *dire*. So dire, in fact, that by the first of the year, we will be faced with two choices: go back to Ireland and move in with your parents, or…" She hesitated, then rushed on. "Or you must marry."

I stared at her.

"Soon," she added, fixing me with a serious gaze. "Before the end of the year."

"Marry?"

"It goes without saying he must be wealthy, Evaline."

"Marry?"

"We only have another month before the bill collectors will take over and we'll be forced to leave Grantworth House. And then we'll have no choice but to return to Ireland." Tears brimmed her eyes and the tip of her nose turned pink. "An engagement announcement by Christmas would keep them at bay."

"Christmas?"

Christmas was only two weeks away.

It wasn't only my breakfast that was ruined. It was my entire day. My week.

My *life*.

"I…" The words didn't come. I felt hot and cold and lost, all at once. "How can this be?"

Lose Grantworth House? The home that had been part of the vampire-fighting Venators' history for centuries? It couldn't be. We couldn't allow that. *I* couldn't.

"Bram didn't want to tell you," Florence rushed on. "But I insisted. He's at his wits' end, trying to come up with a solution…but he's run out of time. And money." Her fingers turned whitish-blue as she clasped them even harder while one tear spilled from an eye. "The only way to save us is for you to marry. You're the heiress to Grantworth House, and your husband would be able to help us. And, of course, a husband of the peerage wouldn't suffer to have his wife's family tossed on the street…it would be terrible for his reputation.

"Florence, I had no idea," I said, trying to make sense of everything she was saying. "I didn't realize… I-I…"

"You're our only hope, Evaline. If you don't find a wealthy man to marry within the next month, we're going to be out on the street—or moving back to Dublin." She rose from the table, pressing a handkerchief to her face, and rushed from the dining room.

I stared after her, suddenly feeling violently ill. The muffin-puff no longer appealed, and the rasher of bacon looked disgusting, sitting in its grease.

Marry?

I couldn't marry.

I didn't *want* to marry—anyone. I couldn't marry. Ever.

But Florence and Bram had been so good to me. They'd raised me, along with their young son Noel, when my elderly parents couldn't—as if I were their own daughter. I loved Bram and Florence and Noel, so very much, and I had always felt so secure knowing we had a roof over our heads, and food on the table.

I couldn't let them down. I had to pay them back for everything they'd done for me. They were family.

And Grantworth House…I looked around the dining room, the familiar room of yellow painted walls with white wainscoting, where my great-grandmother, the legendary Victoria Gardella, had sat and eaten at this very table. It was part of my heritage. Part of my history.

I couldn't…

But I couldn't get married, either.

Whoever heard of a vampire hunter getting married?

I WAS STILL NUMB THIRTY MINUTES LATER, WANDERING listlessly around the *kalari*—the room where I honed my vampire-hunting skills, but where Florence believed I was practicing dancing—when I heard the unmistakable sound of Mina Holmes's footsteps approaching. She always walked quickly and with purpose, and even in a crowded room I could tell when she was coming across the way.

I gave a disgusted sigh. The last thing, the very *last thing* I wanted, was to be around Miss Know-It-All and Miss Lecture-Till-My-Ears-Turn-Numb today. Especially since Miss Adler hadn't summoned us to the British Museum since the big disappointment with the chess queen, and so I hadn't had reason to see my so-called partner.

But Brentwood, the butler (how much longer until we couldn't afford to pay him? Would he be on the streets soon too? And what about my maid Pepper? My throat seized up) had learned to allow Mina entrance without announcing her whenever she arrived. Whether it was because he didn't want to argue with her, or whether he'd just learned over the course of the nine months I'd known her, I wasn't sure.

"Evaline! I'm so relieved I found you at home," she said, breezing into the room. "The most astonishing thing happened last night, and— Oh dear." She stopped, looking at me closely. "Whatever is wrong?"

I drew myself up. "Nothing."

She narrowed her eyes. I felt the weight of the infamous Holmes observation skills as she looked me over. I looked back. She might be related to the most famous detective ever, but even Mina couldn't tell what was on my mind by looking at the frock I was wearing today.

"Are you certain there's nothing bothering you? You appear to—"

"*Yes.* What are you doing here?" I changed the subject, and I didn't care if I sounded rude.

Fortunately, Mina was not one to beat around the bush, especially when she had a purpose in mind. "During your— er—nightly adventures, have you ever heard of The Carnelian Crow?"

"No." I felt a prickle of interest and seized on it. That was better than thinking about getting married. "What is it?"

"That is precisely what I'm attempting to discover." She looked uncertain for a moment. "But I haven't yet determined how to do so. I was hoping you'd heard of it." She hesitated, then pursed her lips as if she'd just tasted a lemon. "Much as I hate the thought, I shall have to resort to asking that Mr. Pix person of yours."

Good luck with that. The pang of worry was back. But then I realized… "Since you're a Holmes, *you* should be able to help. I don't know why I didn't think of that right away."

"Help with what?"

"Pix has gone missing. So if you want to ask him about The Carnelian Crow—what is carnelian, anyway?—we're going to have to find him."

She pursed her lips again. I could tell she was ready to launch into a lecture about what a reprobate he was, and demanding to know why I continued to involve myself with such a disreputable criminal. Either that or she was going to give me far more information than I needed about carnelian. Whatever it was. A gemstone, maybe? Regardless, I was already regretting speaking out.

"You're certain he's actually missing?" she asked.

"I haven't seen him for at least two months. And Bilbo hasn't seen him either. He seems to have disappeared right after the chess queen incident."

"I suppose Bilbo is one of his equally disreputable associates."

"He's the barkeep at Fenman's End."

"The place in Whitechapel where you're always getting into brawls and winning at arm-wrestling?"

I suddenly had a great idea. "I'll take you there tonight. You can begin your investigation then."

"Investigation?" She seemed about to argue, then stopped. "I suppose I have no choice if I want to find out about The Carnelian Crow. If anyone would know what it is and how to find it, that dratted man will. It seems every time we get involved in a case, he's in the thick of it." She paused, then barreled on. "I suppose if I'm going to visit Whitechapel tonight I should find something suitable to wear. Perhaps a visit to Lady Thistle's is in order."

"Yes," I nearly exclaimed. Anything to get out and away from the dull worry that hovered over the household. Besides, I'd never been to Mina's favorite clothing boutique, and I was curious about it. "I'll get my coat."

"Don't forget money for the street-lifts!" she called after me.

But I ignored her. The Stokers were, after all, on a tight budget.

Miss Holmes
~ *Our Heroines in High Fashion* ~

LADY THISTLE'S WAS LOCATED ON THE THIRD STREET LEVEL not far from Fleet-street.

I glanced at Evaline, and of course she'd neglected to bring coins for the street-lift. But despite her argument to the contrary, she seemed so out of sorts that I refrained from mentioning it, and instead fed the appropriate funds into the slot for the lift.

The scrollwork doors opened with a dull grating sound. We stepped into the glass-sided lift, pulling our skirts in to make certain they wouldn't catch as the gate closed. Then, with a subtle jerk, the small cage began to rise, taking us past a walkway at the second level where a horde of trade street-carts were parked: a knife grinder, a cog-smith, a compact knit factory, a brolly repair shop, and a mobile leather repair shop. That particular smithery gave off a rich, *au naturel* scent as the hide was heated, tanned, and stretched into a smooth leather pallet as steam rolled from the mechanism's small chimney.

On the third level, where our lift stopped with hardly a jolt, we were greeted by an expansive array of carts from more street hawkers, but the vast majority of them were for edibles. I cast a sidelong look at Evaline as we stepped out of the glass and scrollwork cage and a rush of sweet, spicy, freshly baked scents greeted us.

But she gave them nary a glance—and that alone indicated how disturbed she was over the events of her morning. I declined to mention it again, although I had by then deduced what was upsetting her.

"Look, Evaline," I said, slipping my gloved hand through the crook of her elbow in that companionable way I'd seen other young ladies do, "there's a cart selling popping tea! I must try one, and you as well. My treat," I added to forestall any argument. I also declined to release her arm when she would have resisted, instead firmly dragging her toward the cart.

Since I knew she was far stronger than I, the fact that she acquiesced and allowed me to do so indicated her willingness to be convinced.

I'd never had a popping tea before. The beverage was a relatively new concept, having been developed by an English businessman who'd married a woman from Japan and brought her back home to London to live. I'd read about the beverage in the *Ladies' Tattle-Tale* (it had been given a mention in one of the gossip columns after Princess Alix was seen partaking of one).

Still gripping Evaline's arm firmly, I perused the flavor options as we waited in line. Jasmine, orange, honeyed chocolate, cardamom-vanilla, and basil-mint. I ordered jasmine, but my companion was more adventurous and decided to try the cardamom-vanilla. I must confess, after I smelled the delicious spice emanating from her beverage, I wished I'd thought to do the same.

The beverages were handed to us in tall, slender paper cups that fluted at the top like a tulip. Each one was set inside a brass holder (to protect one's fingers from the heat, and also to stabilize the flimsy paper insert) with a tiny handle near the base. I belatedly realized the delicate paper cups themselves were infused with the scent or flavor chosen: mine had the floral hint of jasmine, and Evaline's smelled like vanilla.

But it was the popping tea itself that delighted me. The beverage was warm and steaming, but inside was a myriad of small bubbles like large fizzes that shot from the bottom of the drink. Upon reaching the surface of the tea, each pea-sized ball popped enthusiastically, releasing the flavor and scent of jasmine or cardamom-vanilla into the air and lightly dampening one's face as one came near. The flavoring settled over the top of the beverage in a sweet, foamy, milky layer.

Thus, as one tipped it to drink, the smell and flavor was prominent inside the milky tea. It was a sweet, perfumed beverage that warmed its brass holder—and my gloved hands, by extension—and was perfect for a chilly winter's day.

I decided immediately that popping tea was my new favorite indulgence, and that I would endeavor to taste all of the flavors in the very near future. Evaline and I sipped our drinks whilst leaning over the edge of the walkway railing, looking down over the lowest street level, where we were treated to the sight of the tops of wagons, carriages, hackneys, and the hatted heads of passersby as they navigated through the mucky, dark, snow-muddied streets below.

Since Evaline had remained silent and very brooding, I decided I should seize the opportunity to direct our nonexistent conversation.

"I received a visit from Inspector Grayling this morning," I said, feeling strangely uncomfortable about bringing up the topic.

For the first time since I'd arrived at her house, interest flickered in her eyes. "Oh?" she asked in a strange tone, drawing out the single syllable into several that went up at the end. "And what did he want?"

I buried my face in the comfortingly warm, if damp, scent of my tea and inhaled its floral essence. "I'm not certain. He didn't precisely say."

Evaline turned to look at me. An actual smile was beginning to curl at the corners of her mouth, and I was delighted to have at least somehow breached her foul mood. "He didn't say? He just arrived at your house with no excuse whatsoever?"

Because of the way she was regarding me, I felt uncomfortable mentioning the state of my attire when Grayling arrived. Instead, I repeated our conversation (word for word, of course, and with all inflections included) without going into detail about the crow charm. I could get into that later.

Evaline merely looked at me with a widening grin. I was relieved to see that even her eyes had begun to sparkle a little. "You don't know why he came?" she asked at the end, a teasing note in her voice. "Really, Mina, how much of a stone-head are you?"

"I don't know what you mean," I replied stiffly.

Her expression sobered. "He missed you. He was worried about you. He wanted to see you. And now that Dylan's gone…"

All at once, my face was hot—and it had nothing to do with the steaming cup I held in my hand. "Don't be ridiculous. And what does Dylan have to do with anything?"

Evaline merely shook her head, smiling mysteriously as she returned to her drink. Her long eyelashes—so dark and thick and curly—fluttered as she sipped and looked out over the city with all the appearance of a woman in control.

"Why would Inspector Grayling want to see me?" I said, while studiously avoiding looking at my companion. Really, she was quite absurd. I regretted having brought up the topic. Why on earth would Inspector Grayling want to see *me*?

"Unless he wanted my assistance with one of his cases," I decided. "I'm certain that's it…and perhaps he merely lost his nerve for asking me. Although Lestrade never seems to mind asking Uncle Sherlock for help. Though—to be fair—I believe Lestrade is in far more need of assistance than Grayling would be. He's quite… Well, the man is infuriating, and he's always commenting on the fact that I seem to attract dead bodies, which isn't the case at all. How on earth could I *attract* dead bodies? It makes me sound like some sort of—of cemetery or hospital. Why, it's absurd to even consider…" I trailed off when I realized Evaline was shaking with silent laughter.

"Methinks the lady doth protest too much." She giggled.

"Well, I'm glad to be such a source of amusement for you, Miss Stoker," I said frostily, deciding that was the last time I would ever ask her for advice.

Once we'd returned the brass fittings to the beverage cart (and received a rebate of sixpence per cup for doing so),

Evaline and I continued on our way to Lady Thistle's. At least she had lost some of the worry limning her eyes and tightening her expression.

The shop's entrance was down the side alley of a side alley, tucked between a lace shop and a tiny bookstore that dealt with antiquated books. I generally resisted the urge to go into the latter, for fear I'd spend my entire monthly allowance on one precious book—for there were many rare, interesting tomes that were in locked cases throughout the shop. But I'd peeked in the window several times and seen the proprietress moving about. I thought, rather fancifully, I must admit, that she seemed like a sort of otherworldly librarian—with her long corn-silk hair fashioned in intricate braids, and the out-of-date medieval-style gown she wore.

"I've walked past this street dozens of times and never noticed Lady Thistle's before," Evaline said before I had the chance to glance in the bookstore. She was looking at the clothing boutique's narrow doorway. "It's quite well hidden, and cunningly so. There isn't even a sign."

Due to her delicate mood, I refrained from pointing out that her observation was obvious. "Yet, for the uninitiated, the hand-painted thistle on the glass of the door is an indication that we're in the correct location."

The door, which was inset in a small alcove, was framed in pale sage green, and the thistle painted on it was the same green with a lavender blossom on it. It was, as my companion noted, the only identifying marking anywhere. I pushed open the door and followed Evaline inside.

The space was long and narrow, and I heard my companion's swift intake of breath as she looked around the shop. That had been my reaction the first time I visited, with my mother. How many years ago? Three. Perhaps four.

I quickly submerged a pang of grief—it was now over a year since the last letter from her, and she'd been gone for nearly two years. What was even more confusing and troubling was the fact that my mother, Desirée Holmes, had also been known as Siri—and she'd been Evaline's mentor in regards to her vampire hunting.

"This place is amazing," Evaline said in an uncharacteristic whisper.

I couldn't disagree. The place was like no other clothing shop I'd been in before or since.

While the front of the establishment was dim and appeared abandoned—a tactic that was meant, I believed, to discourage people from entering after peeping through the dingy glass window—as one moved toward the rear of the deep, narrow space, alcoves displaying a variety of clothing and accessories became visible along each side.

Each alcove was lit with two bright gas lamps and contained one mechanized dummy modeling a clothing ensemble. The figures moved in smooth choreography: one spun slowly, another counted out the steps to a stationary quadrille, and still another curtsied and rose, over and over again.

There were also mechanized hat racks, shoe racks, and a slowly spinning cone-shaped spiral that displayed gloves, decorative hair combs, and other accessories.

That in itself was hardly enough to cause Evaline's exclamation, for the clothing displayed herein was nothing like the sort of attire one bought from most dressmakers. Everything in Lady Thistle's was of the style known as Street Fashion—which was, as Dylan had once called it, "cutting edge." I had come to understand that phrase described something new and different, and perhaps even futuristic.

To be more specific, Street Fashion was a mode of dress that was slightly scandalous—with specially designed corsets worn on the *outside* of the clothing, and split or slit skirts that were rarely long enough to cover one's shoes. Some of them were even short enough that a hint of the lower extremities might be revealed. (Not that I had ever worn something that beyond the pale. But I'd admired them and their obvious convenience.)

Evaline, who'd often expressed her admiration for clothing I'd acquired from Lady Thistle's, was agog at the options—many of them far more extreme than anything she'd seen on me.

"Miss Holmes, is it you?" came a creaky, quavery voice from the back of the shop.

"Good day, Lady Thistle," I said, bustling past a mannequin who was curtsying while in a frock that barely reached past her knees. The skirt was trimmed with a hem-flounce made from glinting pieces of glass and silver. "It is indeed I, and I've brought my friend Miss Evaline Stoker with me."

I was never quite convinced that Lady Thistle was, in fact, strictly worthy of the title—for what would an elderly member of the peerage be doing, operating a tiny, impossible-to-find clothing boutique? Especially since she didn't look like the sort of person to *wear* an external corset or split skirts that allowed glimpses of ankles, calves, or even knees.

"Good, good," she said in a whispery voice.

It suited, I'd thought from the moment I met her while with my mother some years ago. (Three, it had been. Only three years, though it seemed like an age.)

Yes, Lady Thistle's voice and her figure were as insubstantial as the down of the plant for which she was named. Bird-like in her movements, tiny and hardly more than a bundle of needle-thin bones and with skin as smooth and translucent as moonlight, the shop's proprietor was dressed in a severe black and gray ensemble. There was nary a glint nor a gleam nor even a sparkle anywhere on her clothing—in stark contrast to the items she sold, where everything had some sort of showy, metal- or jewel-like trim. Her snow-white hair was scraped back into a tight bun, and her small, dark eyes darted about, seeming to miss nothing. Though her eyes were sharp, her ears were not, and she wore a device that resembled an Ocular-Magnifyer, but it covered her entire left ear in order to help her hearing.

"Show her around, then, Miss Holmes. Magpie's gone out

to fetch an order from Veller's, and so I'm here alone."

As it turned out, Miss Stoker was in no need of my assistance. She already appeared to have found several articles of clothing that interested her, and when I attempted to show her how to find different sizes and colors in the drawers below the mannequins, she shooed me away.

Very well, then. I'd leave her to her own devices, for I had my own shopping to do. The last time I'd been here, I'd seen an ankle-length split skirt that had a pair of hidden trousers incorporated into its attached petticoat. I thought a one-piece item like that would be extremely useful while going about my business in investigating.

My pleasure at the thought of trying them on ebbed when I was reminded that I had nothing to investigate at the moment, and would likely not have anything in the near future unless I could find Mr. Pix. Nevertheless, I was resolute and determined to at least try on the skirt.

But Miss Stoker had taken over the dressing closet, and there wasn't room enough in there for both of us—especially with my long limbs and tendency to misplace my elbows.

"Is there another place in which I might try this on?" I asked Lady Thistle, who was perched on a backless stool upholstered in cobalt-blue velvet. It looked terribly uncomfortable, but she sat erect and still and didn't appear to mind.

"Back there, Miss Holmes. Behind the red velvet curtain. Mind you, don't step on the cat's tail."

I'd never been back this far into the shop, and it was so crammed with stacks of hatboxes, small chests of lace and ribbons, a long hanging rack, and a plate-sized table and chairs that I could barely make my way through. Probably only a woman the size of Lady Thistle could easily navigate the maze; I wondered how Magpie, who was approximately twice the size of myself, could manage. In fact, I brushed past too close to one side and sent a pyramid of boxes tumbling. Fascinators spilled out—feathers, beads, lace, and gemstones all over the scarred wooden floor.

"I'm sorry, Lady Thistle," I called, hastily gathering up

the mess and settling each of the gorgeous fascinators into the boxes from which they'd fallen. I hoped I had them correct.

I was just stooping to pick up the last fascinator (easier said than accomplished when wearing a corset and toting a bustle at the back of one's waist, not to mention layers of frothy petticoats)—which had partially slid beneath a closet door—when I saw something that caused me to freeze. And to emit an audible gasp.

My breath stopped (partly because I was half bent and the cage of my corset was cutting off my lungs) as I used my finger to trace a small, pale red carving on the bottom of the door.

It was a symbol that looked like the infinity sign.

Or of two Cs facing each other.

Miss Holmes

~ Of Hidden Doors and Unboxed Corsets ~

I NEARLY FELL BACK UPON MY HEELS AS I CONTORTED myself to make certain I was seeing the carving properly. I even disengaged the tiny magnifyer I'd begun to habitually wear on a chain clipped to my bodice like a timepiece.

And upon closer examination, I confirmed my initial impression: the symbol carved near the base of the closet door was the same as the one on the reverse of the carnelian crow pendant.

There was, of course, no question that I would open the closet door.

But I, unlike Miss Stoker, don't generally rush into action without considering repercussions as well as strategies. I took a moment to check the other closet doors in the back of Lady Thistle's, and confirmed that I was quite alone: the proprietress had slid off her velvet perch and was discussing the cut of a sleeve with Evaline, and Magpie— the burly assistant who would certainly announce her presence if she tried to navigate the backroom maze—was still gone.

I turned the closet doorknob and carefully pulled it so the door opened, taking care in the event it squeaked or some sort of alarm went off. To my relief, it moved silently and easily, and I peered inside.

Shelves lined the walls on either side of the space, and there was a large display rack on the back wall. Both shelves and rack were filled with boxes that, though neatly aligned, looked as if they hadn't been disturbed in years.

Hmm. I couldn't help but think there had to be something more to a door marked with a mysterious symbol.

Or maybe it wasn't such a mysterious symbol after all. It could be an infinity sign, and I was manufacturing something out of nothing simply because I was bored.

But after a glance toward the front of the store to assure myself I was still unobserved, I went inside the closet and began to poke around. I was required to leave the door ajar in order to have some illumination for my activities, and although I wasn't certain what I was looking for, I began to randomly remove boxes on the shelves to look inside.

Nothing but outdated or damaged hats, corsets, gloves, and shoes. Not one thing out of the ordinary.

Sighing, I turned to leave, and in my disappointment and haste, my elbow caught the edge of the rack at the back of the closet. I cringed, expecting everything to come tumbling down upon me...but nothing moved. Not even the rack. Not even the box I'd bumped quite roughly.

The hairs at the back of my neck prickled, and I narrowed my eyes, looking more closely at the rack. It took me only a moment to ascertain that it was fake: the items were fixed in place like the piece of a stage set. Curious. My pulse kicked up a bit as I examined the situation more closely, once again wishing I had thought to bring my Flip-Beam Illuminator—the small, hand-held light that required only a few cranks to work.

At last I confirmed the suspicion that had first led me into the closet: there was a cleverly concealed door in the back wall, camouflaged by the faux display rack. And when I finally discovered the mechanism—it was a relatively simple latch that utilized an empty box labeled "gemstones and feathers, misc."—the entire rack slid to the side, revealing an opening. I could see a white brick wall across from me, and little else. But there was a glow to the right that led me to believe there was a corridor or passage angling off into... somewhere. At least it didn't appear to be too dark and gloomy.

I didn't care for dark and gloomy places. Especially if they were underground. I shivered.

"Mina?"

Drat and *blast*. Miss Stoker *would* have to come along at the very moment things were getting interesting. She'd want to go barging into the space without any plans or preparations. And she'd probably leave me behind like she did on the night we descended to the old Thames Tunnel through the old Wapping station.

"Mina, where are you? I want to show you this divine ensemble."

In an effort to keep her from announcing (accidentally or purposely; one could never tell with Evaline) what I'd discovered, and that I'd been snooping, I hurriedly backed out of the closet.

"There you are," she said, looking confused. "Lady Thistle said you'd gone behind the red velvet curtain, and—"

"I was—er—looking for the necessary," I said, then took her by the arm and urged her back out to the front of the shop. I needed to think about how to proceed.

"How did that skirt fit you, Miss Holmes?" said Lady Thistle, adjusting the device at her ear as she perched once again on her blue velvet stool. "Did you find the other changing room?"

"Yes, I did, thank you. I—"

"Your mother, she always preferred to use the one back there, she did. Couldn't understand why, but she claimed she liked to be out of the way and didn't want anyone to walk in on her. Sometimes, she'd be back there trying on clothing for *hours*. Happened a few times I thought she was still here when it was time to close up, but she'd slipped out when I wasn't looking. But then, my ears aren't so good."

I was so stunned by her words and their implications that I was struck dumb, and it was Evaline's turn to maneuver me back out to the mechanical displays and the clothing she'd been mooning over.

"I don't think you should be making any sort of major purchase," I hissed when she practically ran me into one of the hat racks. "Considering your brother's financial situation."

Miss Stoker stopped dead and gave me a most affronted look, then all of the enthusiasm drained from her expression.

I felt a moment of guilt for bringing her so abruptly back to the reality of her situation, but I ignored it. I wanted to leave Lady Thistle's as quickly as possible so I could determine what to do next.

"That was quite rude," Evaline snapped at me as soon as the shop door closed behind us. "Even for you, Mina."

"Rude? I wasn't rude—*I'm not rude.*" It took me a moment to gather my thoughts. "I was just being efficient. And realistic. If your family is about to be thrown out on the street, it's an impetuous and irresponsible action to buy expensive clothing. Besides," I continued firmly, "I really only wanted to get you out of there so I could tell you about something I discovered."

Miss Stoker, who'd been marching along slightly ahead of me in an effort to demonstrate her irritation, came to a sudden halt. "So you *were* snooping back there. I had a feeling. What were you looking for?" Her eyes gleamed, and I shook my head mentally.

That was typical Evaline: quicksilver as mercury and easily distracted by anything shiny and new—especially if it was dangerous or unsuitable for a young woman. Not that I could blame her about being attracted to the dangerous and unsuitable. I had more than once thanked Miss Adler for giving me the opportunity to do more than read and knit and conduct experiments in my laboratory.

"I wasn't looking for anything. But I found a secret door."

To my surprise, my companion hardly blinked. "A secret door? Oh, *pish.* It probably leads to the alley behind the shop. I thought you'd found a drawer of corsets that hadn't been unboxed yet. I really liked that lemon-yellow one, and the boning was very flexible. I might even be able to wear it when I'm hunting the Un—" Suddenly she stopped walking *and* talking, then her eyes goggled.

"How the blooming Pete did you know about Bram's financial problems? I didn't tell you anything about it, and especially nothing about us getting thrown out on the street.

We *aren't* about to get thrown out on the street…at least, not yet, anyway." Her strident voice eased a bit and I saw the worry creep back into her eyes. "How *did* you know?"

I merely tilted my head and shrugged. The evidence had been obvious—I'd seen it all when I arrived at Grantworth House this morning. "I'm a Holmes, Miss Stoker. It's all about observation and deductive reasoning. I—"

"Never mind," she said wearily. "I shouldn't have bothered to ask." Then all at once, she straightened up and her expression brightened once more. (Quicksilver, I said.) "Now tell me more about the secret door."

"Right." My original intention this morning had been to tell her what had transpired with the insistent crow—but both times I'd attempted to do so, we'd been distracted. First by the fact that her family was in dire financial straits (and it was clearly bothering her), and second when she went off on that ridiculous tangent about Inspector Grayling.

But now was my opportunity, and so I launched into a description of how I'd come to obtain the tiny pendant, and about the symbol that was on both the charm and the closet door that hid the secret entrance.

"Carnelian is a rock, isn't it?" she asked as I concluded my explanation.

"Yes, Miss Stoker. Carnelian is a fairly common gemstone from the quartz, or chalcedony, family. Its color ranges from brilliant orange to brownish-red, and everywhere in between. There are pink carnelians as well. The stone is translucent, so light can pass through, and it's usually either polished into a smooth cabochon setting, or is carved into an image. I believe Miss Adler recently discovered a cameo made of carnelian in one of the boxes of antiquities she's been cataloguing for the Museum. An interesting characteristic of carnelian is that wax doesn't adhere to it, so it was often used as a seal to close letters in Roman times." I managed to finish speaking before Miss Stoker's eyes glazed over with boredom.

"Right then. But how do you know the pendant isn't a—a

ruby crow? Or a *garnet* crow?"

"Because Grayling recognized the charm. He gave me very little information, but what I was able to glean is that The Carnelian Crow is some sort of establishment that proper young ladies should avoid." I couldn't hold back a grin as Evaline's mouth curved into a smile.

"And, of course, as soon as you locate the place, you'll be going there."

I smiled. "Precisely."

"Grayling's not going to like that," Evaline said in that annoying, lilting voice she'd adopted earlier when the topic of the Scotland Yard investigator had arisen.

I sniffed. "Inspector Grayling has absolutely no say in regards to any of my actions."

Evaline merely smiled at me.

"We'll need to pay another visit to Lady Thistle's as soon as possible, once I've made certain preparations that will allow us to disappear in the back of the shop long enough to investigate."

My companion was still grinning. "I'd like to be there when Grayling learns you've discovered the location of The Carnelian Crow before he does."

I sniffed. I couldn't care less what Ambrose Grayling thought.

Miss Stoker

~ A Puzzle of Three-by-Three ~

LATER THAT NIGHT, MINA AND I MADE OUR WAY TO Fenman's End.

I was amused and annoyed by the fact that Mina was walking so close that she kept bumping into me. And it wasn't just her that did so. It was also the ungainly satchel she insisted on bringing. With all of her "accoutrements"—as she called them.

It wasn't as if we'd never been in more dangerous places or situations than Whitechapel. But there was no chance of us passing through Seven Dials unnoticed. Mina had armed herself with several different weapons and tools, and they clinked and clunked inside the canvas bag with every step.

When we arrived at the dismal entrance to Fenman's End, I was even more amused by her expression. She was afraid of dark, underground places, but she seemed even less interested in stepping inside the shabby, dirty, and loud pub.

"The place is filthy," she muttered into my ear as we walked inside. "Don't touch anything—or any*one*—and certainly don't eat or drink anything."

"We each have to drink an ale or they'll make us arm-wrestle with one of the regulars—barehanded; gloves aren't allowed—in order to stay," I said. Just to see her eyes pop wide with horror.

I wasn't sure whether it was because she didn't want to drink anything, or touch any of the patrons' hands.

"You're not the least bit amusing, Evaline Stoker," she said when she realized I was teasing her, and she marched past me toward the bar counter in a pair of spindly heeled copper-heel and -toed boots that were terribly impractical for Whitechapel. But I coveted them anyway.

"Oo's this?" Bilbo demanded when I slid onto a stool. Mina took one look at the chair next to mine, the grimy, sticky counter, and the barkeep as he shot a stream of tobacco onto the floor, and swayed as if she'd gone lightheaded.

I, on the other hand, ignored his question and posed one of my own. "Have you seen him?"

"I tol' ye, I ain't seen 'im. And you owe me from last night. You never paid. Two farthings." He stabbed at the counter, and I swear it sounded like he was breaking a sticky seal when he pulled his fingertip off. Then he swiped that same hand over his nose, and when it came away, there was something shiny and glistening on his hand. It looked like a pale gray garden slug.

Mina was looking even more green. Though I was tempted to linger so I could watch her squirm, I decided to get to business. After all, I was expecting her help; I didn't need her fleeing in horror or puking her guts out.

I looked toward the hidden door to Pix's lair, which was set into a wall near the bar counter. If you didn't know exactly where to look, you'd never see it.

As I dug out the coins for Bilbo, I gave a little nod in that direction. "I'm going back there." I set a sixpence on the counter—far more than the two farthings I owed—and held his eyes. He gave a bare nod and the coin disappeared.

"Come on." I didn't need to ask Mina twice; she and her blasted satchel were right on my heels again.

I'd been to Pix's underground lair twice. The hidden door, which was obscured from the rest of the pub behind a structural beam, opened to a set of stairs that led down into darkness. The previous time I'd entered from this direction, when I'd been with Pix, there had been lamps lighting the way. But not now. I sighed as Mina bumped into me from behind and curled her fingers into my arm.

It was slow going through the dark and down the stairs. She stepped on my heel twice. And once her satchel swung forward and clocked me in the hip with a clatter.

At the bottom, I took her by the arm not carrying the bag and felt my way along a rough-walled corridor. There was a dim glow where the passage ended at a door, lit by a single electric light bulb. Its illumination was weak, but enough for Mina to shake free of my hold and walk without breathing down my neck.

But here was where we came to a dead end. The door was locked by a grid of mechanized dials that only Pix would know how to open. I stared at it for a moment—it looked much different than the last time I'd been here.

Someone had been busy.

"Move," Mina said, shoving me aside. She had a slender bronze gadget in her hand about the length of a pencil. With three gritty-sounding twists, she cranked enough energy for the device to shoot out a pale gold light.

I wasn't much of a cognoggin, but I certainly appreciated that tool.

"Hmm. Looks like a combination," Mina said as she surveyed the rows of three by three brass dials with numbers on them. "Each dial has to be turned to the correct position in order for it to open. Get the right settings for each row, and its bolt will unlock. There are three rows, and three bolts to a row. I don't suppose you know the combination."

She wasn't even asking. She already knew I didn't.

I wanted more than anything to prove her wrong...but I couldn't. I didn't have the slightest idea what nine numbers would open the door.

"There is another entrance. From the outside." Not that I was certain I could find it—it was well hidden, of course, and I didn't know the streets and alleys of London like Mina did.

Blast and *drat*.

"Hush." Mina was examining the dials with the help of her illuminator and a hand-held magnifyer that looked positively medieval compared to the one in her lab that strapped over her head. She made a sound of satisfaction and, placing her ear against the door, turned one of the knobs. It made a soft clicking sound that stopped abruptly as it seemed to settle into place. "Right, then," she muttered to herself.

I waited impatiently as she worked on the second knob in

the first row. This was going to take forever. I couldn't see what she was doing, or the numbers she was turning to. I had no way to assist.

Mina turned the second knob a few clicks, listening carefully, and seemed to be satisfied with its position. She paused for a moment, staring at the problem. Then her eyes widened. "Hmm. I wonder…"

She turned the third one on the top row rather quickly into position, without even putting her ear to it. "Well, then," she muttered when it clicked into place, and then a dull *clunk* indicated that a bolt had shot open. "Oh, that is *quite* fascinating." She glanced at me with an odd smile. "One down…two to go."

Before starting on the second row, she stepped back and looked at the grid of dials. I could almost hear the cogs of her mind clicking along fluidly.

Mina nodded, then turned to examining the first dial of the second row with her magnifyer and illuminator.

Then, all at once, she smiled broadly and looked at me with that same funny expression. "Got it." She turned the first dial of the second row, made a satisfied sound, then turned the other two.

But there was no *clunk*.

"Drat," she muttered. "And I thought— No, wait. Of course. It was after midnight, so it was the following day. One must appreciate a man who pays attention to detail." She changed the middle dial one tick, and then we heard the telltale clunk. "Elementary," she said under her breath.

"Now for the third," she muttered, folding her arms over her middle. "Hmm."

It was only a moment before her eyes narrowed and she turned to me. "When is your birthday, Evaline?"

I jolted. "The nineteenth of February."

"Is that so," she muttered, and I watched as she quickly turned the dials. Click, click, click…*clunk*.

I saw the door ease in its frame as its final lock was

released. "You did it!"

Mina gave me an offended look. "Of course I did. It was really quite simple, Evaline, when—"

I didn't want to listen to her tell me how brilliant she was. I wanted to see what had happened to Pix. I pushed past her and stepped over the threshold. As there weren't any vampires about, I pulled out my knife and held it at the ready as I scanned the dark chamber.

Everything was quiet and still, and I didn't sense any other living creature but Mina, who was once again breathing down the back of my neck. I could only make out a few shapes, thanks to the drassy light in the hall.

It took me a minute to find the button for the lights. An array of electric bulbs came on with a pop and a soft sizzle, and I looked around the chamber. Though it was underground and part of a cave, one would never know it. The walls were smooth: paneled and painted, like a parlor room. The furnishings were comfortable and, I knew from experience, well made. Two sofas were arranged in a cluster with a low table between them. A desk and some shelves sat in a corner. Silk tapestries covered two of the walls, and fine rugs from India took the chill away from the stone floor. Pix had created a small dining area tucked off to one side. A massive fireplace yawned across one entire wall, and was filled with old ashes. Two tall-backed chairs in dark red upholstery were arranged in front of it.

I noticed a divider, like a large dressing screen, that cordoned off a corner of the chamber and suspected that might be where he slept—and perhaps even led to a water closet. Pix didn't seem the sort to deny himself the comfort of indoor plumbing.

But, despite its luxurious furnishings, the place looked and felt deserted.

I admit, I'd been more than a little terrified I'd find a dead or gravely injured Pix somewhere in the place. But I didn't smell anything like death. My tension eased a little.

Mina pushed past me and *tsk*ed when she saw the

number of illegal electric lights brightening the room. "I should have known," she muttered, and began to wander around.

I took the opportunity to look behind the dressing screen and felt a strange clutch in my heart. The bed was solid and quite large. It had a thick poster at each corner. The coverings were made neatly, the enormous, heavy quilt and trio of pillows smooth and untouched. For a moment, I imagined what Pix would look like sprawled on the bedding: eyes closed, limbs akimbo, dark hair mussed. His body would be relaxed and at ease.

And with no deception, no masquerade, no facial alterations.

Just him.

Only once had I seen him without some sort of disguise or clothing meant to cloak him in shadows, and even then it had been only a brief moment in faltering light.

He was always hiding something.

Always.

Just then, I felt a familiar chill prickling over the back of my neck.

I whipped the wooden stake from my hidden pocket and hurried out into the main part of the chamber where Mina was digging through the desk drawers.

"UnDead," I told her when she looked up at my sudden appearance.

Her eyes widened and she raced over to where she'd left her satchel. As she began to fumble through it, I rolled my eyes. By the time she found her stake, it would be the next century.

My amusement faded when I realized the vampires were near—and coming from the same direction we had. Had Bilbo told on us? I hadn't sensed any UnDead when we were in Fenman's End, so they must have arrived after we left.

A soft clinking sound drew my attention. It was coming from behind a small panel in the wall, and I recognized it. Why would Bilbo send down an ale from the pub?

The small, lift-like device made a soft ding when it reached the bottom. "What was that?" Mina demanded, looking around nervously.

I pointed as the little panel opened. Unlike the time I was here with Pix, when he ordered a pair of "gatters," there were no glasses inside the compartment. But there was a wooden stake.

A warning from Bilbo.

At least I knew he didn't want me dead.

I estimated there were three UnDead at the most, but I still wasn't perfect at measuring the chill at the back of my neck for distance and number of vampires.

I held a finger to my lips and gestured for Mina to hide behind the dressing screen. I made an emphatic motion for her to stay there. She wouldn't be any use and would probably just get in my way.

The chill was growing stronger, and I eased myself flat against the wall behind the open door.

Then, all at once, I had a terrible thought that made my knees go weak and my body turn to ice. My breath shook.

What if…oh, gad…*what if the vampire was Pix?*

Miss Stoker

*~ In Which Our Heroines Are Bathed in
the Delicate Aroma of UnDead Ash ~*

*No. No. **No.***

I couldn't allow myself to even consider that possibility.

My mouth was dry. I gripped the stake with one hand, and the interior doorknob with the other. The back of my neck was pure ice. My heart raced. I could see Mina poking around the edge of the screen.

And I could smell the vampires: dank, dead, and evil.

Please. Not Pix.

I waited until the right moment, watching through the crack between the door hinges and the wall. As soon as the first one stepped through the entrance, I rammed the door at him as hard as I could, then pulled it back. As the first vampire fell back onto his companions, I jumped out, ready for attack.

It took me only a second to see that, no, none of the three were Pix.

I didn't even have an instant to be thankful. I took advantage of their surprise and flew into action, swiping down with a powerful thrust into the heart of the first vampire. He *poofed* into a cloud of musty, evil ash, and I swirled through it as I swung up and around at the second vampire.

I grunted with fury as I caught him harmlessly on the arm, then ducked as he lunged at me. I bumped into the third vampire—a female—and punched her in the face as I came upright.

She grabbed for me with long-nailed fingers. I tried for a deathblow to her heart, but she laughed and tripped me. I fell backward, but somersaulted away and sprang to my feet.

"Fancy move," she hissed, her eyes red and glowing. Her fangs were distended and seemed more delicate than most. Still, I had no desire to have myself impaled upon them. I spun around when she rushed toward me, causing the wall hanging to billow behind me. From the corner of my eye, I saw her companion rushing in to join the fray, and I angled to face them both.

Two against one, hm?

I yanked the tapestry from its moorings with one vicious pull, and flung it at them in a broad, whipping motion. It snarled the attackers just long enough for me to grab the female by the arm and yank her into my stake.

Poof! She was gone, but my legs had become tangled in the tapestry, and suddenly a cloud of silk weave tufted over my head. I was blinded long enough for two strong hands to grab and fling me away. Someone shrieked (Mina, of course) as I flew through the air.

I crashed against the far wall. The impact knocked out my breath—and it *hurt*. I was shaken, in a big ball of pain, gasping for air in a room filled with vampire dust. For a moment I couldn't move; then I had to. I tried to pull to my feet as the last attacker lunged at me.

I dodged too late. He caught me by the front of my bodice and whipped me against the wall again. My head banged backward and I heard a soft *snap* at the back of my skull. I nearly lost hold of my stake, and now there were black shadows flickering in my vision…and then red lights.

No. The red lights were the vampire's eyes: glowing with fury…and hunger. They caught my gaze, grabbing it like a fist, and held. I couldn't pull away, and his burning eyes tugged and pulled and coaxed. I saw the gleam of his long fangs, curved and malicious, ready to plunge. I pushed against him, trying to hold him off as his hypnotic gaze bored into me…luring me into its hot, red trap.

Though I fought it, the fight began to drain from my body: my knees weakened and my thoughts became mushy. I felt as if I were walking through a thick soup of gray glop. My heartbeat was trapped by his, and his was stronger. I felt my pulse thudding, hard and dull, as the blood in my veins strained to be freed.

My fingers loosened, and I was aware of the stake slipping. Terror flooded me, and somehow I managed to hold on to my only weapon. I trained all my efforts, my thoughts, my intentions on that slender piece of ash. Focusing on the sensation of holding the smooth, lethal wood saved me.

The thrall that held me shivered, straining like a piece of web being pulled too taut. I fought harder, silently and desperately, as his eyes glowed brighter and more captivating.

Just as I broke free—as the web of his control snapped—he plunged toward my throat.

I cried out, going rigid as his fangs drove into my skin. The surge of blood being released from my straining veins was both a relief and a horror, and I felt the last bit of my control sap as the UnDead feasted on me.

But I still held the stake. I was vaguely, softly aware of the slender pike in my hand. I had to hold on, but the world was becoming murky and dark and soft and—

I heard a shriek in the distance, and suddenly a great jolt caused my attacker to lose his grip on me. His fangs dragged free from my neck. I stumbled backward, somehow managing to remain upright as I bumped into the tapestry-covered wall behind me.

Though the blood flowed from my wound, I was free. I was glad I was the one bleeding and not anyone else, since I couldn't actually *see* the blood on me at the time. The sight of blood and gore can…well, it can paralyze me at times.

Someone screamed my name, and I shook the last bit of fog from my head and looked over to see that Mina was *on the vampire's back*, clutching him from behind, around the neck. She held on for dear life as he spun and tried to peel her hands away from his throat—no, it was a stake she held there across his Adam's apple, gripped on either end.

Despite the pain coursing through me, and the black and white lights flashing through my eyes, I grinned at the sight of the awkward, two-headed "beast"—and then I flowed into action.

Just as the vampire was about to ram backward into the wall, crushing Mina, I whipped the stake through the air.

He cried out and froze, then exploded into dust. Mina plunked bonelessly to the ground, but I wasn't paying attention.

I spun around, pulling out a second stake—this time from my boot—prepared for another attack. I stopped when I realized the back of my neck was no longer frigid with cold. That was all of them, then. Three.

Mina pulled to her feet, her chest heaving with exertion. "I am not"—she puffed, leaning against the wall as she held a hand to her front—"ashamed to…say…that…that…was particularly…terrifying."

I realized I was shaking. Hot, wet blood coursed down the front of my bodice. My belly rolled unpleasantly. My knees were about to give out.

I sat down, still breathing hard.

I'd almost died. And Mina Holmes—*Mina Holmes!*—had sort of saved my life.

"Thank you," I managed. "If you hadn't jumped on him…"

"Right."

That was all she said. She must really be shaken if she was reduced to a single syllable.

"You didn't have the chance to interrogate him?" I asked wryly. My breathing was back under control. But my pride—and the rest of my body—ached. "You were, after all, tête-à-tête for several minutes there." I heard a strange, high giggle. It came from me.

Mina gave a sharp bark of laughter as well. "I begin to see your point."

We'd had an ongoing discussion—an argument, really—about why I'd never taken the time to try and get information from a vampire. She'd criticized me more than once for dusting the creatures too quickly. And Mina had even made comments in the past about how "anyone" could stake a vampire. Maybe she was beginning to see my point of view.

"But," she said in a voice that was steadier, "I did have the opportunity to notice something important—and troubling— from my position of attack. That was," she added too smoothly for me to believe her, "the reason I jumped on him in that manner."

"What?"

"Two small marks at the back of his neck."

A chill that had nothing to do with sensing the UnDead rushed through me. "Like the vampires the Ankh was torturing in her underground lair? And the museum guard she killed during the chess queen fiasco?"

"Precisely. Exactly, in fact. One mark, or insertion point, on either side of the nape of his neck. Unfortunately, I had the opportunity for a close examination while you were—er— pulling yourself together. Thank you," she added hastily, as if to forestall any response. "You dispatched three of them, after all. I did very little in the grand scheme of things."

I nodded. We understood each other: we'd both contributed to what might have been a much more unpleasant situation. Possibly a fatal one.

"You do realize what those two marks mean," Mina continued.

Unfortunately, I did. "The Ankh is still working with Pix's small devices—what did Dylan call them? Batteries? To try and control the vampires." A stab of fear caught me in the belly. The Ankh certainly had it in for Pix. She'd killed him by using one of those very same devices. If it hadn't been for Mina's friend from the future, Pix would still be dead.

He could be dead again.

"Yes. I'm certain our UnDead visitors tonight were minions of our favorite arch-criminal the Ankh." Mina slung the satchel over her shoulder. "I've seen what I need to see here."

My body was throbbing from head to toe. I smelled like vampire dust—it had clogged my nose and mouth and frosted my eyelashes and brows—and by the way, I was still bleeding from the bite.

Mina frowned as she looked at me. "You're quite a mess, Evaline. And you're still dripping blood all over and down your bodice. If we aren't careful, we'll attract more UnDead from the scent. Here, put my cloak around you or we'll never get a cab. Don't you have any salted holy water with you? Honestly, I don't know how you can call yourself prepared…" She began to rummage in her satchel. "We should leave as expediently as possible, and I don't believe it would be prudent to make our exit back the way we came, since that was the direction from which the vampires came. Your appearance might cause comment. Here." She thrust a small vial at me. "Use it."

As I poured the salted holy water on my wound, (gritting my teeth at the screaming pain), Mina started toward the other door that I knew led up to the street from a different direction than Fenman's End. Apparently, she'd discovered the secondary exit during her snooping.

"And then there's the consideration that the arrival of the UnDead on the premises so quickly after our arrival has merely confirmed my deductions about Mr. Pix's fate."

My heart sank as I followed her through the opening, which closed and locked behind us with a different mechanism of clicking, clunking cogs. She had cranked up her pocket illuminator and beamed it down the crooked tunnel ahead of us.

"You think Pix is dead. Or captured." I dreaded her answer.

"*Evaline.* How many times must I tell you that it's not a matter of mere *thinking*—at least in the way *you* and everyone else goes about doing it, nattering on with different scenarios and options and opinions. It's a matter of *observation*—"

"And deduction. I *know.* Can you skip the blasted lecture and just tell me?" My voice was high and tight, echoing eerily in the damp stone corridor, but I didn't care. And every time I took a breath, I inhaled more vampire ash. It was disgusting. "I suppose he's probably dead. Or the Ankh took him." I tried to keep my voice neutral. I don't think I succeeded.

"On the contrary, Miss Stoker," Mina said, glancing back at me. "It's my belief that not only did he expect you to come here, looking for him—with my guidance, naturally—but also that Mr. Pix is very much alive."

Miss Holmes

~ *Wherein a Pickpocket's Devotion is Revealed* ~

"YOU THINK PIX IS ALIVE?" MISS STOKER'S VOICE—WHICH sounded far more relaxed and boisterous than it had been a moment earlier—reverberated in the tunnel. Unfortunately, the closed space contributed to the rank smell of dead vampire dust, which wafted from her with every movement. "How do you know that? And why do you think he expected me to come looking for him?"

With this last, however, her tone changed to affront. Apparently, my companion didn't like to be anticipated.

"Evaline." I sighed. Being a Holmes and blessed with impeccable deductive reasoning was exhausting. "It's patently obvious he expected you—obvious, at least, to someone who was paying attention. But I shall endeavor to explain, since you are clearly missing the data to inform your own decision. Once we get out into the fresh air," I added forcefully. "I cannot think clearly when I'm boxed in like this."

I gave my Flip-Illuminator another two sharp cranks, as it appeared to be dimming. It would not do for the light to flicker or waver, for I wasn't fond of dark spaces, especially narrow, close ones underground like this—which was a problem, because it seemed as if every case Evaline and I took on brought me, at one time or another, into dark, deep places. Villains and criminals tended to congregate underground.

That was why I was walking as quickly as possible through this warren of tunnels to get to the exit. Instead of being fixated on my surroundings in the narrow, dim space, I focused on where my beam illuminated the uneven stone floor —for it enabled me to track which direction to go due to a number of different markings and clues (for expediency, I needn't list them here).

To my relief and delight, Evaline not only refrained from

continuing to badger me, she pushed ahead to take the lead on our way out.

It was only another few moments before she warily pushed open a door, poking her head around to ascertain the level of danger or safety, and then—apparently assured of the latter—beckoned me to follow her.

There would be no chance of getting a hackney at this time of night, especially in this neighborhood. I looked at the moon's position and figured the time to be two o'clock. An instant later, both Big Ben and the pink-faced cogwork clock on the tallest spire of the Oligary Building bellowed out in tandem: *bong...bong...*

The two different tolls reverberated over the sleeping city from different directions, clashing and mingling in a pleasant discord. I'd taken two steps out into a street that seemed relatively deserted—and relatively clear of refuse—when Evaline grabbed my arm and fairly whipped me back into the shadows.

"What on ear—"

She didn't speak, but, keeping us both in shadows, pointed soundlessly to the sky.

I looked up. We were in a poor, dangerous, ramshackle part of London that didn't boast the many street levels of the areas I normally frequented—nor did it contain the tall, swaying buildings connected across the street by fly-walks at various levels. Here, though the roads were narrow and crowded, the buildings were no more than three stories high.

Which made it easier for the sleek black airship I saw to glide through the night...closer to the ground than it would normally be able to navigate.

I'd never seen a vessel like it before. Though it wasn't very large, its shape was long and narrow, with a sharp, finlike tail and wings resembling those of a bat. A cold white beam of light that I knew could not be conducted from gas or oil shot from the bottom of the front part of the ship and scanned slowly over the streets and buildings below.

For some reason, it gave me the feeling of a malevolent eye searching for something.

Whatever it was—I didn't know and wasn't yet prepared to conjecture—it spooked Evaline enough that she forced me to remain in the shadows and silent (even though it would be impossible for any of the airship's inhabitants to hear our conversation from that distance) until the vessel had glided off into the night.

"What was it?" I was finally permitted to ask.

"I don't know. I'm not certain. I just know I don't want it to see me."

She spoke as if the airship itself were a sentient being. I had more questions, but contained my curiosity for the time being. Instead I remained silent and contemplative until we located a hackney cab (this required several blocks of ambulation, and I began to regret having put quite so many items into my satchel).

Thankfully, the driver didn't seem to notice Evaline's wounds, and allowed us to climb aboard. Thus we did finally settle into seats inside the cab, and Evaline turned to me as soon as the vehicle lurched into motion.

"Explain," she demanded rudely. "How do you know Pix was expecting me to come, and how do you know he's alive?"

"To be clear, I am *fairly* certain he is still alive—and in hiding—but, of course, until we produce him, you cannot hold me to that particular guarantee. There's always the chance that some unexpected mishap might have befallen him." I saw her jaw move as she audibly ground her teeth, and I hastened to continue. "But he was alive when he left his quarters, and, by all appearances, he left willingly and under his own steam. I suspect he went into hiding because of some danger I cannot yet confirm, but would deduce it's related to the incident with the Ankh when we found him in her underground lair."

"And how did you know he expected me?"

I shook my head. Really, hadn't she been paying attention *at all?* "The locks on the door, Evaline."

Even in the drassy light fighting through the hack's dirty windows, I could discern the blank expression in her eyes.

I sighed again. "There were three rows of locks. Each row had a dial that had to be set at a particular number. The first row of numbers was six-two-nine."

It took her a moment to make the connection. "How coincidental. That's the address of Grantworth House. Six-two-nine Claremont-circle."

I nodded encouragingly.

But she still wasn't fully comprehending, so it was necessary to prod her thought process.

"The third row was one-nine-two," I prompted. When she didn't respond, I looked at her without bothering to hide my growing frustration. "Surely those numbers are familiar to you, *as you just told them to me a short while ago.*"

"Oh! Right. My birthday. The nineteenth of February…" At last the dawning of comprehension began to light her eyes. "I see. And what was the middle row?"

"Two-six-four." I waited. Then, "It's another date, Evaline."

"The twenty-sixth of April?"

"Right." When further recognition didn't seem forthcoming, I was required to coax her along. "What day did you first meet Mr. Pix?"

"Well…it would have been the day Miss Adler first sent the message to meet her at the British Museum. The—er— what was it? Oh, yes. The twenty-fifth of April."

I nodded. "That was my first thought as well, but realize that although the message from Miss Adler *arrived* on the twenty-fifth, we actually met with her at midnight—which would make it the twenty-sixth. And you had your first encounter with Mr. Pix *after* we met with Miss Adler and discovered Mayellen Hodgeworth's body in the museum."

"Of course!" Miss Stoker seemed as pleased with herself

as if she'd come to the conclusion all on her own. "So the entire lock combination was made up of numbers that were…that were…"

"That were familiar to you. He clearly chose those numbers so that you—or, more accurately, *I*—would be able to gain access to his underground lair."

Evaline mulled over that for a moment. I waited patiently for her to catch up with my thought process. She was remarkably quick to do so. "If he wanted us to get inside, then there must have been a reason."

"Precisely." I had been waiting for this moment since I realized how simple and yet cunning were the combinations to his door. Mr. Pix was growing—ever so slightly—in my esteem. I still knew him to be a delinquent and corrupt criminal, but he was also proving to be rather intelligent and resourceful. "And I believe this is what he meant for us to find." I held out my hand to show her the tiny object.

She peered at it. "What is it?"

"This little pendant, my dear Miss Stoker, is the aforementioned sign of The Carnelian Crow."

Miss Stoker

~ A Convoluted Explanation That Includes a History of the Fiction of the UnDead ~

"What does that mean?" I asked. "That he left it for us to find? How do you know he *meant* for us to find that little charm, anyway? Was there a blooming *note* with it?"

Mina's voice became a little frosty. "I don't need a note to know he wanted us to find it, Evaline. Besides, if he left a note, someone else might have discovered it, and—"

"Then how can you be certain?" For all I knew, Pix could have been *hiding* the tiny carnelian crow from everyone —including us.

"Because the charm was hidden inside *Frankenstein*."

"The book?"

"Yes, of course. Isn't it obvious it was a message for us?"

I blinked. Then shook my head sharply. I was hoping to dislodge whatever was keeping me from seeing the "obvious."

Mina sighed gustily. "Very well, then. I suppose I shall have to explain. But it really is very obvious, Evaline. *Frankenstein*, by Mary Shelley, of course, is about a monster created by Dr. Frankenstein when he tries to animate a human—and it gets out of hand. That information alone might draw one's attention to the book—given the activities of our nemesis the Ankh and what she has been doing with her batteries. Surely Mr. Pix hasn't forgotten that she tried to *un*-animate him, and is trying to control the UnDead using her own devices.

"But even more to the point, hiding the charm inside the book was a message for you in particular, Evaline."

"Because…why?"

"Because of 'The Vampyre,' of course."

I blinked again. I was really, *really* trying to follow her… "The vampire? What does *Frankenstein* have to do with a vampire? Because they're both monsters?" I asked.

Mina appeared ready to explode. "First of all, Frankenstein wasn't a monster. He was the *scientist* trying to *create* the monster. It was *Frankenstein's monster*. And 'The Vampyre' was a short story, written by John Polidori, who was…?" She left off, expecting me to fill in the blank.

I shrugged. "Just tell me, Mina. Please. Before I scream."

She drew herself up as if insulted. "Very well. But you *asked*. 'The Vampyre' was the first piece of literature—published, anyway—that ever depicted a vampire realistically. That is, having the appearance of a normal person, but one who is immortal, drinks blood, and is sensitive to sunlight. The short story was written by John Polidori—who, by the way, died under mysterious circumstances…" She frowned. "Now that I think of it, I believe I read somewhere that your great-grandmother Victoria Gardella might have had some involvement in that event."

I gave a frustrated scream inside the back of my throat without opening my mouth, and Mina huffed, but continued.

"John Polidori happened to be the personal physician of the poet Lord Byron. They were also friends with the other poet Percy Bysshe Shelley, who was married to…*Mary Shelley*. They very famously spent a summer together in Switzerland. It must have been around 1819 or so; I'll have to check the date to be—"

"No need," I muttered.

"That summer on Lake Geneva was particularly rainy and dreary, with a lot of storms. And it was Mary Shelley who suggested a contest: that they each try to write a horror story as a way to while away the time. Mary Shelley produced *Frankenstein* during that summer—or a draft of it—and Lord Byron began to write a story about a gentleman vampire."

"I thought you said John Polidori wrote—"

"He *did*. Byron never finished the piece, but Polidori apparently found it very interesting and asked if he could take the idea and write his own story. Byron gave permission, and Polidori wrote what became known as 'The Vampyre,' and modeled its main UnDead character, Lord Ruthven, after

Byron himself. So now, clearly, even you can see the connection, Evaline. Your Mr. Pix cut out a hole in a book that has a direct connection to your vocation as a vampire hunter. He hid the charm inside as a message to you and left the book where we would find it. On his desk—along with a book by Edgar Allan Poe. But I suppose you don't see that connection either." She sighed as if greatly injured.

I ignored that last bit because Mina's explanation did make sense. And Pix was very clever. I certainly wouldn't have known about the connection of *Frankenstein* to vampires, but no one would be surprised that Mina did.

I sat up straight. "How in the world does a simple Cockney pickpocket know all about 'The Vampyre' and *Frankenstein* and their connections?"

Mina's eyes widened, gleaming like marbles in the dim light. I'd actually taken her by surprise.

"That, my dear Miss Stoker, is a very good question. A *very* good question. Perhaps there is more to that reprobate than meets the eye."

I'd been thinking that for months.

"Right, then," I said. "And since he didn't leave us a note—"

"He couldn't leave us a note, Evaline. What if someone else got access—"

"I was *joking*," I fired back, tired of being made to feel less brilliant than a Holmes. But—everyone else was, weren't they? At least I was stronger and faster because of my vampire-hunting legacy. And I healed quickly—which was a good thing, considering the jagged wound on the top of my shoulder. And I'd killed three UnDead tonight while Mina… Well, it was best if I didn't think about how she'd probably saved my life. I was already about to strangle her.

Unaware of my uncharitable thoughts, Mina was still speaking. "One can only infer Pix wants us to locate—and visit—The Carnelian Crow. Perhaps we will find answers there. Tomorrow, I shall make arrangements for our second visit to Lady Thistle's. I shall call for you at three o'clock. Please be prepared and fully equipped for any eventuality that might occur," she added pointedly. "For I suspect we will soon be setting foot inside the mysterious Carnelian Crow."

If Inspector Grayling could hear the zeal in her voice, he would probably lock her up in a jail cell and throw the key into the automated sewers.

We rode in silence for a while. I was feeling a little better about Pix's fate.

But the thought of Pix brought me back to the uglier part of my day. And the impossible decision that loomed ahead of me.

"I have to find a husband," I blurted out.

"A husband? What on earth are you talking— *Oh.*" Mina must have done some of her famous deductive reasoning, for she stopped talking. That alone was concerning—that even Mina Holmes didn't have anything to say about it.

I was truly in a fix. "If I don't get married—or at least engaged before the New Year—Florence told me we'll have to go back to Dublin. And live with my parents." I stared out the window and watched the angular blobs of dark, shadowy buildings pass by. Whenever the hackney approached a gas lamp, the area brightened…then faded as we trundled past.

Just like my thoughts. I had been able to forget about my sister-in-law's plea for most of the evening—but now my family's plight was brought back into the moment and fully illuminated before I pushed it back into the dark once more. I wished I could leave it there.

But I couldn't.

"I don't have any other option." Maybe there was a part of me hoping the brilliant Mina Holmes would come up with a different solution.

"That is most distressing. At the very least, having a husband would put far more restrictions on your participation in our investigative activities—not to mention your nocturnal vampire hunting—than your current situation."

What could I say? She was horribly correct. And certainly wasn't saying anything I hadn't already thought.

To my relief, at that moment the hackney pulled up to 629 Claremont-circle. Grantworth House stood bathed in moonlight, stately and calm. The sight of my ancestral home, and the reminder that it might soon no longer belong to us— and what I would have to do to ensure that didn't happen— brought unexpected tears to my eyes.

I fairly leaped out of the hack so Mina wouldn't see. "Good night," I called softly as I closed the door. As I walked across the thin layer of snow to the tree that gave access to my bedchamber window, I couldn't help but scan the edges of the lawn and along the street.

But there was no sign of Pix loitering in the shadows. Nor were there any footprints other than my own.

As I vaulted myself into the lowest branch of the oak, I sent up a fervent hope Mina was right: that Pix was still alive, and that he'd gone into hiding on his own.

Just as I climbed in through my window, another dark thought—somehow worse than all the others—struck me.

Once I got married, I wouldn't be able to kiss Pix. Ever again.

THE NEXT MORNING, MY EYES WERE GRITTY WHEN I finally peeled them open. It had been another difficult night.

But at least I had an adventure to look forward to later today. The Carnelian Crow—if we did actually find it through the door in the back of the closet at Lady Thistle's— sounded both dangerous and exciting. The adventure could be even more fun than the night Mina and I dressed up like men in order to infiltrate a men's club (of course, that didn't end very well for Mr. Dancy, but it was a rousing success until then).

I checked the clock and was surprised to see it was nearly

noon. I didn't normally sleep that late—if you could call what I'd been doing sleeping.

I pushed the bell to call Pepper, and as I climbed out of bed, I caught sight of myself in the mirror. Good gad! Even though I'd applied salted holy water, the bite wounds on my neck looked *horrendous*. I was going to have to wear something to hide my neck for the next few days.

With that in mind, I began to search through the wardrobe for something to wear for the day's excursion.

"There you are, sleepyhead," said Florence, bustling in behind Pepper, who carried a tray with tea and a small breakfast.

What was she doing in here? I gasped and barely had time to grab a crocheted shawl to pull up and around my neck, hiding the marks there.

My sister-in-law didn't appear to notice. In fact, she seemed surprisingly chipper after yesterday's grave announcement, and a wild ripple of hope rushed through me. Maybe something had happened yesterday to change things. Maybe Bram had come up with a different solution, or sold out a new show, or maybe he'd even sold his novel (which I didn't think was finished) for a lot of money. Or maybe they'd refigured the finances, and realized they'd left off a zero somewhere.

Maybe someone rich had died and left us a pot-load of money.

"I almost came in to wake you two hours ago, but I thought you should get some extra beauty sleep last night." Florence peered closely at me then *tsk*ed—perhaps noticing that I hadn't slept all that well—and turned to the wardrobe. "Well, we'll need to pick out something particularly fetching for today. Something that shows off your dark hair and will bring out the green flecks in your eyes. What about that forest-colored velvet bodice, with the midnight-blue over-skirt?" Her voice became muffled as she poked around inside the closet.

The piece of toast I'd bitten into stuck in my throat. "Why," I managed to say in a dry voice that grated, "do I need to look particularly fetching today?"

"It's Wednesday, Evaline. We are home to callers every Wednesday from two until four." Florence backed out of the wardrobe, her arms filled with petticoats, skirts, and at least two different bodices. "You know that."

"Well, yes, I know, but *you're* the one they come to call on—"

"And they are all coming today. To meet you."

I felt as if the floor was suddenly disintegrating around me. The room tilted. I clutched the shawl tighter around my throat. Maybe if it was tight enough, I'd strangle.

"Who…all?" I managed to ask, but the stricken expression on Pepper's face answered my question.

Florence stilled and her too-bright expression faded. She appeared annoyed. "Evaline, a number of suitable candidates for you to marry are coming to call at two o'clock."

The single bite of toast I'd managed to swallow suddenly became as large and heavy as an anvil in my belly. "Today? I have to— Today? But I-I have a prior engagement this afternoon, Flo. I'm sorry." I forced a smile.

She skewered me with a look she hadn't used since she found out I'd attended the Cosgrove-Pitts' Roses Ball without her. "Does this engagement happen to be with a man suitable —and wealthy—enough to be your husband?"

"Er…" I wish I could have lied, but she would have caught me out anyway. "No."

"Evaline, I thought you understood the severity of the situation—and the necessity of settling on a husband as quickly as possible. You have no idea how careful I had to be in arranging for today's tea without letting on to everyone how dire our situation is. It was a delicate—very delicate— project, but I feel confident I handled it properly."

"Right," I said weakly. My knees felt as if they were about to give out. No. This couldn't be happening. Not today, not so soon…

"A simple, casual word to Lady Veness—hardly more than a hint, really—about how eager you were to settle on a husband. Then she and her big mouth took care of the rest," continued my sister-in-law, completely oblivious to my horror and distress. "She's been wanting to get you off the marriage mart so her granddaughter has a chance to snare a wealthy husband. They've all been waiting for you, you know. You're quite a catch, my dear." Her eyes were bright with pride and tears. "You're young and beautiful, and kind and funny—and you come from a good family."

"I—er—I need to send word to Miss Holmes that I am otherwise engaged this afternoon," I said numbly.

What did she mean, *they'd all been waiting for me*? Who? A slew of boring, stuffy bachelors who would want to control me once I became a wife?

Surely no one expected me to make a decision *today*. I looked at Florence, whose expression had turned steely. My emotions sank.

Maybe she did.

Perhaps Mina could figure out a way to extricate me. Maybe she could contact her father. Sir Mycroft Holmes worked for the Home Office and was considered indispensable to national security (or something like that), and she could have him call me away. No one would deny Sir Mycroft what he needed.

"It's a pity that poor Mr. Dancy died," Florence said, pausing for a moment to look genuinely sad. "He was such a pleasant and handsome young man."

Now my throat burned from unshed tears. Mr. Dancy. If there had been one man I might have *considered* considering for my husband, it would have been him.

This can't be happening.

But it was.

I managed to pen a desperate note to Mina without Flo looking over my shoulder (she was too busy picking out my jewelry). I gave it to Pepper, who would make certain it got delivered to the Holmes residence as soon as possible.

Then I had no choice but to submit to my sister-in-law's edict and get ready to choose a husband—all the while making certain she didn't see the bite marks on my neck.

I felt like I was going to puke.

And that nauseated feeling hadn't gone away when, less than two hours later, I was ensconced in the larger parlor to await my guests.

Florence had pulled out all the stops and sent Pepper off to the market to get the expensive tea biscuits (Ballenger's Biscuits for a Genteel Gathering), along with a stop at the pastry shop for the tiny pink shrimp and salmon cloud-cakes favored by the Queen. Florence had also arranged for one of Pepper's cousins—he was a footman in an earl's household—to come on his day off and help serve. That was to make it look like we had more staff than we actually did.

My sister-in-law was sparing no expense to put on a good show, and a surge of guilt swirled with the nausea in my belly. She shouldn't be spending all this money we didn't have.

But since she was, I had no choice but to do my best. It was in my power to keep us from getting thrown out of Grantworth House and sent back to Dublin.

Maybe it wouldn't be as terrible as I imagined. Hadn't my great-grandmother Victoria Gardella gotten married? I wasn't certain how that had worked, but surely she came up with a way to sneak out at night and do the necessary vampire hunting to keep London safe. After all, it was she who'd chased all of the UnDead out of the city seventy years ago. They hadn't had the temerity to return until now.

Which brought me to the curious—and troubling—information Mina had shared about the two marks she'd seen on the back of the vampire's neck. The Ankh must be at her experiments again—which was another, more serious reason for me to *not* be sitting like a prize mare in the parlor, waiting to be examined and bid upon by a slew of possible husbands.

Fury sliced through me. The Ankh had been right about

one thing: why *did* women have to be subjected to the whims and will of men? Why *did* we have to sit neatly and quietly at home and sew and bear children (I shuddered at the thought) and run the household, while men were able to do whatever they wanted? Even have their own clubs? Live alone? *Travel* alone? Run businesses?

The heat of anger and frustration—and fear—rose inside me, and I felt even more stifled by my restrictive corset (yet another atrocity inflicted on women by the men of society). I couldn't breathe, and my head felt light…

And then the parlor door opened and the first of our callers was announced.

Florence gave me a meaningful look, and I rose. I probably greeted Mr. Broomall and his sister appropriately, but I don't remember. It felt as if I were swimming underwater: everything was muted and slow. And I couldn't breathe.

I'd just begun to take my seat when the door opened again, and more guests entered: two more potential husbands.

And then, moments later, another—this time with an elder sister and her friend accompanying him. And then a trio of candidates. And then another.

It was hardly half past two and the parlor was crowded with nearly twenty people. Lady Veness had apparently come through with spreading the gossip, regardless of her personal motivations.

I knew everyone at least by face, and mostly by name. I'd met all of them at one time or another, as there aren't that many of us who move about in the higher levels of London Society. (I spared a moment of envy that the Holmeses weren't part of this upper stratum of "peerage," so Mina didn't have to deal with being a broodmare on display.)

Florence was beaming over the success of the event. The conversation in the chamber was so loud that I could only hear the people sitting near me. I don't believe the parlor had ever been that filled with people. However, during the entire affair, I was constantly adjusting the unusually high, lacy neckline of my bodice to hide the marks on my neck.

I received offers to attend the theater, to ride in St. James Park, and to attend Christmas fêtes and dances and dinner parties. Each activity would, of course, be chaperoned by sisters, mothers, or maids until I selected a husband and was formally engaged.

Unfortunately, they were all a blur. Not one of the men I spoke with seemed like someone I'd want to spend the rest of my life with.

Ugh. The very thought made my insides churn. *The rest of my life? With one of the men in this room?*

That was far different than agreeing to take a carriage ride in the park, or attend a dinner party.

As the door opened yet again, I thought desperately that this would be the *perfect* time for Pix to make one of his unexpected appearances. Where was the dratted man when I really needed him?

I immediately thrust away that thought. I didn't need Pix —or any other man—to save me. I would figure out this mess myself. And if I had to make the ultimate sacrifice—

"Miss Stoker."

The voice came from behind me. I turned to discover that a man had maneuvered through the crowded room to position himself just behind the settee on which I was sitting. I gave him credit for being clever enough to approach from the rear while everyone else clustered around the table in front of me.

I craned my head to look at him. The restriction of my corset didn't readily allow me to twist, so I rose just enough to adjust my seat so I was facing the arm of the settee where he stood. "I don't believe we've met," I said, readjusting my blasted bustle on the seat. Although he did look familiar...

He was a pleasant-looking man, and I could tell right away he was wealthy—based on the tailoring and stylishness of his clothing. He was quite a bit older than me—perhaps thirty—and boasted a head of wiry, sandy-brown hair. He wore long sideburns and a neat mustache. His gloves were spotless white, and he held a delicate cup of tea in one hand.

"Ned Oligary," he replied with a little bow. "At your service."

"Oligary?" I repeated, swiftly moving my hand out of the way when he leaned against the arm of the settee to lean closer.

He gave a rueful smile. "My older brother is Emmett. I expect you've heard of him."

Who hadn't heard of Emmett Oligary? The richest, most famous businessman in England—and possibly the Continent as well. The Oligary Building, with its sharp black spires that seemed to pierce the sky, was as much of a landmark as Big Ben and Westminster.

I would never forget the Oligary Building, for that was the place I'd staked my very first vampire. At least, as far as I knew for certain. I had had a previous encounter, but I didn't remember what actually happened. And Siri hadn't been around for me to ask.

"I've not only heard of your brother, I've met him," I replied. "When the Betrovians were in town."

"I know." Mr. Oligary's eyes glinted. "At the welcome ball for the princess and her contingent. I attended as well. Unfortunately, I was unable to locate your dance folio, Miss Stoker, or we would have had the pleasure of officially meeting before now. I'm delighted to have rectified the matter today."

My cheeks warmed. I had hidden my dance card at the ball because I wanted to avoid as many dances as possible.

"I'm honored to meet you—even belatedly," I replied with a smile.

"I would consider it an honor if you—and a chaperone, of course—would join me at New Vauxhall Gardens tomorrow night for the unveiling of the Christmas decorations. Emmett tells me you enjoyed your first visit there some months ago. I can't guarantee the weather, but I can promise we won't have to wait in line for any of the attractions." He smiled broadly, revealing a particularly nice set of teeth.

I had to admit, his invitation was the best one I'd received thus far. "That would be lovely, Mr. Oligary."

I happened to look over just as the parlor door opened once more. The new arrival was Mina Holmes.

From her shocked expression, I could tell she hadn't received my message.

Miss Holmes

~ *Wherein a Lengthy Conversation Leaves Much Unsaid~*

THE EVENTS OF MY DAY HAD NOT GONE AT ALL AS PLANNED (it included a row with Mrs. Raskill over my upending a bowl of biscuit batter—an occurrence that required me to change my clothing—among other things), and arriving at Grantworth House to discover that Miss Stoker was completely unavailable to accompany me back to Lady Thistle's was the proverbial icing on the cake. (To be clear, I am a proponent of iced cakes—what is the point of having one without the sugary glaze?—but I speak metaphorically here.)

I wasted no further time at Grantworth House and took my leave, in spite of the desperation in Evaline's eyes that begged me to bring her with me. I might at some point find a way to extricate her from the increasingly imminent nuptials Mrs. Stoker had planned, but today was not to be the day.

I'm not ashamed to admit my mood had gone sour and that I might have stomped a bit as I made my way back to the hackney—on which I had wasted the money to ride over to St. James on a fool's errand. Evaline could have sent word that our plans were altered. (Although, to be fair, I'd been gone from home on a variety of errands for several hours prior to arriving at her house.) I might possibly also have slammed the door a bit harder than necessary once I climbed inside.

And then I stifled a shriek when I saw I wasn't alone in the cab.

"Good gad! What on *earth* are you doing here, you—you —" I couldn't find the right word, for my brains had momentarily deserted me due to shock.

"Ever'thing all right, miss?" called the hackney driver from his perch outside the carriage. He'd started the mechanized vehicle, then stopped it—both times with a violent lurch.

"Er—yes," I called back, then rapped on the ceiling to let him know he could lurch off again. "Carry on."

I turned my attention to the sharp-eyed man sitting in the shadowy corner of the vehicle. A fine hat—too fine for a mere street thief—rode low over his forehead, and I was fairly certain he was wearing a false nose. Definitely the hair that tufted out from beneath the edge of his bowler didn't belong to him. It was bright, frizzy, and red.

"Mr. Pix, do you realize you nearly stopped my heart?"

"Wot's going on 'ere?" he asked, rudely ignoring my more than fair questions. He gestured to the row of carriages we passed as the hack trundled away from Grantworth House. "Ever'thing all right wit' Evaline?"

I folded my gloved hands primly in my lap. This was the first time I could remember being alone with the scoundrel—except for when he carried me out of a burning opium den.

Over his shoulder.

Over his *bare, muscular* shoulder, while he was wearing that bolero-style vest *with no shirt* beneath it.

My cheeks felt hot, and I was a little prickly. Which is probably why I responded in the blunt manner with which I did. "Evaline is just fine. In fact, she's going to be getting married very soon." He might as well know so he'd stop sniffing around Evaline with his irresponsible, disreputable self.

The air in the carriage changed—seeming to be sucked out of it all of a sudden—as if a giant vacuum machine was at the door. Mr. Pix didn't move, other than his eyes flaring then shuttering so quickly I nearly missed it.

"Who?" His voice was deathly quiet.

Honestly, the man was incredibly rude. He sneaked into my carriage, refused to respond to my questions, and now was demanding answers to his own.

"I don't know yet," I confessed. "But she seemed quite enamored with Mr. Ned Oligary. I believe he's going to take her to New Vauxhall Gardens."

"*Oligary?*" A vulgarity I won't deign to repeat passed from between his lips. Beneath the low brim of the hat, his face changed into an expression that made my breath catch. And not in a good way. In that moment, I thought I understood why Mr. Pix supposedly had quite a hold over the criminal underground in London.

He looked terrifying in a cold, powerful way.

But I wasn't a Holmes for nothing, and I gathered my wits. I, at least—not being the criminal type—had nothing to fear from him. "Right then, Mr. Pix. I don't know what you're about, skulking around in my carriage, but if you don't respond to my questions, I'll—I'll get out and leave you here with the bill."

At that, a dart of humor glinted in his eyes, then disappeared. "Wotcha want t'know?" he asked, laying the Cockney accent on very thick. I had reason to believe it wasn't a legitimate one, but I decided not to pursue it at that moment.

"Evaline and I visited your—er—lair last night," I told him. "We found the carnelian crow pendant, as you no doubt intended."

He inclined his head but didn't deign to respond otherwise.

"We also fought off a trio of angry UnDead. They were quite vicious, and Evaline was— Well, it was fortunate I was present. I was able to—er—distract one of them when she—er… Well, it was a very near thing. For both of us." I couldn't think of that horrible, violent battle without feeling queasy. If Evaline hadn't recovered enough to fight off that last UnDead, I knew I wouldn't be alive today.

Pix seemed about to say something, but he presumably thought better of it and remained silent. However, I noticed his fingers (gloved, of course, for the man is quite a master of disguise and adheres to even the smallest of detail, including always covering his hands and ears) curl into themselves, then relax an instant later.

I continued, "You might be interested to know—or

perhaps you already do—that one of the vampires that attacked us had two marks at the back of his neck."

"Like the ones from the Ankh?" He appeared to have given up on the Cockney affectation, a decision I applauded but on which I chose not to comment.

"Precisely. I see you are already aware that the Ankh seems to have continued her experimentations."

"'at's one word for it. Experimentation." His face was hard.

"I can only deduce the reason you've gone into hiding is because you know you're a target of hers. You preferred to go underground—so to speak—before she caught up to you."

"She won't catch the likes o' me again, Miss Holmes. The only reason she did the last time was—" He shook his head and pursed his lips.

"I know her true identity," I informed him.

"I do as well."

I believed him. I had no reason not to, for clearly he and the Ankh had had some sort of shared history—as was evidenced by the encounter I'd witnessed in her underground torture chamber.

Mr. Pix looked at me, and for the first time, I felt as if there were no disguises, no facade, no subterfuge. As our eyes met in the shadowy light of the hackney, a strange, almost intimate understanding snapped between us.

He was the only person to whom I'd confessed my knowledge; I wasn't even certain why I had chosen him to do so. Even Evaline wasn't aware that I knew without a doubt that the Ankh was Lady Isabella Cosgrove-Pitt, wife of the most powerful parliamentarian in England.

"You and I are the only ones who would believe it," I said.

"Well, now, Miss 'olmes," he replied with a trace of his normal jocularity, "at least we 'ave something in common."

"Besides a strong regard for Evaline Stoker." I scrutinized him. His face remained passive, but I was certain I'd seen a telltale flicker in his eyes.

Pix shifted slightly and adjusted his hat even lower. "Then I suggest we keep this charming interlude to ourselves."

"An excellent idea. I concur." I had my reasons for agreeing, but I was quite interested in his for suggesting that I not tell Evaline of our meeting.

At once, he seemed more talkative. "You found the carnelian crow pendant I left. You'll need to use it."

"Quite. And that is the only reason I haven't yet tossed you out of this taxi," I told him frostily. "Because I haven't any idea how to use it, or where the establishment is. Pray, enlighten me."

His brows appeared to rise; it was difficult to tell due to the low placement of his hat and its resulting shadow. "But you've determined the Crow is a place. Well done, Miss Holmes. It took me several weeks to determine that important detail."

I clamped my mouth shut. The only reason I knew that much was because of Grayling.

I had also determined something else about Pix, now that he'd abandoned his Cockney accent. He was American.

"Where is it, then? How do I find it? Have you been there yourself?"

"Apparently there are a number of ways to find the place, and to access it—depending upon who you are. Wear the pin."

Before I could continue my interrogation over his cryptic comments, he moved—slipping from the corner of the carriage, throwing the door open, and leaping out—all in one smooth motion.

One moment he was sitting there insouciantly, and the next he was gone.

The hackney door slammed in his wake, and I barely had the wherewithal to grab and latch it as the vehicle continued on its journey.

I looked out of the window, but even then I didn't see him among the many people and carriages traveling along the street.

I sat back and took a deep breath. I was beginning to understand Evaline's misguided fascination with the man.

He was quite something.

I WAS IN SUCH A STATE WHEN I CLIMBED INTO THE TAXI AT Grantworth House that I had neglected to change my ultimate destination with the hackney driver, so when we lurched to a halt and the green light inside the cab indicated we had arrived, I found myself alighting near the street-lift to Lady Thistle's.

Despite my burning curiosity, I had no intention of attempting to locate and infiltrate The Carnelian Crow on my own. As I have pointed out numerous times, I am not the impetuous sort.

Nor am I like those foolish young women in the gothic-horror novels by the likes of Mrs. Radcliffe or Wilkie Collins —the females who investigate a dangerous noise in the dead of night on their own in their *night frocks.* (Evaline was the only woman I knew who could make a case for investigating danger on her own, and she would never do it clad only in a night frock. At least, I don't believe she would.)

The first time I read—or, rather, attempted to read—one of those stories, I'd thrown the tome against the wall. For fiction reading, I remain content with *Frankenstein* and stories by Mr. Poe, Mr. Verne, and Mr. Twain. Though many of those tales are far-fetched, at least they don't feature imbecilic characters that do little to exemplify the intelligence and resourcefulness of my gender.

I will admit, however, that it was in part due to the raw intensity and concern that had blazed in Inspector Grayling's eyes that stayed my hand in regards to The Carnelian Crow. It was clear this mysterious establishment must be taken very seriously, and breached with all caution. For obvious reasons, I would have been far more confident had Evaline been with me—she'd proven herself valuable a majority of the time.

However, I did decide to pay another visit to Lady Thistle's. I would poke around that back closet a little more (under the guise of trying on a new split petticoat) and see what else I could find.

It was briskly cold and the air was damper than usual—as if it were attempting to snow, but Mother Nature couldn't quite form the flakes, so the precipitation merely hung there in a cold, gray glaze. There were few pedestrians about, which meant I had the street-lift to myself and my voluminous skirts.

As before, I rode up three levels and disembarked near the popping tea cart. An aromatic drink to warm my hands and insides appealed, and I was considering which flavor to sample this time when I heard a familiar bark. This was followed by a quiet metallic clicking and the clop of approaching footsteps on the fly-way bridge.

I couldn't control a rush of something—pleasure, surprise, perhaps even bashfulness—when I turned to see Inspector Grayling being towed along by the incorrigible beagle Angus.

Apparently, the beast, who was leashed, had scented or otherwise sighted me, for he was clearly making a beeline as fast as his mechanical leg—and master—would allow. Though as a rule I find animals best left to their own devices and certainly not beneath my hands—or skirts, as Angus was wont to be—I couldn't resist him.

I crouched (with difficulty, due to the blasted corset) and greeted him with a pat to the head. His long ears flopped over my gloved hand and he sniffed excitedly at the white puff of my breath in the cold. He even attempted to slurp at my face, and I confess I allowed him to get close enough that I felt the barest whisk of tongue across my chin.

"No, sir, I'm quite sorry, I'm fresh out of Stuff'n-Muffins today," I told him when he redirected his damp nose to sniffing around the ruffles of my hem and along every inch of my shoes. He then moved on to my reticule, but by that time, my lower appendages were protesting and I realized I was going to need assistance returning an upright position. Drat.

"Good day, Inspector Grayling." I glanced up at him, then over to determine whether the lamppost was close enough to use as a prop to pull myself up. Dratted corset and skirts and petticoats!

"What an unexpected but delightful pleasure, Miss Holmes." He sounded like he meant it, and suddenly a large hand (apparently he *did* own gloves) appeared in my line of vision. "If you've finished greeting the obnoxious beastie, may I help you?"

"Thank you," I said, feeling a little breathless when he pulled me up easily, with no effort on my part. It was such a smooth, powerful movement that I nearly bumped into his chest from the momentum.

"Popping tea?" he said, turning to look at the cart. I noticed the cold had made his cheeks ruddy.

"It's quite delicious. I tried the jasmine flavor yesterday, but I thought I would sample a different one today. I was attempting to make a decision when I heard Angus's greeting." I looked down as I realized the creature had flopped on the ground next to me and was gnawing on the button of my thick-soled, fur-lined shoe.

"Angus!" Grayling exclaimed, yanking—but not too hard —on the leash. "Behave yourself, or there'll be no ham bones for a month. You'll be stuck with gruel, and you know how inedible Mrs. MacPherson's gruel is. And I won't feel the least bit sorry for you about it."

I heard someone giggle (surely it wasn't I) and turned my attention to the tea cart. I decided upon the cardamom-vanilla flavor, but before I could open my reticule, Grayling elbowed me aside.

"Allow me, Miss Holmes," he said, then commenced with ordering his own popping tea (honeyed chocolate) and paying for both.

"Why thank you," I said, burying my heated cheeks in the

warmth and aroma of the beverage. The exotic scent of cardamom filled my nostrils as the little fizzes popped with alacrity. "That was unexpected and very kind."

"It was my pleasure, Miss Holmes. I've been— Blast it, Angus, *no!*" His voice rose in horror as the beast lifted his leg to urinate on the lamppost.

I turned away, hiding a smile, and leaned against the same railing upon which Evaline and I had done yesterday—and where, coincidentally, the topic of our conversation had been none other than Grayling himself.

"What brings you to this part of town?" asked the man now, resting his elbow on the rail next to me. "Especially on such an unpleasant day."

He was one of the few individuals who towered over me, and I found myself having to twist a bit to look up at him. His excessive height used to annoy me, but I was becoming accustomed to it.

"A clothing boutique I frequent is located off Meckler's Alley. Lady Thistle's."

"I've not heard of that establishment," he replied, sniffing audibly at his beverage. "Quite interesting," he muttered, sticking his nose into the cup. His eyelashes, a slightly darker shade than his gingery hair, brushed against the edge of the vessel. I'd never noticed a gentleman with such long, curling lashes before.

"I shouldn't think you would have heard of it," I replied lightly. "After all, it's for ladies' clothing. What need would you have to frequent a shop for young ladies' clothing?" Then I realized what I had said, and the assumptions therein, and I immediately began to stammer. "I mean to say, as far as I know, you don't have a—a need to shop with a lady, or for—"

"No," he said, looking steadily across the fly-bridge to the other side of the street, "I have—at the moment—no reason to shop for or with a lady, Miss Holmes." Then he turned suddenly to me. "Although I am hopeful that might change."

I found myself unable to swallow. And all at once, my heart was galloping off in a very queer manner. My knees felt a trifle unsteady. "Right then," I muttered, and took a large drink from my tea.

Too large of a drink, in fact, which resulted in my needing to battle back a choking cough, because it went down too large and too fast. My cheeks were flaming by the time I got myself under control.

Fortunately, Angus had wrapped himself and his leash around an air-cart mooring, and Grayling had discovered this just as I brought the cup to my lips. If he noticed my actions, he gave no indication.

"Perhaps we should walk a bit," Grayling said, offering me his arm. "At least that might keep Angus from causing further disruptions. Did you say Meckler's Alley?"

I found it unexpectedly pleasant to be strolling along the walkway with the inspector and his four-legged companion as we sipped our respective beverages.

I became accustomed to the feel of his leg brushing against my skirt, and I discovered I rather enjoyed the slight movement of the muscles in his arm beneath my hand. His proximity made one side of me quite warm despite the wintry day. In fact, the chill in the air no longer seemed unpleasant, and to my surprise, the two of us conversed readily on a number of topics.

I happened to mention a new exhibition at the British Museum, expressing my interest in seeing the display of woodcut *ukiyo-e* prints from Japan, and Grayling verbalized a similar desire.

"Perhaps we could—er—coordinate the day so we are there at the same time," he suggested.

"That would be quite enjoyable," I said without thinking. "I can't imagine Miss Stoker would be interested in my position on *kabuki* theater—which is one of the popular subjects of those types of print, and has many parallels to our own Shakespearean theater. She would likely shush me if I attempted to educate her. Miss Adler might be able to give us a guided tour, however."

"Miss Adler? But...she is no longer employed by the museum."

I halted abruptly. "What did you say?"

"I assumed you were aware. Miss Adler is gone. She is no longer at the British Museum."

"How do you know this? Why? Where did she go?" My thoughts were a jumble, and tucked deep inside them was a glimmer of hope. Perhaps that was why I hadn't heard from my mentor. I began to walk again, with, I confess, a bit of a spring in my step.

"I believe it's been more than a month that she's been gone," he replied. "But I only discovered this information a few days ago, when I called on her there."

"You called on Miss Adler at the museum? Were you working on a case?"

"Er...no, I was not. I—er— Well, blast it, Miss Holmes, I am usually tripping all over you during any given investigation of mine. And when I hadn't—er—encountered you—or Miss Stoker or Miss Adler, for that matter, I...well, I thought perhaps something might have...happened." The wintry chill had turned his cheeks dark red.

"How astonishing," I murmured, still engaged by the tantalizing thought that Miss Adler's silence had not been due to her disappointment in me. Then I realized what he'd said. "You thought something might have happened? Such as?"

"Well, it does seem that every time there is a dead body, there you are," Grayling said rather forcefully. "What was I to think? You were, after all, consorting with that Eckhert bloke. If something had happened, I— Well, I was concerned."

"I see." I wasn't certain what to make of his speech, but I couldn't deny there was a sort of bubbling warmth blossoming in the center of my person. Perhaps it was the way he said *that Eckhert bloke*.

"But apparently he has gone away as well," Grayling said after a moment of silent walking through the slush.

"Mr. Eckhert? Yes, he's gone—gone home."

Grayling glanced at me now, for the first time since we'd

gone off on this strange tangent. I felt the muscles in his arm tighten beneath my hand. "Does that— Well, Miss Holmes, are you quite—quite despondent about that?"

"Despondent? Certainly not. Of course, I wish he hadn't gone, and I do miss him—strange as it may seem to *you*, he was a friend—but it was for the best. I knew it and so did he, and Miss Adler agreed. I could have gone with him—but, of course, that wouldn't have done."

His arm relaxed a trifle. "I see. You—er—could have gone with him?"

"Traveling to—as far as he was going, to a place I didn't belong, would not have been the best choice, as interesting as I might have found it. Despite all its faults, my world is here, in 1889 London."

"1889 London?" he repeated thoughtfully. "Quite. Well, one cannot argue that, at least."

He lapsed into silence, and I wasn't inclined to break it. He'd given me several things to think about, including the sobering reminder that the last time Miss Adler had disappeared without a word, she'd been in a particularly tenuous position at the hands of some bloodthirsty—literally —UnDead.

I now had a real missing person to investigate (as, clearly, Mr. Pix's disappearance was intentional and not of a sinister nature), as well as The Carnelian Crow. I couldn't help but feel a thrill over the fact that my life seemed to have returned to its previous busyness.

As we approached Lady Thistle's, Grayling spoke again, bringing up the subject that I was certain had been lurking in the back of his mind since we began walking. I was surprised he'd waited this long.

"And so what have you learned about The Carnelian Crow since yesterday?" he asked. He pitched his voice low as a precaution, but as we had just turned down the side alley from Meckler's, no one was in the vicinity. "I'm as certain as the sun will rise tomorrow that you've been busy investigating —despite my warning to the contrary."

"I'll have you know, Inspector Grayling, that I've taken your warning exceedingly seriously."

"Indeed? That's quite remarkable." A little smile flickered in his face. "But certainly you've been busy. And I'm just as confident you've learned something of note."

"As a matter of fact, I have. But, quite extraordinarily, it was completely by accident."

Grayling stopped and looked down at me with an expression that was a mixture of exasperation and disbelief. "I find that impossible to believe."

"Believe it, sir. Incidentally, I discovered something very interesting when I visited Lady Thistle's yesterday."

We'd reached the tiny ladies' boutique, and I indicated the door framed in sage green and its thistle symbol on the glass.

"This place?" He peered through the door's window. "It appears deserted."

"It's meant to, so as to not attract too much of a clientele, I suppose."

"Too much of a clientele? What sort of boutique doesn't want to attract new customers?"

That was a fair question, and one that I hadn't contemplated until now—perhaps because it had always been that way, since my mother used to bring me here. "Would you like to discuss the tenets of good and bad business practices, or would you like me to tell you what I discovered, Inspector Grayling?"

"Och, well... Though the topic of business practices might be fascinating to the likes of Emmett Oligary, I believe I should limit my purview to criminal activity. What did you learn, Miss Holmes?"

I hid a smile, taken off guard by his little jest, then went on to tell him about the hidden door inside the closet in the back room of Lady Thistle's.

Grayling was both impressed and mystified, and expressed those opinions. "Due to the marking on the closet door, one would make the logical assumption that the hidden door somehow provides access to The Carnelian Crow," he said, stepping back from the shop's entrance in order to study the buildings surrounding it.

"I have confirmed your understanding that there are different ways to access the establishment, depending on who the individual is attempting to do so," I said, also looking at the architecture of the adjoining shops.

"Indeed. And where did you come by that particular bit of information?" Grayling looked at me sharply.

I hesitated, then explained (although I did not mention our visitation of Pix's lair, nor the acquisition of a second carnelian crow pendant). After all, Grayling had been involved with the rescue of Mr. Pix from the clutches of the Ankh, so the individual was not unknown to him.

"This Pix character," said my companion, appearing none too pleased at the information. "He seems to be possessed of quite a bit of information of the criminal sort. Perhaps I should speak with him myself. Where might I find the bloke?"

I shrugged, then prevaricated. "I have no idea, Inspector Grayling. He comes and goes as he pleases."

He muttered something unintelligible, then returned to his perusal of the building. "If, as you suspect, the hidden door in the closet leads to an entrance to The Carnelian Crow, one must consider where precisely that establishment is located. Are one or more of the neighboring businesses merely a front for the Crow? There is an antiquarian book-shop here—hmm, I might be persuaded to look inside in short order—and Lenning's Tannery next to it. And on the other side, Madame Facing's Lace Shop..." He continued to himself. "We're on the third street level, so at the rear of the buildings, where the hidden door would have led, there's no alley or mews access...only space."

Angus gave a sharp yip, drawing the attention of both of us. Apparently, we'd been standing in one place for too long.

"I shall venture inside as planned, Inspector. I'll check the closet and perhaps even look through the hidden door to see whether your estimate is correct—I won't go any further," I added hastily, as I could see him gearing up to launch into a lecture. "You have my word."

He didn't appear the least bit mollified by my promise. "Perhaps it would be best if I accompanied you inside, Miss Holmes. I can tie Angus at this lamppost for a moment." He dug in one of the voluminous pockets of his overcoat. "I usually save this for riding on the Underground, but it will do to keep him busy for a few moments." He produced a package wrapped in butcher paper.

Angus immediately plopped down on his behind and fixated his eyes on the packet. His mouth was clamped closed and his nose quivered. I do believe a parade with booming drums and tooting horns could have floated by and the beast wouldn't have noticed.

"Och, then. There's a good boy." Grayling unwrapped the object and produced a small ham bone, which he offered to Angus. The beagle took it with an enthusiastic swipe of teeth and settled himself down to gnaw on it.

"Right, then. Shall we, Miss Holmes?"

Startled from my affectionate regard of the adorable canine, I looked up to find a similar expression in Grayling's eyes. This disconcerted me, and I stumbled over my feet as I turned to the door. "Yes, of course."

But when I reached for the door latch of Lady Thistle's, I made an unpleasant discovery.

The door was locked. I pulled harder, jiggling it in its frame, then looked through the window.

Grayling had been more correct than he realized: the place was closed and deserted.

"*Caw!*"

I started and looked up. A huge crow had settled on the top of Angus's lamppost, and he was looking down at me with a disapproving eye.

I couldn't be certain, but I suspected he was none other than my bold nocturnal visitor.

Miss Stoker

~ In Which the Requirements of Friendship Are Debated ~

"WELL? DID YOU FIND IT?" I DEMANDED. "THE Carnelian Crow?"

I could hardly believe I'd had to miss out on Mina's plan to investigate the secret door at the back of Lady Thistle's in favor of meeting potential husbands. I'd been going back and forth between fuming and sulking ever since Mina poked her long nose into the parlor, then disappeared without even trying to help me escape!

She was a *traitor*.

Fortunately, Florence had been so pleased with how the afternoon had gone, and the number of gentlemen who'd arrived to call on me yesterday, that she'd allowed me to escape from the house early the next morning to visit Mina.

My sister-in-law might have been pleased, but I alternated between being terrified and shocked at what was happening —and so quickly.

It felt as if I were in a boat tumbling down a wild river, with no way to paddle or even slow down, let alone get to shore. I'd been trapped for hours with the prospective suitors and whichever of their female relatives they'd drummed up to bring with them.

Then I had a short while to freshen up before having to accompany Mr. Broomall, his sister, and his sister's husband's sister to dinner and the theater. We attended a play at the Lyceum, which in Florence's mind did double duty by putting ticket sales in Bram's pocket while bringing me closer to finding a husband. It hadn't been as dull an evening as I'd feared (Mr. Broomall actually made several witty remarks, and at least his breath didn't stink like that of Sir Buford Grandine), but it wasn't the type of thing I wanted to repeat on a regular basis.

"As a matter of fact, I did not find The Carnelian Crow,"

Mina told me. She had a ring around her eye from the magnifying device she often wore while in her laboratory, which was where I'd found her after Mrs. Raskill answered the door.

I sat up straight. "You didn't go to Lady Thistle's—but you left me by myself at the mercy of all those *suitors*? How could you do that?"

"And what, precisely, was it you expected me to do, Evaline? I couldn't very well drag you out of the parlor from under the noses of all those people. Can you imagine the scandal—along with the number of individuals I would have had to push out of the way? Someone—probably me—would have landed in the tea and scones, and that currant jam would have stained everything it touched.

"I must say, you really do have your pick of the young—and not so young—bucks of the peerage. Everyone who is worth any sort of money was there, drooling all over your elegant hand."

"This is *not funny*," I snapped, too upset to even appreciate that Mina Holmes had made a joke. "You could have done something. Had your father call me away on important Home Office business"—she scoffed at that—"or you could have—I don't know—set fire to the house so we all had to vacate. I could have dashed off in the confusion. You're a blasted *Holmes*, as you are constantly reminding me. You could have *deduced* something to do."

"Even if I would have extricated you from that situation," she replied, "what good would it have done? You'd simply be required to meet them the next day, or the next day, or the next day. Evaline, the problem you face is far bigger than simply sitting down for tea on a particular afternoon and missing an adventure. It's not going to go away if you avoid it."

"But I don't want to get married!" Sudden tears stung my eyes, and I roughly dashed them away. I'd managed to hold them back for over a day. "At least, not now. I'm only seventeen."

"Nearly eighteen," Mina unhelpfully reminded me. "You're two months away from attaining the age by which most young women have already been wed."

"You sound like Florence," I retorted. "And that is *not* a compliment."

"Evaline. If you want my help… Do you want my help?"

"Yes! Isn't that what I've been saying? What do you have in mind?" A rush of hope had me sitting up straight again. After all, what was the point of being friends—I supposed we were friends—with a Holmes if they didn't use their brains to *help* you when you needed them?

Mina, who seemed to be using a different sort of hand-held magnifyer to compare the two carnelian crow pendants, looked up at me without raising her face. Just her eyes moved. She looked like an irritated fish.

"It's quite simple, Evaline. You have three choices. You either find a man you can tolerate, and agree to marry him—of course, that would then create a number of issues related to vampire hunting and other activities, which we would need to address once the nuptials occur—or you find a way to *remove* the *necessity* and urgency for you to marry at all, *or*," she continued in a firm voice when I began to object, "you refuse to marry and leave your brother and sister-in-law to handle the repercussions of their poor financial management. And whatever happens happens."

I gaped at her. "That? That's your solution? That's your assistance? That's you *helping* me?" I had the sudden urge to yank the hair out of my head.

(Oh, that was an idea. If I cut all my hair off, and maybe started dressing in trousers, perhaps that would put off all the interested suitors. Hmm…)

"I might not be a blasted Holmes, but I know all that already."

Mina merely looked at me. "Then why are you asking me for assistance?"

I did that little scream of frustration inside my closed

mouth, but managed to keep myself from kicking the stool out from under her. Just because *she* didn't have a family she cared about disappointing, and parents who cared about her—

I spewed out a long breath. A twinge of shame squeezed my belly.

I did have a family I loved. And they loved me, without a doubt. And it was true—Mina did not. Her mother had abandoned her, and Sir Mycroft was completely engrossed in his work for the government. Mina even called him "sir" to his face, instead of Papa or even Father.

And because I had a family I cared about, and who loved me, that meant I really only had two choices: I either had to marry so that my wealthy husband would help settle our debts, or I had to help find another solution. I couldn't—*wouldn't*—let my brother and Florence down.

Time to change the subject.

"So why didn't you go to Lady Thistle's?"

"I didn't say I didn't go to Lady Thistle's," my ever-exacting friend replied in her precise voice. "I went there, but the establishment was closed."

"Closed? Do you mean permanently?"

"I don't know," she said, examining the two crow pendants with yet another tool. "But the fact that the door was locked, and from what I could discern of the interior, it was completely deserted, I do find it more than interesting that the day after I found the secret door, the place was locked up." She looked back up at me. "And then there's the fascinating bit of information Lady Thistle shared about my mother going to the back to try on clothing, and being gone for some time. It—"

"She must have been going through the secret door—maybe even to The Carnelian Crow," I said. "I wonder how long that establishment has been around."

"Indeed. Those are my suspicions as well. Grayling said he's been hearing about a secret red crow for several years now—five, I believe he said. But the bigger question I have is whether Lady Thistle *knew* what my mother was doing, and if she was attempting to give me the information without appearing to do so—or whether it was purely the insignificant ramblings of an elderly woman who has few people with whom to speak on a daily basis."

"Right."

"And there is also the chance that something untoward happened because Lady Thistle was so free with that information, and she was forced to close down the boutique and possibly go into hiding—"

"Or worse."

"Or worse. Evaline, you are always the bloodthirsty one. Regardless, and therefore, I intend to take matters into my own hands. I was hoping you'd be able to assist—"

"You're going to break in?" A spike of glee shot through me. "When? Tonight— Oh, *blast*. Tonight I've got an engagement with Mr. Oligary. What time—"

"Mr. Oligary?" She looked at me with a funny expression. "Do you mean to say you're being escorted by Mr. Oligary? So you've truly caught his attention, then. I only said that in order to dissuade— Right. Er—you do mean the younger Mr. Oligary, correct? Ned, I believe is his given name? That was he who was speaking to you when I arrived yesterday, correct?"

"Yes." I frowned. I'd missed something, but I wasn't certain what, and before I could ponder further, Mina went on.

"I'm certain Florence is beyond delighted over the possibility of you getting a marriage proposal from Ned Oligary."

Delighted was an understatement. Mr. Oligary's invitation to be his guest at New Vauxhall Gardens tonight had made Florence so ecstatic that I thought she was going to burst her corset with excitement. That was the only reason she'd allowed me to visit Mina this morning without giving me a hassle.

"Perhaps you can get Mr. Oligary—since you seem to have caught his attention—to escort you to the fête at Lord and Lady Cosgrove-Pitt's home on Saturday. Surely he's been invited." Mina's eyes gleamed. "He and his brother."

"I don't particularly want to go to Cosgrove Terrace on Saturday—or ever, to be honest. A fête at Cosgrove Terrace won't be an adventure. It'll be filled with stuffy people talking about uninteresting things like politics and fashion and—"

But Mina wasn't listening. "Drat. I wish I could find a way to go with you."

"I'm not going yet, Mina. And for all I care, you can go *instead* of me. I'll let Mr. Oligary know you're interested," I added snidely.

"Believe me, if I could wrangle a way to go, Evaline, I would do it in a minute. So you'll have to go instead."

"Why?" I grumbled. "The last time we were there—"

"The last—and only—time we were there together was the first night we met the Ankh, as you recall. The reason you should go to Cosgrove Terrace is so you can snoop around. Look for clues."

"Clues?" I felt a flicker of interest. I always liked snooping around. But we weren't really investigating a case at the moment except that of the crow pendants—and Pix's disappearance. "Wait. Don't tell me you think Lord or Lady Cosgrove-Pitt know something about The Carnelian Crow. That's ridiculous. Why would two respected, premier members of Society have anything to do with a place like that?"

Mina wore a strange expression, and I don't mean because of the apparatus she'd placed over her head—although it was odd all on its own. It had a large telescoping lens over one eye, and there was a set of tiny clamping hands that extended from the sides of the device and held the two pendants close to the lens. From the top of her head, two small antenna sort of things curved out and down, shining a pair of tiny lights onto the pendants. Mina looked like a strange sort of insect-like Cyclops with hands coming out of her temples.

She pulled off the apparatus and still wore the odd expression. "Evaline, what I'm about to tell you is of a very confidential nature. I'm aware of only one other person who has this information. If you were to divulge this to *anyone*, it could seriously jeopardize—"

"Just tell me what it is."

"Lady Cosgrove-Pitt is the Ankh."

I gaped and then burst into laughter. "Are you mad? There is absolutely no way that's true. I know you suspected it for a time—"

"I *deduced* it from the very first, from my many observations of both individuals, Evaline. I was certain of it before we even went into the opium den during the scarab affair. However, it's true there was a time when I began to question what I *knew* had to be true, and that did frustrate and stall my investigations."

"It's impossible for Lady Cosgrove-Pitt to be the Ankh, Mina. First of all, she was hosting the Roses Ball at Cosgrove Terrace on the night we met the Ankh for the first time. We were underground, on the other side of the city, remember? In the Thames Tunnel? But we saw Lady Cosgrove-Pitt at the ball when we returned."

Mina sniffed. "An elementary sleight of hand, Evaline. If you recall, the Lady Cosgrove-Pitt who was supposedly at the ball was standing on a balcony, speaking with someone, and waved to us from a distance. That Lady Cosgrove-Pitt was obviously a decoy, and she was set up at a distance so no one would notice. I suspect she has a maid or some other individual who plays her stand-in in situations like that."

I rolled my eyes. "I don't buy it. What about the fact that when the Ankh was flying off *with me* after the fire in the opium den, and you and Grayling were speeding over to Cosgrove Terrace on his steamcycle? Lady Cosgrove-Pitt—

good *gad*, could she not have a name that's less than a mouthful?—was there when you arrived."

"Once again, simple, Evaline. First of all, there was a bit of a delay before Grayling and I set off on the cycle. Secondly, as I recall, *you* were blacked out and couldn't know who was with you and who wasn't—and for how long—when they abducted you from the burning opium den. And third, it was several minutes after Grayling and I arrived and asked for her that Lady Cosgrove-Pitt was fetched for us.

"There are, as you are well aware, several illicit ways to travel speedily through London: via underground tunnels on motorized vehicles like the one Mr. Pix has, and even small airships—smaller than the black one we saw two nights ago. Either of those could have assisted Lady Cosgrove-Pitt to get back home in a speedy manner. She could have removed her disguise and changed clothing during the travel time as well." Mina folded her arms over her middle and lifted her nose at me as if to make a challenge I couldn't combat.

"Fine, then. Even if *all* of those things are true, there's absolutely one thing you cannot argue: Lady Cosgro—I'm just going to call her Lady C-P—was there, in Queen Elizabeth's Tower of London bedroom, when the Ankh appeared to steal the chess queen."

To my chagrin—because I was certain I'd had the stopper for Mina's argument—she merely smiled like a very satisfied cat who'd found a dish of cream.

"Actually, Evaline, that incident is how I know with absolute certainty that Lady Cosgrove-Pitt is the Ankh."

"I beg your pardon?"

"You see, when the Ankh was in the tower room making her speech, I looked over and saw Lady Cosgrove-Pitt. I'd told her several times previously—when she was the Ankh—that I knew her identity. Not only was Lady Cosgrove-Pitt watching me, she was waiting for me to look over at her in astonishment. And when I did, she acknowledged, once and for all, that I was correct by nodding at me. She actually *smiled* with triumph."

"But that doesn't necessarily mean——"

"She looked right at me and said, 'Checkmate.' There was no mistaking her meaning, Evaline."

I sagged back onto my stool. My head was spinning. Could it be true? The elegant, demure, wealthy Isabella Cosgrove-Pitt…really the Ankh?

Why?

"She'd planned the whole thing—the entire ruse—to make certain anyone who would have any credibility was there and saw the Ankh in the same room as Lady Cosgrove-Pitt. Note that even my father was in attendance, as well as several other important personages.

"But she made a mistake. What I think will ultimately be her downfall. She had to let me know I was right—but that she had, after all, won. However, now that she's confirmed what I knew all along, I only need to find proof."

"So the Ankh who was in the Tower of London room… that wasn't the real Ankh?" I was still trying to take in the information.

"Keep up, Evaline, please. It's not that difficult."

I glared at her. "You're correct. Deductions are not nearly as difficult as fighting off vampires and killing multiple UnDead while being outnumbered by them. And bleeding all over the place." I shivered.

Mina sniffed, but she softened her tone. "Right, then. So now that I know Lady Cosgrove-Pitt is the Ankh, I just need to find proof. Which you could do if you get an invitation to Cosgrove Terrace. Hmm. Maybe the idea of you getting married isn't such a bad one after all——"

"Are you *mad?*"

"Well, Evaline, one must take advantage of all circumstances—even if they aren't the least bit preferable."

I snarled to myself for a moment, then gave in. "What sort of proof do you want?"

Mina shrugged. "Whatever you find. You'll know it when you see it."

"That's helpful," I grumbled. But I had to admit, I felt a bit more interested in attempting to wrangle an invitation to the party. It would be a lovely affair—probably with a lot of really good food. I certainly could appreciate good food.

I couldn't help but remember the last time I'd been to Cosgrove Terrace—with Mina, when we were investigating the missing girls related to the Society of Sekhmet. Pix had been there at the ball, the dratted scoundrel. That evening, he'd been dressed as a waiter. But I'd recognized him.

It would be just like him to show up again like that. I felt a little prickle of hope at the thought of encountering him unexpectedly. Perhaps even in a dimly lit—

"Evaline, are you paying attention?"

"Yes."

"You didn't hear a word I said, did you?"

"Erm...something about proof? And—oh, yes, Mr. Oligary. What about him?"

Mina seemed slightly appeased. "Since you'll be with the younger brother—tonight, is it?"

"We are going to New Vauxhall Gardens. I'll try not to fall into the pond," I added slyly.

Mina sniffed. "My goodness, your social calendar is becoming quite booked up, Miss Stoker. The theater last night, New Vauxhall tonight, possibly the Cosgrove-Pitt fête on Saturday—"

I snarled so she could hear me this time, and she stopped teasing me.

"Right, then. When you are with Mr. Oligary, perhaps you could do some detective work there as well. Young men seem to fall all over themselves when you give them your full attention, and you could easily get him speaking, I'm certain. It's quite an advantage, really. You did a remarkable job coaxing information from Mr. Ashton during the spiritglass case."

I supposed that was a compliment. "What kind of detective work?"

"One of Inspector Grayling's *few* unsolved cases is that of the accidental death of Mr. Emmett Oligary's business partner, Mr. Bartholomew. I thought I might—well, since I'm not working on anything else at the moment, perhaps I would offer my assistance with that." Her face lit up. "Perhaps that was why Inspector Grayling visited my residence. I had previously offered to assist with the investigation about Mr. Bartholomew. He must have intended to take me up on that offer."

I resisted the urge to roll my eyes. For someone as smart as she was, Mina could be a complete rock-head. "So…what about Mr. Oligary?"

"Right, then. Perhaps you could attempt to find out what he knows about that night—the night of the accident. That's how Mr. Oligary the elder got his limp, you know."

That task didn't sound nearly as exciting as digging through Lady Isabella's house looking for clues. (My pulse was already bumped up from excitement—but that was two days away.) However, Mr. Ned Oligary and I had to talk about something while we were strolling through the amusement gardens. "I'll do my best."

I slid off the stool, and the weight of my bustle and petticoats fell into place. I suddenly felt ten pounds heavier, and not just because of the fabric. "I promised Florence I'd be home by noon."

"One more thing." Mina offered me one of the carnelian crow pendants. "Wear this when you can."

"Why? It's not really my style." It was too small. And bright red.

"*Wear it.*"

I huffed. But when I left, I had the tiny pendant in my hand.

Miss Stoker

~ A Sparkling Evening ~

"Miss Stoker, you are very punctual. And you look incredibly lovely." The warmth in Mr. Ned Oligary's eyes matched the admiration in his voice when he greeted me at the gates of New Vauxhall Gardens later that evening.

I admit it—I felt particularly pleased. I normally didn't much care what potential suitors thought about my looks or attire because I didn't want to attract their attention. However, Mr. Oligary didn't strike me as the sort to layer on meaningless compliments.

He was a more serious person than the type of young man I normally needed to fend off. He seemed more mature (of course, he was nearly thirty, which made him quite a bit older than many of the other potential husbands). And he was different from the other males I encountered at balls and parties—most of them titled "lord" and "sir"—because he wasn't a member of the gentry. He was from a family that had *worked* to become wealthy—a fact that most of upper-crust Society looked down upon.

Perhaps that was why Florence had allowed me to go to the Christmas Lighting Extravaganza at New Vauxhall Gardens with Mr. Oligary, taking Pepper as my chaperone. My maid and one of her friends, Hillie, would be following us at a proper distance, along with Mr. Oligary's footman.

I also assumed my sister-in-law was being unusually accommodating in order to make it as easy as possible for Mr. Oligary to fall in love with me and offer for my hand. She didn't seem to care whether my husband had a title, as long as he had a bulging bank account.

I wondered if it even mattered to her whether I loved my husband. Whoever he might end up being.

She loved Bram, didn't she? Surely she would want the same for me...

As I slipped a hand through the crook of Mr. Oligary's arm and back into my fur-lined muff, I caught a glimpse inside the gates of the amusement gardens. I couldn't contain a gasp. "I've never seen anything so beautiful," I said, quite honestly. Of course, I had seen New Vauxhall Gardens several months ago, but it looked so different decorated as it was for Christmas.

"But it is only a proper setting for one as lovely as yourself, Miss Stoker. You sparkle as brightly as the lights and candles," he replied, leaving a puff of white in the frosty air. "I confess, I haven't looked forward to an outing like this for quite some time. If ever. Thank you again for accompanying me."

Despite the chill, I felt my cheeks warm and a small squiggle in my belly when our eyes met. Then I was immediately irritated. He was flirting with me, and I found myself wanting to respond in kind. But I didn't want to give him the wrong impression.

Or did I? I was supposed to be looking for a husband, after all.

Ugh.

"It's rather more cold than I'd anticipated," he said, "although I see you've dressed for the weather."

Indeed I had. Somehow, Florence had managed to come up with an incredible ensemble of luxurious pine-green velvet, lush sable fur, and glittering gemstones (probably faux) around the cuffs and hem...and that was just the hooded cloak and muff.

"Oh, this way, Miss Stoker," Mr. Oligary said when I began to walk toward the main entrance. "We—er—go in through the private gate here."

Right. I should have known. His brother owned the place, so of course we weren't normal, paying guests. We didn't have to wait in line, either—a queue that stretched three blocks.

"As I was saying," he continued as we approached the small side gate, tucked unobtrusively behind a gas lamp. "It's rather more cold than I'd anticipated, so I took the liberty of arranging for a more comfortable way for us to view the Lighting Extravaganza."

I was hardly listening, for the moment the private door had swung open, I found myself in a wintry world of frosted trees, twinkling lights, and glowing orbs of all sizes. Two women dressed in gauzy, glittering gold offered peppermint sticks to everyone who passed by. A trio of young boys sang a carol just inside the entrance. As I watched, the small platform on which they stood began to carefully trundle along the path. When they passed us, I noticed they were safely enclosed by a railing, though I couldn't tell how they were being propelled along.

"Our carriage awaits, Miss Stoker."

I turned. There was an elegant two-seater open sleigh fashioned of bronze, copper, and brass scrollwork that made it appear as delicate as a snowflake. A small lamp dangled from the front, casting its own circle of gold. The driver sat beneath it—holding not reins, but a small steering device that looked like it belonged on a bicycle.

On the back of the horseless sleigh was a neat, comfortable bench seat with a foot rest where Pepper and Hillie could sit comfortably. This arrangement provided the proper chaperonage, but also gave the occupants of the mechanized sled a bit of privacy.

The footman had already opened the side door, and Mr. Oligary helped me up into the sleigh. I wrangled my petticoats, skirts, and cloak into place, then sank onto a plush, chocolate-colored velvet seat. I immediately realized *it was warm*.

Before I could speak, Mr. Oligary climbed in next to me. As the sleigh was hardly the size of a landau, this put him quite close on the bench—a fact that was both slightly disconcerting and exciting.

"Thank you, Greer," said Mr. Oligary as the footman produced a thick blanket made from gold-tipped brown fur that settled over our laps like a cloud, but provided immediate warmth. It felt as if it had been pulled from an oven, and I removed my fingers from the muff to burrow beneath the heated covering.

There was another few moments of activity while the two maids were settled on their bench and buckled in, then also offered a warm blanket (not as thick and likely not preheated).

"Very good, sir," said the footman. "Shall we be off?"

"Yes, of course," said Mr. Oligary, checking his pocket watch—which appeared to have its own illumination. "The extravaganza is to begin in only a quarter of an hour."

The sleigh began with the slightest of lurches, and though its self-propelling engine was a trifle too loud, the ride was smooth as the vehicle's blades slid over the snow.

I settled back in my seat and looked around the amusement gardens, struck with awe. Everywhere I looked were tiny, twinkling golden lights: suspended from trees like streams of glowing raindrops, hanging in curtain-like swaths that were pulled back from the pathway as if to beckon us on through, and dancing in the air on tiny mechanized dragonflies.

We passed decorative orbs arranged in clusters on the ground. They were as large as carriage wheels, as small as dinner plates, and every size in between. Each was illuminated from within by a coppery, silvery, golden, or bronzy glow. Many of them moved, rolling along gently, shivering, or even spinning in their place.

There were more singers along the way, in trios, quartets, and even a quintet. When our trail ended in a T-intersection, an actual *piano* was sitting in the middle of the snow! It was being played by a man wearing a black topcoat and tailcoat, as well as black gloves. An array of candles in golden glass bottles hung from the tree just above the musician and instrument, creating a sort of glittery canopy over his head.

"The Lighting Extravaganza is this way," Mr. Oligary commented as the sleigh turned to the right.

I could see the shadowy shape of Oligary's Observation Cogwheel and its suspended carts in the distance in the opposite direction, and I had a pang of disappointment we weren't heading in that direction. It would be an amazing sight to ride in the massive wheel and look down over the glittering carpet of gold, bronze, copper, and silver lights.

"But the lights have already been lit," I said as the view before us in this new direction turned into a wonderland of frosted silver and white forestry. Either side of the path was studded with a row of identical saplings (they might have been artificial, they were all so perfect), painted white and gilded with matching glitter. Each was decorated with a dozen lit candles, and topped by a silvery-white star. Swaths of sparkling fabric were strung in wide, filmy garlands across the path above our heads. The scents of pine and burning logs were strong, and I suspected they were somehow being piped into the air to add to the atmosphere.

"Oh, you've not seen the best of it," Mr. Oligary told me with a smile. "This is just the introduction. The best part will be turned on during the Lighting Extravaganza. See?" He lifted his gloved hand to point off to the right.

I looked and saw that he was correct: the area was dark and shadowy, unlit and unremarkable. As we drew closer, however, I could hear the low rumble of voices and make out the crowds of people that gathered in the drassy area.

Good heavens. There were already so many people here, and there were still three blocks' worth of others waiting in line to get in. I also realized there would be an entrance fee for each of them.

Mr. Emmett Oligary was going to make a great amount of money tonight.

A little niggle of frustration clawed at my insides. So much money here, and my brother and sister-in-law were struggling to keep a roof over our heads. If the Lyceum Theater could have a *third* of the people gathered here tonight for only one performance, things would certainly turn around for the Stoker family.

And I wouldn't have to think about giving up my life.

The sleigh eased into an area in the shadowy section that

had been cordoned off—like a box at the theater for the higher-paying guests.

"Greer," Mr. Oligary called as soon as the driver had turned off the mechanism.

"Yes, sir?" Greer extinguished the small lamp dangling from the front of the sleigh, eliminating even that bit of light from the area.

"Please bring the girls on the back any refreshment they might want. Miss Stoker, would you like a beaded hot chocolate? Or a peppermint froth? I believe there is tea as well."

I had no idea what a peppermint froth was—or a beaded hot chocolate, for that matter—but I didn't care. I never turned down chocolate anything. "Yes, please. A hot chocolate would be very nice."

Mr. Oligary nodded at Greer, who nodded in return, then moved around to the back of the sleigh to ask Pepper and Hillie what they wanted.

"Now we wait," Mr. Oligary said to me, shifting so he was angled slightly toward me as if he were preparing to converse. Our knees nearly brushed, and I felt a bit of a draft from where he'd been so close to my arm a moment ago, but I was not the least bit uncomfortable. "The Lighting Extravaganza isn't due to begin for another…eight minutes."

The drinks arrived almost immediately, however— perhaps Mr. Oligary had had it prearranged. I wasn't complaining at all, and when he handed me the bowl-sized cup, I took it eagerly.

"I've never seen a cup of hot chocolate—or any other cup —this size," I said, inhaling a breath of pure chocolate. "It smells heavenly."

"It tastes heavenly too." He sipped—he'd received a peppermint froth—and I followed suit, getting a large taste of whipped chocolate cream before I even got to the beverage itself. "It's… What are those little crunchy things in the cream?"

"Yes—those are the vanilla and cinnamon 'beads.' They'll

dissolve and flavor the chocolate, or you can just crunch them if you like. The chef wanted to try something different for tonight." Mr. Oligary used a handkerchief to brush away a bit of minty cream that clung to his mustache, then used a very long, corkscrew-shaped peppermint stick to stir his beverage.

We enjoyed our drinks for a moment, then my companion said, "Emmett mentioned that you were involved in the scare with the Princess of Betrovia that night at the ball. He said you and your friend—Miss Holmes, was it? Is it true she's the detective's niece?—were quite helpful in calming her down." He smiled again, and his eyes seemed to twinkle in the dim light. "The princess, I mean. Not Miss Holmes."

"Mina—Miss Holmes—and I were showing Princess Lurelia around London during their visit, so we were familiar to her. I'm certain that helped ease her mind."

I was glad Mr. Oligary had brought up the subject of his brother so I didn't have to. I didn't want to sound like I cared about his family's money—which I suppose I did (or, rather, Florence did)—by asking about his rich brother. But Mina wanted me to find out what I could about Emmett Oligary's partner's death. I would rather seem gauche by asking prying questions than face Mina's wrath by not at least trying to get information. After all, she still groused about me not interrogating the UnDead before I staked them.

"I heard about the tragedy that caused Mr. Oligary's limp," I said, ignoring the fact that it was really stretching the bounds of propriety to mention it so bluntly. "Is it true he was injured while trying to save his partner's life?"

"Unfortunately, yes. Hiram was working late one night—I believe he and Emmett were considering a plan to bring electric machinery into one of their factories—"

"Electric? But isn't that dangerous? And I thought Mr. Bartholomew's name was Edgar. Are there two Mr. Bartholomews?"

"Right. Yes. Er, no. His name was Edgar Hiram Bartholomew. But having a partner named Emmett, he generally went by Hiram. Except my brother often called him by his given name. Which created some confusion of its own."

By now, the two other sleighs that had been pulled into the cordoned area were filled with people. It was too dim for me to tell whether I recognized any of them, but I was certain Mr. Emmett Oligary was one. Surely he'd want to watch the festivities—unless he was managing the lighting himself.

"Your brother and his partner were considering an electric machine?" I said, realizing I was actually curious about the story now.

"This was before Moseley-Haft, you understand. In fact, it was this catastrophe that changed my brother's mind from embracing electricity to realizing the dangers of it. You might not be aware that Emmett was instrumental in getting Lord Moseley to sponsor the bill that outlawed electrical power in England. And then there was the matter of bringing Mr. Haft on board—ah, but I'm certain the inner workings of politics is not the most exciting topic for you, is it, Miss Stoker?" He gave a little laugh.

He would be correct. If Mina were here, she might be interested. But not me. I wanted to hear about the actual tragedy. Oh, not because someone died, but because Mr. Oligary had clearly been heroic, and I would rather hear about that than the details of some old, rich men making laws in their offices.

"What happened? How did Mr. Oligary injure his leg?"

"As I said, Mr. Bartholomew was working late. He'd had a meeting with a representative from Boston, I believe it was. Or maybe New York? I can't recall. Someone from the Edison family from over there, who was a proponent of electrical power and would help set up the electrical system we needed. And there I go again—giving too many details."

If Mina were here, she'd be kissing his feet and begging for more. As such, I knew I had to be patient and try to remember everything he was saying. It was too bad there wasn't such a thing as a small recording device so I didn't have to.

"No one is quite clear on what happened in the meeting, but obviously things went badly. My brother, who was returning to his office—which was down the hall from Hiram's—to pick up some work he'd forgotten when he went to a dinner meeting, heard a loud disruption from down the hall. The way he described it, the noise was like a large fish, flopping about on the floor as if it had been pulled from the water.

"Emmett rushed down the hall and burst into Hiram's office to find his partner being—well, there is only one way to describe it: being electrofied."

"How terrible!"

"Emmett still can't talk about that moment without turning pale gray," Mr. Oligary said with a frown. "He tried to disconnect Hiram from the machine—he was vibrating and flopping all over, as if he were having a seizure. It appeared he had fallen into or against the machine, with all its wires poking out. Some of them were lying against his skin, burning into it or poking in it, and— Oh, *dear*—Miss Stoker, I'm sorry." His voice rose a little, then eased. "Forgive me for being so—so insensitive. You surely don't need those sordid details. I apologize."

"Mr. Oligary," I said frostily, "I am not a delicate flower about to expire simply because you mention a wire searing against someone's skin, or poking into their arm." (If he only knew.)

"Yes, yes, of course you aren't." He smiled, but ruefully. "I just— It's unseemly to talk about such ugly things."

By now, I could see the preparations being made for the ceremony to begin: several people were moving around purposefully and the crowd had become quieter. But I couldn't, for the life of me, see what was going to be lit. There was nothing but an empty space in the center of the gathering.

"How did your brother injure himself?" I asked in a low voice.

"Apparently, during his efforts to free his friend, Emmett

stepped on a loose wire. The electrical power was so strong, the wire zapped him along the foot and up into the leg. By the time he was able to extricate himself, Hiram was gone. And Emmett's leg was…well, it'll never be the same."

"How terrible," I said. After all, I had seen poor Mayellen Hodgeworth electrofied by the Ankh. I knew very well what it looked like when someone was flopping around, thudding helplessly as the pain of hot electricity seared through them—

"Miss Stoker, I do apologize. I should never have been so blunt. I could have kept some of the more sordid details to myself."

"Not at all. I'm certain you could have been more detailed if you'd tried."

Now what? I obviously needed to ask more questions. If this had become a case investigated by Scotland Yard, there must have been some indication it was more than an accident. "So it was a horrible accident with electrical wires. How did Mr. Bartholomew get himself—well, falling against the machine?"

Mr. Oligary drew himself up. "Oh, it was no accident."

"Truly? Why do they think that?" I asked, uncaring who "they" were in this situation. I had finished the last bit of my hot chocolate, and Greer appeared at my elbow to take the empty cup.

"Excuse me for being blunt, Miss Stoker, but Hiram is no fool, and he would never have gotten so close to that open-wired machine so carelessly. There was nothing for him to have tripped over—and he'd fallen backwards against it, which would have been an odd place for him to be standing in the first place. And even if he had fallen accidentally, why was the machine turned on and the bare wires exposed? No, there was simply no way it could have been an accident. Someone had to have done it—someone pushed him. And we all know it was the man from Boston."

"Or New York."

"Or— Right. Yes."

"The representative from the electricity company killed

Mr. Bartholomew—with electricity?" Something didn't seem quite right about this theory. "With the same sort of machine he was trying to get them to use? Why would he do that?"

"Emmett believes something happened during their meeting that caused the agreement to fall through. And that the American—I don't recall his name—was angry and decided to take out his anger on Hiram."

"Why, that's terrible," I said. "What happened to the American representative?"

"He disappeared. No one ever saw him after that. That's why the case was turned over to Scotland Yard. They've been looking for him—but he's probably returned to Boston by now."

A sudden hush went over the crowd.

"It's about to begin," said my companion unnecessarily as he shifted back to looking straight forward. Then he gestured to Greer. "Have the two girls on the back come around so they can see. There is a small bench over there."

I found it endearing that Mr. Oligary had thought about Pepper and Hillie. Another man might have ignored the two maids and left them to their own devices—or even stuck in a position where they couldn't see.

Everything became quiet and still, the crowd hushing with anticipation. The night was moonless, brushed with clouds that obscured any of the stars, and the large circular area in which we gathered was ringed by tall trees. They formed a sort of barrier from the rest of the amusement garden, but someone had begun to extinguish the other lights through which we'd already traveled as well.

It became very dark.

From behind us, I heard the soft sound of a violin as it began to play "Silent Night," smooth and clear in the darkness. And then, to my astonishment—and that of the rest of the crowd—a golden light began to glow on the ground in the center of the empty circle. Everything remained the same until the song finished.

The world lapsed into expectant silence until the sudden joyous sound of trumpets announced "Joy to the World."

At that, the golden light began to spread across the ground. It radiated from the center of the space like dozens of wheel spokes shooting out toward the crowd—and beneath their feet. People exclaimed and jumped back or to the side as streaks of light shot through the snow under them. The effect was stunning: the entire circular area was now glowing from the ground up. The snow was gilded like a heavenly cloud.

"There's more," Mr. Oligary murmured near my ear.

And he was correct. As "Joy to the World" ended, the musicians (hidden somewhere behind us) began to play "O Christmas Tree"…

And that was when the center of the area began to rise.

More gasps and exclamations filled the air as the golden glow slowly spiraled up and out from the ground, the funnel shape growing wider at the base as it rose. It was a tree—a pine tree—massive in girth and completely covered with sparkling lights of gold, silver, bronze, and copper. It shuddered slightly as it grew taller, higher and higher, broader than any tree I'd ever noticed.

And it moved: ornaments made from tiny cogs and clock-workings buzzed and spun and clicked, blinked and flashed and bounced, swayed and shivered, and fluttered.

The sight was incredible to behold: this living, moving creation of light and machinery that expanded to a height of three stories above us. By now, the crowd had gone utterly silent, awestruck and filled with wonder…and then as we watched further, hand-sized mechanical angels appeared, flying out from the depths of the tree carrying glittery fabric buntings of gold and copper that were draped around the statuesque display.

Somehow, the angels wrapped the shimmery garland along the branches, then settled themselves, each in their own perch on a bough still holding their section of the bunting.

I realized I'd ceased to breathe, and at last remembered to exhale.

"There's more," my companion whispered again.

There *was* more—more lights blinking on around us on countless smaller trees, all decorated with the same wild, mechanized, moving parts—but my favorite part was and would remain the massive Christmas tree and its dancing, moving, glittering parts.

"That was incredible," I said when everything was finished. "I've never seen anything like it."

"I'm so glad you enjoyed it," Mr. Oligary said. "Now, Greer will drive us around through the rest of the amusement gardens—and if you like, we can sample some of the vanilla biscuits and cinnamon popcorn balls at one of the refreshment carts."

Of course, I had no argument with this suggestion, and settled back contentedly in my seat as Greer navigated the sleigh along a pathway decorated in blue and purple lights.

"That's it! Smith!" exclaimed Mr. Oligary suddenly.

"Pardon me?"

"Smith. That was the chap's name, the representative from America who was meeting with Hiram Bartholomew. Edison Smith. Some relation to that Mr. Edison everyone talks about—his sister's son, I believe it might have been."

Smith? Something inside me dropped low and heavy. I tried to dismiss it.

Surely it was a coincidence. Surely it didn't mean anything. Smith was a ridiculously common name.

But Smith, I'd recently learned, was also Pix's real last name.

Miss Holmes
~ Wherein a Scotsman is Ahead of the Game ~

"You do realize this is highly illegal, Miss Stoker,"
I said in a hushed voice.

We were huddled in the alcove-like doorway of Lady
Thistle's in the dead of night.

My partner in crime held my pocket illuminator angled so
I could see the lock on the door—which I was engaged in
picking—while at the same time Evaline stood so as to block
as much of the light as possible from anyone who might look
down this side alley and wonder what was going on here.

The city clocks—Ben and the Oligary Tower—had just
bonged out two chimes. I paused in my work to yawn hugely,
gusting out a cloud of white air in the frigid night. I'd been
rousted from a sound sleep by Evaline almost an hour ago.

"What on earth are you doing here?" I grumbled, once I
got over the surprise of being shaken awake. Fortunately for
her, I'd assumed it was Mrs. Raskill who invaded my
bedchamber, and therefore didn't shout or strike out at the
invasion. "I thought you were at New Vauxhall Gardens for
the Lighting Extravaganza and other festivities."

"I'm not," she replied. "I got a convenient headache and
Mr. Oligary brought me home early. Mina, we have to find
Pix—if he's still alive."

The urgency in her voice washed away the dregs of my
slumber. "Did something happen to make you come all the
way over here to wake me up in the middle of the night?"

"Mmm...maybe," she prevaricated.

"And presumably you have a plan?"

"I don't have a plan. That's your job. But I've got the
muscle. Let's see if we can find The Carnelian Crow behind
Lady Thistle's. Maybe Pix will be there. I need to talk
to him."

I'll admit, it didn't take much effort for her to convince me to climb out of bed, though I did regret it the moment I flung back my warm blankets and set foot on the cold floor.

Now, thirty minutes later, we were engaged in illicit activity in a side alley in London in the deepest part of the night. As it had been nearly two months since our last adventure, I found myself exhilarated to be back on the job.

"Hold it steady," I reminded her as I crouched next to the door. (Since I was wearing a flexible style of corset, lower-heeled shoes, and a split skirt, I was able to hold this posture with relative ease, considering.) "I can't see what I'm doing and my fingers are cold and numb."

"I'm trying to block the light *and* keep an eye out for anyone coming," Evaline retorted. "And I'm freezing, so if you'd hurry things up a bit, I'd be very appreciative."

"Shhh. I need to be able to… Ah. Here we go. And… there." The lock snicked open. I shoved my pick (given to me by Uncle Sherlock on my eighth birthday, along with a jumble of practice locks) into its sheath in my leather toolkit and pulled to my feet with a small groan.

"Ready?" I said.

"I'll go first." Evaline handed me the small pocket illuminator and pushed through the door. "No vampires around, but there could be other threats."

I opened my mouth to argue, but she'd already disappeared into the darkness. Once inside, I turned the Flip-Illuminator back on and cupped it with my hand.

Evaline had moved swiftly and unerringly to the rear of the shop, leaving me to wonder whether the ability to see in the dark was yet another of her skills.

"Mina!" she hissed. "Oh *blooming Pete*! Oh…Grayling's going to have something to say about this."

My heart sank a little as I hurried toward the rear of the shop, for I had a strong suspicion I knew exactly what she meant. "What is it?" I asked.

I was moving so quickly I bumped into one of the free-standing hat displays—which I was certain hadn't been there the other day—and nearly sent it and its contents tumbling to the floor.

"What are you *doing*? Hurry up!" Evaline called back.

"Who is it?" I asked with grim acceptance as I attempted to disentangle myself from a trailing hat ribbon and the levers of the display—all of which seemed to be particularly adept at finding nooks and crannies on my attire and satchel to which they could hook and cling.

"How did you kno—oh, never mind. It's Lady Thistle, Mina. She's dead."

My heart sank even lower and I broke free from the mechanical claws of the hat rack. Drat it. Oh, *drat* it.

The scene was much of what I'd anticipated from the moment Evaline had first reacted: the small, crumpled, bird-like body of the shopkeeper lay still and cold on the floor next to her blue velvet perch. She looked hardly more than the size of a child, or a bag of slender, delicate bones. Her hearing apparatus was a crunched jumble of metal on the ground.

"Shine the light here," I whispered as I crouched (again, with less difficulty than usual due to my criminally appropriate clothing) next to Lady Thistle. She lay on her side, nearly facedown on the floor in a small heap. My eyes were damp and stinging as I touched the soft, bony hand flung out from her on the ground. "Stiff and cold," I murmured. "I need better light—"

"We've got to report it," said my companion, standing so close that her boots threatened to clutter the crime scene.

I knew the only reason she *was* so close was because there wasn't any evidence of blood so far; Evaline cannot stomach the gore associated with death and violence. It was a good thing vampires, when she staked them, simply poofed into dust instead of collapsed into piles of blood and guts.

And *of course* it was a crime scene. I didn't believe for a moment that Lady Thistle had just keeled over—and conveniently the day after I discovered the secret door in the closet.

"Right. There probably isn't a telephone in here; you'll have to go—"

A sound from the front of the shop, along with a swish of the door opening and a larger spill of light, had us both looking that way.

"What's going on in here?" asked a man, whose silhouette clearly showed the bobby hat worn by the Metropolitan Police. A second man was right behind him. Both held night sticks, and one carried a large lantern.

Evaline, who actually appeared to be thinking quickly for once—instead of acting without thinking—rushed forward to meet them. I heard her put on a quavery, shocked female act as she explained that we'd just happened to walk by and saw the door slightly ajar, and thought we'd best check and make sure nothing had happened, for we were both regular patrons of this site and knew Lady Thistle, and—

"Send word to Grayling," interrupted the bobby, speaking to his partner, and clearly not falling for Evaline's somber, if convoluted, tale. "He was expecting something like this to happen and wanted to be notified immediately—anytime, night or day."

Oh he was, was he?

Infuriating man.

The second policeman went off on his task, and despite my irritation at being anticipated by the too-smart-for-his-own-good Scotland Yard detective, I continued with my examination of poor Lady Thistle. I wanted to get as much data as I could before the bobbies came traipsing back here, contaminating the scene.

"Excuse me, miss, but you're going to have to let us see to it," said the policeman who'd remained. He was standing so that he cast an obliterating shadow over my work and didn't have the decency to shine his lantern over it to help.

"Evaline, would you *please* turn on a lamp?" I said, choosing, at the moment, to ignore the buffoon who would certainly make my investigation more difficult given the chance. Which I had no intention of giving. "There's no reason to be in the dark any longer."

"Miss," said the buffoon again. His lantern, still in probably the most unhelpful position possible, swung gently in his grip.

"Please step back," I said rather sharply as I made a matching gesture. "If you don't remove your feet from the vicinity, you're going to destroy any hope of clues. But you could shine that dratted lantern over here."

"Look, miss," he said, "it's not your place to be— It's not *right* for a lady to— Miss, *please*. This is a…a dead body. It could even be a break-in."

My advantage in this instance was the fact that he wouldn't dare put his hands on a lady in order to physically move her, though he *was* beginning to fray my nerves. I hadn't yet been able to turn Lady Thistle onto her back or establish a cause of death, and he was certainly not helping.

"Oh, Evaline, darling, please don't cry," I said earnestly. "I know it's terribly upsetting, finding her like this."

My colleague is nothing if not dramatic. She caught on immediately and began to sob loudly in a manner that was so obviously fake that I was astonished the policeman fell for it.

But then again, this was the same policeman possessing such a lack of common sense that he trod all over the scene of the crime and didn't bother to even try to illuminate it.

Evaline helped matters along by practically throwing herself into the man's arms, wailing with wild, racking sobs and raving on nonsensically. She even knocked his bobby hat askew. I might have felt sorry for him if he hadn't been so easily duped. I managed to reach up and snatch the lantern from his hand—since Evaline was otherwise occupied and hadn't found the lamp—and at last I got a good look at the body.

Though I didn't turn Lady Thistle over immediately, I could see there was no blood. It would have pooled beneath her onto the floor if she'd been cut or shot. If she'd been struck with some blunt instrument, there would be signs of blood and matted hair on the back or side of her head—none of which I observed.

That left asphyxiation, poison, or some sort of accidental or natural death, and though she could be considered elderly, I immediately dismissed the last possibility as being far too coincidental.

As I went about my examination, I managed to block out the sounds of my colleague carrying on, noting with approval that she'd managed to maneuver the bobby away from the area. I'd just finished a close study of Lady Thistle's fragile hands when a pair of boots appeared in my periphery.

I recognized them from the teeth marks and the frayed shoelace. I didn't bother to look up.

"Asphyxiation," I said, "by strangulation."

Grayling crouched next to me, having enough common sense not to disrupt the area with his feet. He brought with him the scent of cold night air, along with spearmint this time, wood smoke, and starched cotton. "What on earth is wrong with *her*?"

I hid a smile. He was referring to Evaline's caterwauling. "It's her way of offering assistance."

I believe he might have laughed if we hadn't been positioned next to a dead body. Instead, his demeanor was sober as he withdrew a small measuring device that I had secretly coveted since we'd first knelt next to a dead body together— that of Mayellen Hodgeworth, on the floor of the British Museum.

"Lady Thistle herself, I presume?" he said.

"She's been dead more than a day," I said, even though I knew his gadget would give a more accurate time of death. Which was why I coveted it. "Rigor has come and gone. She was—she was probably already gone when we were here yesterday."

"Yes," he murmured, and went about with his calculations. "Approximately forty hours," he said after a moment, tucking the gadget back into one of his large overcoat pockets and pulling out a magnifyer...*that had its own illumination.* "Is anything wrong, Miss Holmes?"

I smothered my moan of envy over his seemingly unending array of devices, and gave myself a sharp mental talking-to. Uncle Sherlock didn't rely on so many cognoggin gadgets and machines. I could, and would, do the same.

"Not a thing, Inspector Grayling. I was simply—er— Presumably you've noted the marks around her neck. Whatever was used to strangle her was—"

"Rough and patterned. Like this length of lace." He reached over into the edge of the shadows and procured a string of lace. I had seen it myself, of course, and had already noted the markings on the back of Lady Thistle's neck, which was the only part clearly visible. As I suspected, the width and scalloped edges of the abrasion matched the size and decor of the lace.

"Precisely. Naturally, her fingers have traces of skin beneath the nails—"

"And corresponding marks on her neck, as she attempted to free herself from the—"

"Naturally. And she was sitting on her stool over there when the killer came up behind her. The heel of her shoe got caught on one of the rungs of the stool, and it became loose during her violent struggles." I indicated the heel in question, which was crooked where it was tacked into the sole of her shoe. "She couldn't have walked on it like that, so it had to have happened during the struggle."

"Brilliant, Miss Holmes," he murmured without a trace of irony.

I smiled modestly.

"The killer appears to be a female," he went on, using forceps to draw a long, dark hair from the crease where Lady Thistle's shoulder met her neck.

"Likely a customer who came up behind her—perhaps after using the changing room in the back. Lady Thistle was hard of hearing, and it would have been simple to take her by surprise. And just as simple to overpower her."

"Did she have a shop assistant? Or anyone else who might have been inside regularly? If so, why wasn't the attack reported before now?"

"Magpie." I considered. "She's possessed of dark brown hair, and is certainly large and strong enough to be able to do the deed. And Lady Thistle wouldn't think anything of it if she were in the back room and came up from behind her." I didn't like the idea—Magpie had always seemed harmless as well as rather dim. But it was possible, and I knew better than to reject any possibility. "Shall we turn her over now?"

I allowed Grayling to do so, noting the gentle reverence of his large, freckled hands against the fragile bones of the elderly woman. Something stung the corner of my eye, and I realized this death was affecting me more than any of the others I'd come upon.

Perhaps it had something to do with the fact that visiting Lady Thistle's boutique was one of the few memories and connections I had of my mother—and that now I'd never have the opportunity to ask the shopkeeper for any more stories or memories about Mother.

I privately snapped at myself to buck up. My maudlin thoughts were contributing nothing to the situation, and were, in fact, focused too much on the past tense. There was no reason to deduce my mother was actually *dead*.

Though there was no reason to deduce otherwise, either.

I wrenched my thoughts from that circular path and continued my observation and examination, with Inspector Grayling assisting.

Unfortunately, there was little else to find on Lady Thistle's person, although I'd hoped for more personal traces from her attacker besides a single strand of hair. Grayling made notes with a mechanical ink pen in his fancy copper-wired notebook. It had metal pages which could be written on, then erased.

Grayling lifted the sagging knot of hair to expose the victim's throat and shoulders. "The abrasions here, on the left side of her neck, are slightly darker and deeper."

"Naturally. The killer was left-handed, and thus pulled more strongly with that hand."

"Precisely. The markings don't go all the way around her neck, so she—the murderer—didn't pull the lace crisscross at the back."

"She simply came up behind Lady Thistle, holding each end of the lace, then slipped it down and over the front of her face and pulled back—and slightly upward."

"Correct. If Lady Thistle were sitting on her stool, as you have noted, then the height of the killer would be…" His eyes tracked as he did a mental calculation. "Approximately sixty-seven inches. One moment, and I'll measure it for an exact number."

I pulled to my feet, using the wall to leverage against my corset's restrictions. "The lace, please, Inspector. I'd like to ascertain whether it's a stock she carries—er, carried—here."

Grayling obliged, and I went about the task, enlisting Evaline (who'd stopped wailing shortly after the inspector's arrival) to assist in combing through all of the drawers and boxes of ribbons and other fripperies, feathers, and furbelows.

By the time we'd finished—and discovered another length of the same lace—Grayling had covered the dead woman with a cloak he'd presumably taken from one of the displays.

The front door opened, and this time, the newcomers were two men with a stretcher who'd come to take the body away.

Soon after, the shop was deserted but for Evaline, Grayling, and myself.

"Very well, then," I said. "Thank you very much for your assistance, Inspector. I suppose we'd best be off—"

"Not so fast, Miss Holmes," Grayling said firmly.

Evaline made a squeaky noise that sounded almost mirthful and darted off into the shadows.

"What do you mean, Inspector?" I replied. I might have attempted to adopt the demeanor I'd seen Evaline do when she wanted to appear innocent, but when I widened my eyes, they began to water and dust motes flew into them, making it quite difficult to maintain that ingénue-ish expression.

"Och now, Miss Holmes. You're far too intelligent to think I'd believe your story of just happening to walk by the shop in the middle of the night with the door ajar. It's quite fortunate for you that I'd anticipated this sort of circumstance and made arrangements to be called to the scene. Otherwise, Officer Dagwood would have certainly been within his rights to arrest you both for trespassing, breaking and entering, and, quite possibly, *murder*."

I sniffed and lifted my chin to look down at him—an impossibility due to his excessive height, but I made the attempt nonetheless. "It wouldn't be the first time a Holmes had been falsely accused of villainy while in process of investigating a crime."

"I don't even need to ask what you were doing here," he went on, blithely ignoring my very salient point. "So let's get on with it, shall we? I'd like a bit of sleep before I have to report in."

I pursed my lips. "Very well. The closet with the hidden door is this way. I don't suppose you have a bigger illumination device in one of your pockets."

His only reply was to beam a clear, long, steady stream of light beyond me and into the depths of the shop's rear.

The backroom was no more cluttered or disorganized than it had been previously. And as I was wearing slightly less complicated attire tonight, I managed to navigate my way to the closet with the double-C carving on it without knocking into or dragging anything along with me.

Without comment, Grayling shined his light at the marking I'd noticed at the base of the closet door, then followed me inside the small space. I moved directly to the box marked "gemstones and feathers, misc." and reached inside to release the latch to the secret door…

But there was no latch. The box was not only actually filled with gemstones and feathers and miscellaneous, it was no longer attached to the shelf.

"What on *earth*?" I stared at the box, which wore the same innocent look I'd attempted to don only moments before.

"What is it, Miss Holmes?"

"The lever to open the door. It's gone." I removed the box from its position, explaining, "Only two days ago, this box—or one exactly like it—was affixed to the shelf and was empty of everything other than a small lever that opened the door. As you can see, that is no longer the case."

I thrust the box at him and turned to examine the shelf where the box had been positioned. The latch had been on the platform beneath the bottomless box—but the shelf was smooth and unmarred from anything resembling a latch.

"There's nothing here. It's *gone*." I began to examine the stack of shelves—which only days earlier had slid away to reveal the secret door. It no longer was anything but what it appeared to be.

"Someone killed Lady Thistle and removed—or, more precisely, blocked—the secret door," I said, stepping back away from it.

Grayling was standing…well, quite close to me in that small space, and as soon as I realized it, I momentarily felt my thoughts shimmer and threaten to evaporate. But it was only the flash of an instant before I recovered myself.

"May I?" he asked in a voice that sounded more low and rumbly than usual. "Perhaps I can determine whether the door is still there, and only obscured by a recent alteration."

I insisted on removing everything from the shelves on the back of the closet, and we did so quickly and efficiently, with me handing him the boxes one by one, and Grayling setting them on the floor.

He offered me the illuminator, and I beamed it around the area that had moved.

"There's no sign of a door," I said, frustration tight in my voice.

"May I?" he asked again, and this time I moved out of the way.

To my surprise, he began to pry the shelves from the wall. When he'd finished, he felt around the edges of the bookshelf, the wall, and even the floor. At last, he made a satisfied sound, and then there was a sound of groaning wood and protesting metal as he pulled away the back wall of the closet. It took several moments of rough activity before everything fell away.

"Your secret door," he said, not at all out of breath due to his exertions—although he had paused to remove his over-coat, and then his jacket.

"It's not *my* secret door," I said, moving to peer around him to see what had been revealed. "A *brick wall*? How…how extraordinary."

"Indeed. Someone," he said, brushing a hank of thick hair from off his forehead, "did not want anyone to come through here any longer."

I pushed past him, brandishing the illuminator. "The mortar is fresh. Barely set. Within a day or so."

"As I said, someone did not want anyone—most likely you, Miss Holmes—traversing through this route to The Carnelian Crow."

Drat.

"We could break through the brick wall—"

"We?" he said with a quirked eyebrow. "I hardly agree with your choice of pronoun, Miss Holmes. Aside from that, I've already done enough damage to private property this evening. I'm not inclined to break any more laws—at least at this point in time."

For obvious reasons, I declined to point out that *he* hadn't actually broken any laws prior to tearing away the false back wall of the closet.

"Someone does not want The Carnelian Crow to be easily discovered. Which, of course, means," he said, taking me firmly by the elbow to direct me from the dismantled closet, "you will not rest until you do."

"I hardly—"

"Miss Holmes," he said, "the sun is not long from rising,

and I do believe it's time for all of us to return to our homes. I would offer to give you a ride on my steamcycle, but I expect you'd prefer any other mode of transport."

I closed my mouth. I *might* have agreed to climb onto the rear seat and cling to him from behind as we tore through the streets, but since he'd taken on *that* sort of attitude, I certainly wasn't going to give him the satisfaction of commenting.

Infuriating man.

And so I made no argument, moving toward the front of the shop, where Evaline had occupied herself by modeling several hats that had fallen from the display when I became entangled in it earlier. I was rather surprised she hadn't been in the thick of the action when Grayling was tearing walls away and pulling nails from their moorings, but I can't claim to understand my colleague's decisions. Most of the time, she leaves me baffled by her impulsiveness.

She gave me an odd look, rolling her eyes and making them do all sorts of strange calisthenics—she appeared to be having a seizure—then huffed out a breath and shook her head. "For someone so brainy," she muttered, "you can be oblivious."

Grayling assisted us to find a hackney—not a simple prospect at nearly four o'clock in the morning—and bundled us inside. I was mildly surprised Evaline didn't argue or decline the ride in favor of patrolling the streets for UnDead —or Pix.

I, for one, was quite tired, and declined to speak during our ride home, preferring to restrict my activity to reviewing everything that had happened tonight.

It wasn't until I arrived home after dropping off Evaline (so I could pay the taxi fare, of course) that it occurred to me how almost pleasant my interactions had been with Inspector Grayling.

We'd examined and studied the crime scene without antagonizing each other, trading theories and observations with more camaraderie than my uncle ever did with someone from Scotland Yard.

It also occurred to me that not once during the entire evening had Grayling commented about my penchant for attracting dead bodies.

Fascinating.

Miss Stoker

~ In Which Our Heroine is Carried Wildly Downstream ~

FRIDAY, THE MORNING AFTER MINA AND I FOUND LADY Thistle's body, I was awakened just before noon when Pepper bustled in. She carried a tray with breakfast—a signal from Florence that it was past time for me to rise and face the day, as she put it.

I hated it when she said that. "Face the day." It was too chipper and too sunny, and worse yet, I knew that Florence's idea of "facing the day" was more like "meet more men who could be your husband."

I groaned and rolled over, burying my face in the pillow. Couldn't I just stay in bed? For about five years?

Not only was I not at all interested in "facing the day," but I also realized, as I had every morning for the last two months, that yet another night had gone by without hearing from Pix.

The deeply buried hope that he might sneak into my bedchamber—as he'd done in the past—was squashed every single morning when I opened my eyes and realized it hadn't happened.

"Mrs. Stoker says you 'ave a busy schedule today," said Pepper, giving me a sympathetic look as I lifted my head. She was aware of my vampire-hunter calling, and had been a great help in outfitting me. She'd also helped hide my true purpose from Florence. My maid's wild, pale carrot-colored hair poked out in frizzy tendrils from the edges of her cap and her brown eyes were sober as she continued, "She's going to be up in thirty minutes, and 'as a 'ole stack of inv'tations."

I groaned again, louder and more violently into the pillow. Unfortunately, I inhaled a feather afterward, and that had me sneezing loudly for a few minutes.

"What am I going to do?" I wailed softly. Though I didn't

really expect a response from my maid—after all, what could *she* do?

Nor could she fully understand what it was like to have one's main purpose in life limited to being married. Yes, she worked as a maid, doing considerable manual labor serving the more comfortable upper class, but at least she could decide whether she wanted to find a husband or not. And at least she could look for a new position with a different household if she chose.

Freedom, I was coming to realize, was more important than wealth and status.

With all of this on my mind, I was grumpy all through my morning bath. Pepper seemed to realize I wasn't in the mood for her normal chatter—which often included gossip about her friends who worked "downstairs" for other Society households.

(Why they called them "downstairs" people was always confusing to me, as most servants I knew had sleeping quarters in the uppermost levels of the households where they lived and worked. I suppose the term came because though they lived in the attic, their main work area was in the lower levels of the large houses—the kitchens and stables and pantries, which were on the ground or cellar floors.)

Pepper also liked to go on about ideas for how to better hide the tools of my trade (mainly stakes) in my clothing.

I sat at my dressing table as she did my hair, braiding it in a long plait, then twisting it into a figure-eight-shaped coil. Pepper was an expert at jamming in the hairpins to keep my heavy coiffure in place without them digging too painfully into my scalp.

At any rate, Florence was due in at any moment, and my mood was growing more and more dour. Maybe that was how it happened—maybe I was rubbing off on Pepper, sharing my glumness with her. It doesn't matter how or why my normally very efficient maid managed to knock over my entire jewelry case. But she did. It dumped to the floor, spilling necklets, chokers, earbobs, rings, and other items in a tangled, glittering mess.

We were both on the floor, scrabbling about to pick everything up, when Florence knocked and then came sweeping in.

She didn't make any comment about the situation—it was obvious what happened—but she was also as excited as a teakettle at full steam. "Evaline! You've just received a message from Mr. Oligary." I sighed and pulled to my feet as Florence continued to prattle on. "I do believe the man is becoming attached to you. That makes three days in a *row* since your first meeting.

"It was flowers the day after New Vauxhall Gardens—it was a shame you had to decline his invitation to the dinner party that night, but one must keep one's prior commitments. Besides, I believe it's best that he know how much in demand you are, Evaline. We can't make it *too* easy for him. It must be the perfect balance of availability and being in demand, you understand. And yesterday, he came to call and stayed longer than anyone else—even Mr. Broomall. Now today he's sending you a message—surely it's another invitation." She thrust it at me.

Shockingly, she hadn't broken the seal.

I was, of course, completely aware of everything she'd just said. Including her opinion that I needed to not be particularly available to Mr. Oligary—but I couldn't dissuade him, either. She'd been saying such things for days. Whenever possible. I'd even dreamed about it. In my nightmare, she'd had a *list* and kept going through it over and over and over again until I woke with a start.

Listlessly, I opened the invitation. "He's inviting me to the Yule Fête tomorrow night. He'd like to send a carriage."

Florence's eyes grew so wide I thought they were about to explode from her face. "*He wants to take you to the Yule Fête?* At Cosgrove Terrace? The biggest event of the holidays?"

All at once, she began dancing around the bed, laughing

and clapping and even giggling. She was swinging her skirt and petticoats as if she were a little girl.

"Evaline, do you know what this *means*? Do you realize what a statement he's making by taking you? Everyone in Society will know that he has serious designs on you if you show up on his arm at the Yule Fête!"

If there was any chance I might have misunderstood the implications, it was gone.

Well, I thought sourly, *at least Mina will be happy about me going to Cosgrove Terrace.*

Before I could stop her, Florence snatched the message from Mr. Oligary out of my grip. Oh, drat. Things were about to become even worse…

"*And he has invited* me *to come as chaperone!* Evaline!" Flo's blue eyes were bright and filled with tears of joy. Her cheeks flushed pink with happiness. "Good *heavens!* I'm going to Cosgrove Terrace! *I'm* going to *Cosgrove Ter—* Oh my goodness, what am I going to *wear*?"

With that, she spun from the room, leaving the rest of the invitations in a sprawled mess on my bed.

I looked at Pepper, our eyes meeting in the mirror: mine filled with misery, and hers quiet with understanding.

The wild, downstream situation was feeling more and more out of my control. The river was going faster and faster, and I felt as if I was not only unable to navigate it, but that up ahead was a big waterfall drop-off.

A big drop-off called *marriage.*

The only good thing—and it was a very small good thing, hardly even worth noting—was that surely Florence would leave me alone. She wouldn't expect me to do any other social activities today or tomorrow.

She'd be too busy planning our clothing for the Yule Fête.

I WAS MISTAKEN ABOUT ONE THING.

For the rest of the day and most of the next, Florence was indeed in a tizzy, planning our clothing (and hair and accessories and shoes…) for the Yule Fête. And I was correct—she didn't expect me to attend or host any social activities between the time we received Mr. Oligary's invitation and the moment his carriage was due to arrive Saturday evening.

However, I was wrong if I thought I'd be left to my own devices during that time.

No. In fact, I'd hardly had a moment to myself—except when I was sleeping Friday night. And even then, my dreams were filled with the same activities as my day had been: trying on clothing, sampling fabrics, traveling to Bond-street to visit a lace shop, a milliner, and several modistes.

Thus, by the time eight o'clock rolled around on the day of the event, I was desperate for Mr. Oligary's carriage to arrive. I could hardly wait to be whisked away to the fête. Maybe then I'd have some relative peace.

The carriage arrived precisely at eight o'clock, a full hour before the party was due to begin.

"There will simply be a *crush* of carriages," Florence said nervously as we waited upstairs for Brentwood to open the door to Mr. Oligary. It would never do for us to appear eager, or even waiting in the parlor—even though we'd been ready for well over thirty minutes. No, Florence informed me.

We must Make an Entrance.

I didn't think I'd ever been fussed over, poked and prodded and primped, as carefully and as forcefully as I had been for the last three hours. (That is not an exaggeration.)

I hated to think what I'd be subjected to on my wedding day, if I ever did get married. (Yet another reason for me not to go over that waterfall…)

"We'll surely be waiting at least an hour in the carriage to get to the top of the line. And, Evaline, you've never looked lovelier. I have a good feeling about tonight," Florence said, carefully smoothing her watered-silk skirt for about the dozenth time. "A very good feeling."

All at once, my grumpiness faded and was replaced by a

surge of affection and guilt. Though I would have happily missed tonight's ball, the event was a very special occasion for my sister-in-law. She'd never attended anything at Cosgrove Terrace, which was one of the fanciest, most exclusive homes in London. And she'd be mixing with the crème de la crème of the peerage as well—something I didn't particularly care about doing, but she certainly did. Bram was so busy at the Lyceum in the evenings that he rarely, if ever, was able to escort her to parties or balls. Since I made every excuse to avoid them, poor Florence hardly ever got out.

And, in all fairness, I suppose her anxiousness about the financial situation probably kept her and Bram up at night. If she thought it would soon be resolved by my marriage to a wealthy, powerful man, then no wonder she was so eager— and nervous.

Despite the fact that I felt like a sacrificial lamb going to the slaughter, I could understand her feelings. And because I did love and care about her and Bram, I resolved to stiffen my upper lip and be prepared to do what I must for the sake of my family.

Even if it meant giving up my limited freedom.

Yet even as I made this decision, even though it was made for a selfless reason, my stomach pinched painfully.

Surely there had to be another way.

It wasn't until we were settled in the carriage with Mr. Oligary that a completely different thought crossed my mind.

The last time I'd been at Cosgrove Terrace, Pix had been there, dressed as a servant. He'd been snooping around (just as I had been doing, although I'd had a non-criminal reason to be doing so).

I couldn't help but wonder—even hope—whether that might happen again.

Miss Holmes

~ Meanwhile, Our Other Heroine is on
a Runaway Locomotive ~

HOW EXTRAORDINARY.

That had been my reaction when, on the day after we'd found Lady Thistle's body inside her boutique, I received a message delivered to my door shortly after noon.

Due to the late hour in which I'd returned home after our nocturnal adventures, I hadn't risen from my bed until nearly eleven o'clock. And then, after my toilette, I had been debating whether to visit the British Museum to see whether I could discover when Miss Adler had left and where she'd gone—and whether I should be concerned about her absence —or whether to continue to badger Miss Stoker into trying to obtain an invitation to the Cosgrove-Pitts' Yule Fête.

It was a pity I wouldn't be able to find a way to attend. For not only did I want Evaline to try and ferret out a clue— any clue—that could prove Lady Isabella's identity as the Ankh, but I also wanted to come face to face with the woman herself now that I knew *she* knew that *I* knew for certain she was the Ankh.

I was doing all of this internal debating while in my laboratory, closely examining a second strand of long, dark hair that Inspector Grayling had removed from Lady Thistle's body—which presumably belonged to the elderly lady's murderer—when Mrs. Raskill interrupted with the message, which had been delivered. The messenger, she informed me, was waiting for a response.

My first reaction, as I have indicated, was one of shock and delight, tied up with a bit of bafflement—for the message read:

MISS HOLMES,

137

I would consider it an honor if you should agree to be my guest at the Yule Fête to be given at Cosgrove Terrace tomorrow night. If you are in agreement, I shall call for you at quarter past eight.

(Inspector) Ambrose Grayling.

How extraordinary, I thought more than once throughout the rest of the day, and even while I was preparing for the ball.

(Naturally, this was after I'd sent the messenger away with an acceptance of his kind invitation.)

The Yule Fête was not the sort of event I would expect a Scotland Yard investigator to attend—despite the fact that he was "my husband's cousin's nephew by marriage," as Lady Cosgrove-Pitt had once explained.

I gnawed over the implications not only of the surprising fact that Grayling was attending the ball, but that he had invited me to accompany him. I came up with a number of possible explanations for both, including the most likely being he wanted my assistance with the investigation into some case on which he was working—most likely the Hiram Bartholomew/Emmett Oligary incident. Or the Lady Thistle affair. Or perhaps even the mysterious Carnelian Crow establishment, despite his protestations to the contrary.

After all, I was the one who'd received the crow pendant —which Pix had told me to "wear."

Regardless of the reason for my unanticipated but greatly appreciated invitation, I was going to the fête. Therefore, with the help of Mrs. Raskill (who could be quite a genius when it came to hair and if she was so inclined), I was ready and waiting well before the appointed time on Saturday evening. So when a carriage pulled up out front, I saw no reason to waste time waiting for Grayling to alight, stride up the walk, and knock on my door.

"Good evening, Inspector," I said as I opened the door and came out to meet him.

He appeared startled by my sudden and brisk appearance. His gait hitched and he halted in seeming confusion only a few steps from the carriage.

"Miss Holmes. Why, there you are. How—er… I expected it would be necessary for me to—mm—wait for you to—er— be ready to leave."

"As you indicated you'd be here at quarter past eight, I made certain to be prepared to depart promptly at that time. Why on earth would I be so inconsiderate as to keep you waiting?" I asked, breezing past him to the carriage.

When I saw that our mode of transport was a nicely sprung but several years outdated horse-drawn barouche instead of a hackney cab, I immediately deduced that Grayling had somehow managed to borrow it from a friend or acquaintance. To my knowledge, his only form of vehicular transport was that wild steamcycle, and of course it wouldn't do to arrive at a formal occasion after riding astride on such a thing. He certainly couldn't afford to own a private carriage—especially with the amount of money he obviously spent on gadgets and devices.

I nodded to the driver, and would have clambered in myself, but Grayling insisted on offering a hand—which, in retrospect, was probably a good thing, considering my tendency to catch my feet on everything from petticoats and cobblestones, hat racks and door thresholds, and sometimes even themselves.

As always, it took me far longer to settle into my seat and arrange all the yards of delicate fabric that made up my complicated, glittering evening costume than it did Grayling. When I had finished that task, I looked up and across at him and realized with a start that he looked quite, *quite* handsome.

Even in the dim light from the lamp that dangled inside the carriage, I could see that he'd shaved closely and carefully, trimmed his dark copper sideburns, and tamed his thick, curling hair into a fashionable style. I could smell the lemon-rosemary remnants of pomade, and noted with appreciation that he hadn't overused the product like so many other men did, leaving their hair slippery, stiff, or, worse, with remnants of the dried pomade falling off in flakes. (Not that I'd actually *touched* such overly pomaded hair, but it wasn't difficult to visually assess such a condition.)

He was wearing a correct black topcoat with tails, and over it a heavy dark gray overcoat I hadn't seen before. It was made from fine Betrovian wool and looked far too expensive for a Scotland Yard investigator's salary. Perhaps Lord Cosgrove-Pitt had assisted in his nephew by marriage's correct attire for this affair. Beneath, Grayling's shirt appeared to be perfectly starched white cotton, and the waistcoat was a luxurious green and black brocade. His necktie matched the vest, and his gloves were so white they appeared to glow in the drassy light. A satin top hat and copper-fitted walking stick completed his ensemble. From his person wafted the gentle scent of peppermint mingled with the pomade, along with some other essence that I found particularly pleasing...yet I couldn't define what it was.

As I finished this study of his person, my attention went to his eyes, wherein I discovered he'd been giving me the same close examination. Our gazes met, and all at once I found it difficult to draw in a breath. And though I had meant to say something, suddenly no words came to mind. My mind had gone strangely blank.

"You—er—you look very pretty, Miss Holmes," he said in a voice that sounded as if a frog had lodged near his uvula. He cleared his throat. "That is to say, particularly lovely. Tonight."

"Thank you, Inspector." I subdued a strong compulsion to shift in my seat and fuss with my skirt while looking anywhere but at him. Instead, I gathered my unusually scattered thoughts and said, "Now then, which one is it?"

"Pardon me?"

"Which one? Which case?"

Grayling looked at me as if I were speaking some strange language he couldn't translate. "I'm afraid I'm not following your question."

"Which case are we investigating tonight? I deduced that's why you're going to Cosgrove Terrace. You must have some sort of clue to follow up on. And of course you are in need of my assistance. Do you have a lead in the Lady Thistle murder? Or perhaps—and, may I remind you, I've offered my help previously—it's the Hiram Bartholomew incident. In fact, Evaline did a bit of investigation on that when she was with Mr. Oligary at New Vauxhall. Perhaps her conversation with him might shed some new light on the subject—you know how witnesses can remember different things later on." The words tumbled from my mouth like a wild locomotive whose brakes suddenly stopped working as it careened down a mountain. "And I did spend some time in my laboratory examining the hair you discovered on Lady Thistle's body— the one presumably belonging to her attacker. It is most definitely a real hair, not from a wig. Nor is it horse hair."

Grayling seemed to be having difficulty finding his words now. "Case. Right. Er…Miss Holmes, I regret to inform you that…och, well…that I had no particular case in mind to investigate tonight. I merely—that is to say—I merely thought it would be pleasant to attend the Yule Fête. With—er—you."

I blinked.

And suddenly, just as my bedchamber had seemed to shrink in size when he'd gone in to investigate the crow markings outside my window, so did the interior of the carriage all at once become much smaller.

Not in an uncomfortable way, but in a very…*aware* sort of way. A strangely pleasant way.

"I see. I—"

He rushed on, "I do hope you aren't disappointed, Miss Holmes."

"No. No, no, no, I'm not disappointed," I said quickly, aware that my face had become undeniably warmer. I certainly hoped he couldn't see what surely must be a bright red tint in my cheeks. "Not at all."

"I'm relieved to hear that." He hesitated, then continued, "After all, we had discussed perhaps meeting at the British

Museum to take in the Japanese woodprint exhibit. And when Lady Cosgrove-Pitt insisted I attend the fête tonight, I...well, I thought of you."

Now my cheeks felt as if they were on fire, and I shifted on the bench seat in an effort to move out of the small circle of light so as to hide the glow beneath my skin. Though it was so bright he probably could see it in the dark. "I am most obliged, Inspector."

"However," he went on as his lips curved into a smile (why had I never noticed before what a nice shape they were?), "if you'd like to discuss either the Lady Thistle murder, or the Hiram Bartholomew-Emmett Oligary case and what Miss Stoker might have learned, I do believe we'll have ample time to do so."

He gestured toward the carriage window, which revealed the very long line of vehicles leading up to Cosgrove Terrace.

"Right," I replied, and was relieved to be able to focus on something I fully understood: mysteries. "Perhaps you'd care to enlighten me as to whether you've uncovered any suspects in the death of Lady Thistle. Have you been able to locate Magpie?"

"The individual known as Magpie—apparently her real name is Mary Kay Maggie—hasn't been seen at the small room she lets for several days. Her two fellow boarders—three of them rent the small room at a boarding house—claim to have no idea of her whereabouts. However," he added as the carriage lurched forward a few feet, "I was able to obtain a hair from the pillow on which she normally sleeps."

"And?"

"It is long and dark, and under a hyper-magnifyer, it appears to be identical to the ones found on Lady Thistle's body."

"Interesting." Then I narrowed my eyes. "A hyper-magnifyer? I suppose it's a new gadget of yours." I tried not to sound wistful, but am not certain I succeeded.

He grinned, which had the pleasant effect of making his eyes light up and attractive crinkles appear at their corners.

There was even the hint of a dimple in one cheek. "Indeed. It's quite extraordinary, and I've found it immeasurably helpful when studying crime scenes. Perhaps you'd like to try it out yourself, Miss Holmes. You could compare the hair you've been examining to the other two."

I beamed back at him as my cognoggin heart gave a pleasant little thump. "Would tomorrow be convenient?"

"Why, yes, of course," he replied. "Any time you like. I can meet you at my office. Angus would be delighted to see you as well."

"I've become rather fond of the little beast," I confessed.

We smiled at each other for a moment before I realized it.

"And as to the other cases?" I prompted. "Perhaps we should discuss them. The Bartholomew-Oligary affair?"

"Clearly you've previously familiarized yourself with that incident." By the way he was looking at me with an exasperated and almost affectionate expression, I realized he was referring to the time I'd nearly been caught digging through the files he kept in his office desk.

Drat. I didn't think he'd noticed. But if he had, he then knew that *I* knew he also had a file called "The Individual Known as the Ankh," as well as "The Possible Evidence of Vampires in London." Which meant he knew more than I thought he did.

And then there was the file I had decided I would never mention—the one named "Melissa Grayling." His mother, whom he'd found stabbed to death when he was nine.

"I am aware of the particulars of the Bartholomew case, yes," I replied blandly. "My understanding is there is an individual known as Edison Smith who is the prime suspect for what happened in an electrical accident."

"That is correct. Mr. Oligary is certain Smith had something to do with the accident—and that it wasn't an accident after all, but a business deal gone bad. But the man seems to have disappeared. No one has seen him since then, and it's been nearly four years."

"Do you have any leads on his whereabouts? One would

assume if he were involved in such an accident—if it was truly an accident—he would have returned to America as expediently as possible."

"One would assume." Then Grayling frowned. "Did you say Miss Stoker was with Mr. Oligary? That seems… Well, he is quite a bit older than she."

"Miss Stoker was with Mr. Ned Oligary—the younger. He appears to be courting her, and I anticipate seeing both of them here at Cosgrove Terrace tonight." I sighed, suddenly reminded of the unpleasant reality my colleague faced. "It's become apparent that Miss Stoker is going to be required to marry very soon. She is not at all pleased."

"Required? Pardon me for saying so, Miss Holmes, but it sounds as if you disagree with that—er—necessity as well as Miss Stoker."

"I should say I do." I realized my tone was rather sharp, but I saw no reason to hide my feelings. "Miss Stoker has no desire to wed, and neither do I."

"You don't?"

I hardly heard his faint, shocked response, for my locomotive was barreling along once again. "There might be some women who wish to marry and have a family and manage a household, but I have other things I intend to do, such as solve murders and investigate crimes and—and any number of interesting things. Travel. Experiment. Perhaps go on an archaeological dig.

"A husband would only be a nuisance. And Miss Stoker is of the same mind. Inspector Grayling, once a woman is wed, she is no longer considered her own person. She belongs to her husband, who is able to make all decisions for her: where she goes, what she does, how much money she can spend— even if it's *her* money—and on what. She's expected to sit at home and accept callers in the parlor and serve them tea and biscuits, and to wear clothing that is more restrictive than a yoke or horse bridle, and to have no thoughts of her own about politics or science or law or—or anything. She—"

I stopped suddenly when I observed his stunned expression. Clearly, I'd rendered him speechless and, most likely, utterly appalled at my point of view. Not that I cared about his opinion, when it came down to it.

And then there was the fact that Dylan Eckhert had told me that in the future, in the twenty-first century, women were free to do whatever they wished and when—and that they'd had the vote since the early twentieth century. I knew I was just a hundred years before my time.

If I had hoped a man of my time might understand my opinion and feelings, I was bound to be disappointed—as was evidenced by the baffled expression on Grayling's face.

"I see," he said after a moment. "I suppose I'd never thought of it quite that way."

"Most men haven't, I venture to say," was my dry retort.

I might have continued my lecture, but at that moment, our carriage pulled up to the main entrance of Cosgrove Terrace.

"Miss Holmes," Grayling said when I made a move to scramble to my feet unassisted, "you might not be in need—or in want—of a husband, but you might nonetheless wish to avail yourself of some leverage while disembarking from the carriage. I would hate to see your lovely gown tear or otherwise be ruined."

He'd risen and now loomed over me in the low-ceilinged carriage as he edged toward the door, which had been opened by the Cosgrove-Pitts' footman.

"Of course," I said, mildly embarrassed at my show of overeagerness. "Thank you, Inspector."

His hand was, as always, strong and steady as he helped me down. He waited patiently while I collected all of my hems, ruffles, and gathers and made certain they fell into their proper arrangement beneath my cloak.

Then he offered me his arm and we walked up the broad expanse of stairs that led to the front entrance of the house. The previous time I'd come to Cosgrove Terrace had been in June, and the Roses Ball had taken place on the rear of the house, where an entire wall had been opened so the party could spill out onto a terrace.

As it was winter, and a brisk, cold evening being sprinkled with fat snowflakes, this fête would obviously take place inside.

As we waited in line to be announced by the butler, Grayling assisted me in divesting myself of my cloak, and saw to it that we received a tag for both pieces of our outerwear. The tag was a number that would be typed into the automated coat-check machine that clicked through to the proper location and retrieved the garments, rather than having maids and footmen digging through piles of clothing at the end of the night.

"Miss Alvermina Holmes and Inspector Ambrose Grayling," announced the butler.

I groaned inwardly at the use of my formal name, and glanced at Grayling, who, thankfully, didn't seem to be offended by it. Nor did anyone else in the grand spread of the ballroom ten steps below us seem to notice or care. The noise from the crush of people was deafening, and I didn't see how anyone would be able to make their way across the room with it being so tightly packed.

Despite the roar of conversation, exclamations, and laughter, however, one smooth, throaty voice did reach my ears as Grayling and I stepped away from the butler.

"Ambrose! You did make it…and you've brought a guest. Why—Miss Holmes, is it?"

As my heart beat rapidly and my insides churned, I turned to face Lady Cosgrove-Pitt…also known to me as the cunning villainess the Ankh.

Miss Stoker

~ Our Two Heroines in a Night of Déjà Vu *~*

I THOUGHT I'D MISUNDERSTOOD WHEN I HEARD THE butler announce "Miss Alvermina Holmes and Inspector Ambrose Grayling," but when I turned to look, there they were.

Apparently she had wrangled herself an invitation after all. I suppose I shouldn't have been surprised. Mina was not one to be thwarted in her desires.

"Evaline, look!" whispered Florence as she elbowed me in the ribs. "Those wreaths on the walls are made from *fur*! And did you see the tables of food? They're longer than Fleet-street!" She hit me in the exact same place she'd done thrice already. I would have a bruise that even my Venator vampire-hunting blood couldn't immediately heal.

Fortunately, Mr. Oligary had stepped away for a moment to fetch us something to drink, for Florence hadn't stopped gawking and whispering since we'd arrived. She was beginning to embarrass me.

Not that I could blame her. I was probably gawking a little myself—and so was everyone else in the room. The Yule Fête had turned the inside of Cosgrove Terrace's high-ceilinged ballroom and dining room into a stunning, glittering blue-and-white forest.

Pine trees of every shape and size had been brought in and draped with silver and blue tinsel. The scent of evergreen was so thick in the air that poor Miss Hasherby was sneezing uncontrollably. But a bit of discomfort was not about to keep her from the Event of the Year, so she put on a brave—if not red-nosed and watery-eyed—face and kept a handkerchief in her hand.

Tiny blue lights twinkled from icy white bunting strung along the trio of balconies that overlooked the ballroom. More swaths draped overhead, creating a cloudlike, silvery canopy above us. Delicate ice-blue tapestries fluttered softly on every wall, fringed at the top and bottom with a darker shade. A huge ten-foot wreath made from white feathers and snowy fur hung in front of each tapestry. Elegant tree branches painted silver arched over every doorway and alcove, and were strung with matching round ornaments.

More blue and white sparkled beneath our feet, for a clear glass covering had been laid over the permanent bleached pinewood floor. This revealed a spiral of flickering sapphire lights that glowed from below, frosting the bottom of each gown and pair of trousers with icy blue. I stared down at it for quite some time before I realized each light was a candle inside a blue glass holder. I couldn't begin to imagine the cost and labor associated with only installing the floor!

Mechanical snowy owls with huge sapphire eyes flew silently from tree to bunting to balcony, somehow either invisibly wired or currently managed by some unseen hand.

There was more…so much more. Everything was ice blue and silver: the livery of the servants (I looked carefully at each footman I passed, hoping to recognize Pix beneath some obscure disguise), the trays (silver), the goblets (filled with some fizzing blue beverage), the orchestra (the piano and violins were white; the flutes and trumpets were silver; the musicians were dressed in sapphire).

Even the food: vanilla-white macaroons, tiny blue frosted cakes no larger than a whole walnut, bite-sized pyramids that I discovered were cheesecakes coated with silver fondant. I also saw plates of blue cheese and pale crackers adorned with blueberries, as well as some other biscuit-like items I was told were blue corn cakebread. They were apparently brought from Mexico.

"Where on earth did they find blueberries in December?" Florence whispered.

I didn't know, but before I could respond, Mr. Oligary had returned. He was carrying a fancy metal contraption. It had four silver champagne flutes securely fitted into place at their tops, which kept them safe from the constant jostle of elbows and shoulders.

"One for each of you," he said, carefully detaching them to present Florence and myself with a glass of champagne (*champagne!*), "one for me, and an extra for— Ah, isn't this your friend Miss Holmes?"

But I had already seen her, as she barged her way through the crowd with Grayling in her wake. As most always happened, I was immediately struck by the absolute gorgessity of her ensemble.

For one who was so completely cloud-headed when it came to feminine wiles and social engagement, Mina Holmes had a shockingly flawless sense when it came to fashion. I supposed that was one thing she'd acquired from her mother Desirée.

The best way to describe her gown was a froth of gold and copper. Though it was a winter ensemble, everything about it appeared light and airy—putting one in mind of a golden snowflake. It was made from layers of some crisp, shiny fabric I couldn't identify but that made me think of thin, golden ice, along with tulle sprinkled with sequins that peeked from the petticoats beneath, as well as between the layers of ice fabric.

Lush, almond-colored fur edged the bottommost hem of her underskirt and the gossamer wrap she'd draped across her throat, which dangled behind over each shoulder. There was a cunning little train that cascaded behind her, which was probably just asking for trouble when it came to Mina Holmes and her ability to trip and catch over nothing but her own two feet. Though I couldn't see them, I guessed she was wearing shoes with slender gold or bronze heels (again, not a good idea).

Her hair, already golden brown with glints of copper and bronze in it, matched the dress and was piled in a lovely array of curls at the top and back of her head. She wore an evening hat of almond fur, which was decorated with copper roses, gold mums, and a wide bronze velvet ribbon. Her gloves were a matching bronze velvet, covering her from upper arm to their fingerless tips. Tiny seed pearls and topazes glittered from all over her heart-shaped bodice, which was partially covered by a Street Fashion over-corset.

"Evaline," she said abruptly, "you look very nice. I must speak—"

I laid a hand on her velvety glove and squeezed, quite firmly, to silence her. "Miss Mina Holmes, may I introduce you to Mr. Ned Oligary. Mr. Oligary, please meet Inspector Ambrose Grayling of Scotland Yard. Inspector, I'd like to make my sister-in-law Florence Stoker known to you as well."

"Of course Grayling and I have met," said Mr. Oligary. "He's the detective on the case regarding my brother's business partner's murder." He gallantly offered the fourth flute of champagne to Mina.

She didn't seem to notice, she was so intent on getting my attention and dragging me off. Fortunately, Grayling rescued the glass before she knocked it out of Mr. Oligary's hand.

I had a brief moment to admire how nicely Inspector Grayling was presenting this evening, and what a handsome couple the two of them made—and how he couldn't take his eyes from her—before Mina said, "Please excuse Miss Stoker and myself for a moment," and hustled me away.

"Blooming Pete, Mina, what is wrong with you?" I said, while managing to avoid her stomping on my foot. Then my eyes widened. "Is it Pix? Did you see him here?'

"Pix? No, of course not. Don't be silly, Evaline," she replied. "What would he be doing here? I saw Lady Isabella."

I lifted my eyebrows then spoke slowly, as if leading a child. "It's her fête."

"I know that," she snapped. "It's— Something's going to happen tonight. She practically told me so."

My skepticism evaporated. "What did she say? What do you think is going to happen?"

"I have no dratted idea. But it was the way she looked at me as we came through the receiving line. And she pretended not to be certain of my name. 'Miss Holmes, is it?' she said—

as if she'd never met me before and wasn't quite aware of my identity. Which is complete rubbish, of course. She knows *precisely* who I am."

Mina was quite steamed, and I avoided a stray elbow as she continued on. "Then she took my hand and leaned toward me, saying very softly, just so I could hear, 'I'm so very glad you're here tonight. It's going to be a very *triumphant* evening.'"

I waited for more, but she'd stopped speaking. (A triumph in itself.)

"All right," I said after a moment of Mina staring at me with fish eyes, as if she expected me to whip out a stake or some other weapon and go charging off to fight some battle.

"Evaline, she was *warning* me that something is going to happen. Something big."

"What do you think it is?" I asked, feeling quite at a loss. "I'm not sensing any UnDead in the vicinity."

"I don't suppose you thought to bring a stake anyway," she muttered.

"As a matter of fact, I did," I replied haughtily. Pepper had managed to hide one cunningly beneath my skirts.

Mina was flummoxed. "Miss Stoker, you *are* beginning to learn. Perhaps, one day, you'll even concoct a *plan*."

I rolled my eyes. Planning took time. When one was a vampire hunter, one didn't have the luxury of time. One had to *act*.

"Right, then. So what do you think is going to happen?" I asked again. "Are you certain she wasn't just talking about the party being a triumph because—well, look at this place. Everything here is utterly perfect. People will be talking about this fête for years. Maybe that's all she meant."

"I don't know," Mina replied, clearly frustrated. "I have no idea. If I did—well, we'd have to try and stop whatever it is. But I don't know."

"What do you want me to do?"

"Keep an eye out, of course. For anything that seems odd."

I couldn't help a grin. "Seeing you and Grayling together without arguing or trying to one-up the other seems pretty odd to me. How did you manage to arrange that?"

I'd never seen Mina blush before, but she certainly did right then.

"He sent me an invitation yesterday," she said, lifting her nose. "I assumed it was because he wanted assistance in a professional manner, but apparently he was simply in need of a guest to accompany him."

I barely restrained my laughter. "For a Holmes, you can be completely brainless sometimes. Of course he wanted to bring you to the biggest Christmas party of the year. He's smitten with you."

"He is no such thing," she retorted, with her cheeks going even redder. "Smitten? Why that's a word no one would ever apply to me, in any way. Don't be ridiculous."

"Dylan was smitten with you," I reminded her. I was very much enjoying her discombobulation. "He even kissed you."

"That was—well, that was different. Dylan didn't belong here. In our time. He didn't think of me as strange for wanting to be on my own and do the sorts of things you and I have been doing." Her eyes had gone a little sad. "Just think of it, Evaline. If we lived in the future—like Dylan—you wouldn't *have* to get married. No one could force you to do it. It wouldn't be *expected*. You wouldn't be considered an old maid or on the shelf or unworthy if you chose to remain single."

My enjoyment faded at the reminder of the fate awaiting me. I glanced over and saw Florence engaged in earnest conversation with Mr. Oligary and Inspector Grayling. She was probably doing her best to get Mina married off as well.

It was true. An unmarried woman was considered useless in our world. There was a reason spinsters were considered "on the shelf"—like a useless old toy.

I looked back at my friend, who was watching me with an expression of pity and entreaty. "Have you decided what to do?" she asked, her eyes flickering toward my beau.

"No. Of course not. It's only been a few days. I've got time."

"But what if he asks you? Evaline, it's been all over the *Ladies' Tattle-Tale*—you and Ned Oligary. I even saw a mention in the *Times* about you going to New Vauxhall with him."

"I don't care about the *on dits*," I snapped, feeling my lungs tighten. "Those gossip notes don't mean anything except that some newspaper person was bored and had to write about something."

"Lord Bells-Ferry only knew Leticia Spring for three days before he proposed to her," Mina said. "And what about Baron Qualley? He asked Jemmy Richards the day after her debut. You debuted into Society almost two years ago, Evaline—despite the fact that you've dodged as many events as possible. From what I hear, they've—all of the husband prospects—been waiting for you to show some sign of wanting a proposal. And now you've done."

"*I* haven't done," I said, my eyes stinging with fury. "*I* haven't done at all. It's Florence and Bram. It's their fault, and now I'm going to have to—to sacrifice myself—my *life*—to fix their mess." I could feel my nose starting to drip and the angry flush warming my cheeks.

"Evaline—"

But I had already turned away, blind with angry tears I knew I had to hide before I found myself written up in the gossip *on dits* for a different reason than being on Ned Oligary's arm and on the marriage mart.

Keeping my face averted, I pushed my way along the edge of the ballroom, anxious to get somewhere I could collect myself in private. I bumped into a maidservant dressed in the ice-blue livery, and nearly sent her tray of glasses tumbling. I didn't pause, but dodged around one of the silver-painted trees and along one of the fluttering tapestries that covered the wall.

The orchestra had begun to play, and the swell of music distracted many of the partygoers because it was time to find a partner and dance. I walked even faster; the last thing I wanted was Mr. Oligary—or anyone else—to intercept me for a dratted waltz or blasted quadrille.

Finally I broke free from the ballroom, slipping past a dividing screen that blocked a short corridor. The passageway was empty of everything but a small table and one painting above it. Tucked away from the roar of the crowd, it was much quieter here. Unfortunately, it didn't seem to lead anywhere; there was a double door at the end that probably opened into a study or library. That meant I couldn't make the escape I'd fantasized about making: of walking down a hall, finding another way out of the house, and running away.

Running away from *everything*.

I looked toward the doors speculatively, then began to walk toward them. Maybe there was a terrace outside the window and I could—

No. That was cowardly.

Running away wouldn't help.

Venators didn't run away. Grandmother Victoria surely never ran away.

Just as I reached the door, I heard the unmistakable rustle of skirts and starched petticoats. I spun, ready to shout at Mina to leave me alone—but it wasn't her. It was the maidservant I'd nearly bowled over. She was still carrying her tray, though the glasses were missing.

"I'm looking for the ladies' retiring room," I said, averting my face so she wouldn't see the tinge of red in my nose and eyes. Servants were the worst gossips, mainly because no one ever paid attention to them.

Without a word, she set the tray down on a half-table. To my surprise, she murmured, "In there," and pointed to the door I'd been about to open.

I didn't have to be told twice. I slipped inside and closed the door behind me.

It was not, however, the ladies' retiring room. As I'd expected, it was a study. The heavy maroon leather furnishings and faint scent of tobacco told me it belonged to Lord Cosgrove-Pitt and not his wife. It didn't matter; no one was here and I'd have a few moments to compose myself.

But I'd barely stepped away from the door when I heard the knob turn behind me. I whirled, ready to send the nosy maidservant away in no uncertain terms.

She slipped inside and closed the door behind her, then turned around to face me. "Evaline."

I gasped and looked at her closely for the first time. It wasn't a maidservant at all. It was Pix.

Miss Stoker

~ Two Skirted Figures in an Unsatisfactory Tete-a-Tete ~

WE STARED AT EACH OTHER FOR A MOMENT.

"You look surprisingly attractive in a dress, Pix," I managed to say, even as I battled back the rush of relief.

He's alive. He's well. He's here.

"Blue is a very flattering color on you." I fervently hoped he couldn't see the remnants of my tears or my red nose.

"What is it, Evaline?" He came toward me, rustling like a woman, but moving like a man. "What's wrong?"

I didn't have the chance to step away before he took me by the arms and brought me close enough that I could feel his warmth and the faint smell of tobacco and whoever had worn the maid's dress previously. It was incredibly strange looking into a face topped by a female wig and mobcap, along with some sort of makeup that made him appear feminine and slightly altered the shape of his cheeks and jaw.

But his dark eyes bored into mine, and they were all Pix.

I had no words to respond to his heartfelt question. I was afraid if I even tried to speak, all the emotions I'd packed away for weeks would come rolling out: fear and anger at him for disappearing without a word, fury about my situation and how helpless I was to change it, and—most of all—the realization that I cared more for this cunning, mysterious, disreputable thief than I should…and that, very soon, once my future was set, I was never going to be able to see him again.

At least, not in the way I wanted to.

So I pulled from his grip and stepped away. I kept my voice and expression cold and hard. "What are you doing here?"

"Evaline. You were crying. What—"

"What happened to your damned accent, *Mr. Smith?*" I shot back, unashamed by the unladylike word, fighting to keep the frustrated tears at bay.

He looked at me, holding up his hands as if he expected me to lunge at him. "All right, then." He put some space between us. "All right."

By now, I'd collected myself. "Nice to see you again, Pix." I was very proud of my cool, flat tone. "Sorry I don't have time to chat. But it's time I returned to the party. I was a trifle warm. Needed some air."

"Right." The weight of his gaze, the seriousness in his eyes, told me he had plenty more to say. But for some reason, he remained silent, just looking at me as if he'd never seen me before.

Or as if he'd never see me again.

With a pinched heart, I started for the door as promised.

I could have insisted he tell me what he was doing here, and why he'd disappeared without a word.

I could have teased him about wearing petticoats and maybe even a corset, and needled him about his choice of face powder.

I could have interrogated him about The Carnelian Crow and the Ankh.

I could have demanded to know whether he was Edison Smith. Whether he was wanted for murder.

But I didn't.

I wasn't brave enough.

My hand was almost to the doorknob when I heard his swift intake of breath behind me.

"Evaline." He said my name in a tone he'd never done before. In a sort of tight, strangled whisper.

I wanted to turn back, but I knew better. I felt the prickling at the nape of my neck—not that portent of the UnDead, but of something more intimate. More pleasant, and familiar.

"Don't do it." His words were almost unintelligible. But somehow I heard them, and I knew what he was referring to.

And it wasn't about me leaving the room.

"I have to," I replied, staring at the door only inches from my face. My vision was beginning to blur. "I have no choice."

More rustling behind me. He'd moved closer. And though I felt him, very, very close, he didn't touch me.

"Why? Why does it have to be him?" His voice was filled with loathing. "*Oligary?*"

And that very question—the tone of it, the fact that he'd asked it—answered my own unspoken one. Numbness overtook me, but I managed to move my fingers toward the knob.

"Goodbye—"

"*Evaline—*"

The knob turned without me even touching it, and I stumbled back as the door opened.

"Miss Stoker?"

"Mr. Oligary!" I was barely able to keep from shrieking with shock.

"Is everything all right?" He was there now, in the study with Pix and me, his voice and expression filled with concern.

"Yes, yes. Yes, everything's fine." I had the urge to babble, and I had to use every bit of control to calm myself. Why was I so nervous? I hadn't done anything wrong. "I—er—there was a problem with my gown, and—er—she was helping me attend to it." I gestured carelessly toward Pix behind me as I moved forward to slip my hand through Mr. Oligary's arm in an effort to keep him from coming completely into the room.

"Your gown," he said, stepping back a trifle so as to give himself a better look, "appears absolutely perfect to me. Have I mentioned how lovely you look in it, Miss Stoker? The belle of the ball—at least in my eyes."

I made a noise that I hoped was taken as a sound of gratitude for his compliment, but the fact that Pix was standing there, watching and hearing all of this, made me feel ill. He'd gone utterly silent and still, yet I was more aware of him than ever. My entire body was prickling unpleasantly.

"Right then…er, is that a waltz I hear?" I said, once again moving closer to Mr. Oligary in hopes of backing him out the door. My skirt and petticoats spilled over his shoes as I looked up coyly.

"I believe it is," he replied, smiling down at me from behind his trim mustache. "Have I also mentioned how much I've been looking forward to our first waltz, Miss Stoker?"

"Mm, no…I don't believe you have," I replied, trying to inch us out of the chamber.

"For nearly a year now, Miss Stoker. And it seems at last I am to get my wish."

"Right then," I replied. "Shall we?"

"After you, Miss Stoker."

The door swung closed softly behind us, but we were only two or three steps away when I was certain I heard the sound of glass shattering—as if something had been knocked off a table.

Or thrown against the wall.

Miss Holmes

~ In Which Miss Holmes Willingly Relinquishes Control ~

"IS EVERYTHING ALL RIGHT, MISS HOLMES?"

I turned to find Grayling at my elbow. He was dividing his attention between me and looking off after Evaline, who'd stormed away while fighting obvious tears.

I sighed. There was little I could do at the moment to help Evaline; she must come to terms with her decision—whatever it might be. Aside from that, I couldn't be distracted from whatever was going to happen tonight. There was no doubt in my mind that Lady Isabella had some nefarious plan tucked inside her dainty glove.

"Miss Stoker appears distraught," Grayling added—quite unnecessarily, I thought.

"She—er—I believe a pine needle got into her eye, and she went off to see to it. She's got a bit of an allergy like Miss Hasherby, you know."

He didn't seem wholly convinced, but at that moment, the orchestra began to play. Grayling glanced over, cleared his throat, then offered me his arm.

"If I were to allow you to lead, Miss Holmes, would you do me the honor?"

"Of course, Inspector, but I hardly think it necessary for you to relinquish the lead," I replied, a trifle frostily. *Smitten?* Miss Stoker was clearly addled if she thought that was true. "It would look quite strange if *I* were to be directing our steps across the dancing floor," I added.

"I venture to say it would look more strange if we were both attempting it," he responded. There was a pleasant glint of humor in his green-flecked brown eyes. "Therefore, I shall demur to your very capable abilities. You are, after all, a woman of sharp mind and particular forethought."

My flicker of irritation died in light of his self-effacing

gallantry, and I smiled. "I believe I could bear to relinquish that responsibility for at least one waltz this evening."

"I am most complimented, Miss Holmes. Shall we?"

Grayling and I had waltzed before, more than once—and the first time had been here at Cosgrove Terrace. However, I must confess, this was the most pleasurable spin we'd ever taken around a dance floor. I was no longer offended by his height, nor did I attempt to pull or push the direction of our pacing (though it was a struggle at first) while he was intent upon doing the same.

Thus, we made rather graceful box steps in gentle spirals between and around the other couples. I neither trod on his foot, nor did he trounce on my hems, and there was a very long moment when it felt as if no one else was in the entire room other than the two of us. It was a divine feeling.

"You're quite an accomplished dancer, Inspector," I said after several measures—once I was able to actually relax and enjoy being maneuvered through the paces by his capable hands.

"Thank you, Miss Holmes. I confess, it's much easier to be accomplished when one isn't fighting with one's partner."

I looked at him in surprise, saw the horrified expression that flashed across his face when he realized what he'd said, then, absurdly, I found it all quite amusing. "One cannot argue with that," I replied with a laugh. "There can only be one captain on a ship, the single driver of a carriage."

His horror had evaporated when I chuckled, and now he was looking at me with a very warm expression. "I don't believe I've ever had the pleasure of seeing you laugh," he said, and I felt his fingers tighten slightly at my waist.

My mouth went a little dry and I did stumble at that moment, but he didn't even flicker an eyelash when I stepped on his toe. "Thank you," I said uncertainly.

I felt unaccountably warm all at once, and focused my eyes over his shoulder because I wasn't certain where else to look. I felt…well, quite in the spotlight. And that was a place I didn't particularly care to be.

I reminded myself firmly that there was work to be attended to, and it didn't include giggling girlishly while being squired around the dance floor—although, as Grayling had once pointed out, being on the dance floor offered an excellent and varying view of the entire room.

Perhaps halfway through the dance, I noticed Evaline had returned from wherever she'd gone off to. She and Mr. Ned Oligary were just joining the waltz. Even from across the room, however, I could tell something unexpected had happened, for her face was set in a tight expression.

As Grayling directed us in a small circle to the left, I saw Lady Isabella. She was still standing near the entrance at the top of the ballroom where she'd continued to greet latecomers as well as employ her own expansive view of the event. I didn't recognize the woman and man to whom she was speaking, but I did notice Mr. Oligary the elder standing nearby conversing with several other businessmen. I hadn't realized he was here tonight, and I wondered if Evaline had ridden in the same carriage as both Oligary brothers, or only the younger.

After one more twirl, I spied Lord Cosgrove-Pitt in one of the balconies that overlooked the huge, high-ceilinged room. When I noticed him above, I was reminded of the first night Evaline and I had encountered the Ankh in the Thames Tunnel, beneath the streets of London. We'd rushed back to Cosgrove Terrace after my companion had nearly gotten us killed after announcing our presence at a meeting of the Ankh's Society of Sekhmet.

At the time, I had not made the connection between Lady Isabella and the Ankh—that they were one and the same. But I did distinctly remember returning to Cosgrove Terrace— after that harrowing experience being chased by the Ankh's guards—and wanting nothing more than to make my excuses to our hostess and return home.

I hadn't spoken with Lady Isabella upon my return, but I had waved to her up in the balcony, where she'd been standing exactly where her husband now stood. At the time, she was speaking with a cluster of other guests, but tonight Lord Cosgrove-Pitt was there alone, surveying the activity below.

I wondered for a moment whether he was like me in that way—preferring to be a spectator rather than in the midst of the activity, and that he'd sought a moment of solitude without actually leaving the fête.

"What is it, Miss Holmes? You've gone unnaturally—er, unusually quiet."

I tipped my head back slightly to look up at Grayling, noting as I had done earlier what a smooth and perfect shave he'd acquitted of himself this evening. And whatever sort of lotion he'd used afterward was pleasantly scented with bracing lemon and rosemary. It suited him well. As did the glossy, dark auburn curls that brushed the nape of his neck.

"I was merely noticing that Lord Cosgrove-Pitt seems to have needed a moment away from the crowd." I made a facial gesture in the appropriate direction, up and over to the balcony in question. "I suppose even the leader of Parliament requires a moment of solitude at times."

"I would agree. And one can only imagine how different the view of this crush from above must be than the one we have here on the floor," Grayling commented.

"Indeed. I— Oh my goodness!" I stopped dead still, and my partner bumped into me soundly, nearly rattling my teeth. "What on *earth* is he doing?"

Grayling turned and looked up to see what I had noticed: that Lord Cosgrove-Pitt was climbing up onto the railing of the balcony!

"Good gad. Is he in his cups?" said the inspector, releasing me from his grip. "Excuse me, Miss Holmes."

I didn't mind that he left me standing in the center of the waltz as he went off through the crowd—presumably to see what on earth was happening with Lord Cosgrove-Pitt.

I began to make my way off the floor in his wake, of necessity more slowly than Grayling due to the weight and circumference of my costume. But I didn't take my eyes off the dignified man, who had never looked *less* dignified than he did now, perched as he was on top of the balcony's railing more than twenty feet above us.

Who would have believed the leader of Parliament, one of the most somber and grave men in London, would do such a thing?

By now, others had taken notice of the strange activity. The room was beginning to go quiet, as if a silencing wave passed through it while turning the attention of its occupants to look up at the balcony.

"Good evening, ladies and gentlemen," said Lord Cosgrove-Pitt cheerily as he gripped the edge of the balcony wall. "I hope you're all having a marvelous time tonight."

There was a smattering of murmurs in response, but the majority of his audience remained silent, watching with goggling eyes and arrested expressions.

"I encourage you to take advantage of the food and drink, and enjoy the beauty of my lovely wife's Winter Garden theme decor—did I get that right, Isabella? Winter Garden? —because it's the last party I'll ever be hosting at Cosgrove Terrace."

A more intense murmur rippled through the crowd, and though most of us had turned to look for Lady Cosgrove-Pitt upon his mention, everyone's attention snapped back to the man on the balcony when we heard the last part of his sentence.

Where was Grayling? I stood on my tiptoes, trying to see if there was any movement behind Lord Cosgrove-Pitt in the balcony, but I could see nothing to indicate Grayling had gained access to the chamber.

"Yes," Lord Cosgrove-Pitt continued, "this will be my last fête at Cosgrove Terrace. And I regret to inform you all that I will not be returning to Parliament on Monday either. This is my farewell—to all of you. Please give the prime minister my regards."

He released his grip on the edge of the balcony wall, and, as the spectators gasped in one communal breath, he teetered there on the railing before grabbing at the wall and regaining his balance.

As I was certain Grayling was doing everything in his power to get to Lord Cosgrove-Pitt before he did—well, whatever he was going to do—I forced myself to turn away from the spectacle and seek out Lady Isabella in the crowd.

She was still standing where I'd last seen her—across the room from the balcony where her husband floundered about on the railing. Her face was a mask of shock: eyes wide, mouth agape, body still as a statue.

She even mouthed, silently but obviously enough that it was noticeable, "Belmont!" as if to beseech him not to go on with whatever it was he meant to do.

I began to push my way through the crowd—not in the direction of the balcony this time, but toward Lady Isabella. And as everyone else was so stupefied by Lord Cosgrove-Pitt's speech and activity, it was relatively easy to maneuver through the stock-still partygoers.

I had expected something to happen, and this had to be it. And somehow, Lady Isabella was involved. She'd fairly told me so.

Behind me, someone gave a soft shriek, and the entire room drew in a great, shocked gasp.

"And so...farewell, my friends," cried our host in a robust voice.

"Look out!" someone shouted.

There were the sounds of running, a tumbling noise... and then a dull, ugly *thud* that seemed to reverberate in the silence.

I spun around to see that Lord Cosgrove-Pitt was gone from the railing and the balcony. I knew precisely what had happened, and though I wanted to continue watching the scene of chaos, I didn't need to know the details. The *thud* had been terrifyingly final.

For it was Lady Isabella at whom I'd been looking— purposely—when it all happened, and so it was only I who saw the flash of triumph over her face as someone shouted, "Look out!"

And then the flash of triumph was gone, and she screamed.

Right on cue.

Miss Holmes

~ A Startling Revelation ~

I'D SEEN ALL I NEEDED TO SEE—THAT MOMENT OF satisfaction on Lady Isabella's face—so I changed my direction and charged back through the crowd toward the place below the balcony where Lord Cosgrove-Pitt's life had ended.

As I made my way through the still stunned and mostly paralyzed crowd, I observed several things, which in turn led me to a number of conclusions:

First, Evaline had reappeared, and she was helping a rather stout man to his feet. Based on their location and the disheveled look of her hair and skirts as well as his rumpled coat and askew necktie—along with the fact that Mr. Ned Oligary was nearby—I surmised that it had been her running footsteps I'd heard, and that the immediate tumbling sound after was her knocking the stout man out of the way from beneath Lord Cosgrove-Pitt's swan dive.

It was a good thing she'd acted so quickly, for surely the man would have died—or at least been gravely injured—by the weight of a two-hundred-pound man falling atop him from twenty feet in the air...slamming him onto a cold marble floor.

Second, I saw that Grayling had accessed the balcony, but too late to do anything to stop his distant relative from this strange and uncharacteristic action. Grayling took one look down, his face pale and grim, then spun back into the depths of the balcony—presumably to race down here.

Third: Lord Cosgrove-Pitt was most certainly deceased, but whether it was an accident or suicide...well, I had my suspicions. I pushed my way through the frozen throngs of people, ignoring a few hands that attempted to stop me, until I got to an open area around the body where the spectators seemed unwilling to broach.

A pool of dark red blood was quickly spreading from his

nose and ears, puddling beneath his misshapen, clearly shattered head. He'd landed facedown, and his limbs were akimbo. I was the only one who moved close enough to examine him, for the others appeared to still be in shock. Many of the women clutched their male counterparts, burying their faces in shoulders and arms (although several eyes did peek out slyly).

I did hear a few murmurs directed at and about me: "What is she doing?" "How vulgar!" "Step back, miss!" "A young lady has no business…"

I blocked out the hissing and muttering and crouched down to study the body—not at all certain what I was looking for. The entire ballroom had witnessed the event; clearly Lord Cosgrove-Pitt had acted on his own.

"What on earth are you doing!" Someone had broken from the crowd and was standing over me. He sounded infuriated. His shoes were shiny and his feet fat, but I declined to look up any higher to see more. "You have no business interfering in this—this tragedy. I demand you remove yourself at once!"

I ignored him, confident that whoever he was, he wouldn't dare place his hands on me to forcibly move me away. However, he was encroaching on the scene, as well as my pooled hems, which so far I'd been able to keep free of the spreading blood stain.

Apparently the man didn't get the hint, for he continued to harangue me. "Miss! I must insist that you leave this to the police! It's unseemly for a young woman to view such a horrific scene—"

"It was unseemly for Lord Cosgrove-Pitt to *create* the scene," I snapped without looking up.

"Good *gad*! What a horrible—"

"Scotland Yard! Let me through. Excuse me, let me *through*, sir."

I was still kneeling in my froth of layers of shimmery gold

fabric when Grayling arrived at my side. Naturally, he took care that his shoes avoided treading on my gown.

"*She's* not Scotland Yard," someone grumbled, to which Grayling replied over his shoulder, "She's a *Holmes*. If you please, give us some room. *Sir,*" he added to the man still looming over me in his fat shoes.

I was so stunned by Grayling's endorsement that I almost didn't hear his murmured question to me: "What have you found?"

I glanced at him from the other side of Lord Cosgrove-Pitt and discovered our faces were quite close together. I replied in a low tone, "Nothing unusual yet. No strange mottling of the skin. He doesn't smell like spirits, either. Or almonds, for that matter. No frothing of the mouth, no bluish tint to the skin—and obviously he wasn't in any pain."

Grayling nodding, appearing to concur with my unspoken but obvious conclusions: Lord Cosgrove-Pitt didn't seem to be poisoned; nor did he appear to be intoxicated.

But he had certainly acted uncharacteristically. And yet he'd shown no signs of being under any sort of duress. He'd been upbeat and calm during his so-called farewell speech. As if it were the most normal and natural thing for him to do— to climb onto the balcony railing and give a sort of suicide note in the form of a speech.

Grayling's face was grim when he looked up and pointed to Ned Oligary. "Send word to the Met, if you please, and have them notify the morgue so they can dispatch a wagon. And everyone, I insist—you must step *back*."

Two of the other gentlemen began to help clear the area of weeping, gawking, whispering partygoers.

"Miss Stoker," I said, looking up and projecting my voice over the throng. She wouldn't be lingering near anything with a lot of blood or gore, but she could be useful in another way. "Ah, there you are. I'm certain Lady Cosgrove-Pitt is in need of some comfort," I suggested firmly. I couldn't see the newly made widow anywhere, but then again, I was crouched on the floor in the midst of a crowd.

"Right." After an odd glance at one of the maidservants, Evaline pushed off into the people in search of Lady Isabella.

I sat back on my heels and managed to keep from tipping off balance as I considered the body, the distance he'd fallen, and everything that had occurred.

Was there some reason Lord Cosgrove-Pitt would have wanted to take his own life—and in such spectacular fashion? Was it possible he was having financial problems—like Bram and Florence? Or did he have some other reason for ending his life—a terminal illness, perhaps?

How could Lady Isabella have known this would happen? Or, more specifically, how could she have *made* it manifest?

Perhaps she hadn't known *what* would happen—just that something would? If I hadn't seen that moment of pleasure and triumph in her face, I would be asking myself far different questions. But the fact was, she'd hinted at an unexpected event, and the expression on her face had not been surprise or shock but satisfaction.

It was as if she had planned it. But that was absurd. I stared down in the vicinity of the dead man, no longer seeing him or Grayling's long-fingered hands as he continued to adjust and examine the body.

Did Lady Isabella have some sort of incredible control over Lord Cosgrove-Pitt?

My eyes flew open wide.

With a stifled cry of comprehension, I lurched forward while still in a crouch and lost my balance, barely missing slamming my hand onto the poor man's corpse.

"What is it?" Grayling gave me a startled look as I attempted to right myself.

I didn't respond immediately; instead, I maneuvered so I was next to Lord Cosgrove-Pitt's head while still managing to avoid kneeling in the congealing blood. Grayling had allowed him to remain facedown—likely in deference to the many people still hovering about, looking for the opportunity to satisfy their curiosity about what the results were when a man landed on a marble floor after falling twenty feet onto his face.

Lord Cosgrove-Pitt was wearing a high, stiff collar held in place by a necktie, which made it very difficult for me to pull it away from his person—especially considering the fact that I wasn't very well versed in assembling and removing male attire.

"What are you doing, Miss Holmes?" Grayling asked as I fumbled beneath the man's chin in an effort to unfasten the tight clothing around his throat.

But the tie came loose before I had to respond, and I pulled the shirt collar away. "A light, if you please, Inspector?"

He obliged quickly and efficiently, shining a light down over the back of Lord Cosgrove-Pitt's shirt. I moved the dead man's thin, graying hair away, baring the nape of his neck and where it curved into the back of his shoulders.

He and I must have seen it at the same time, for Grayling drew in his breath sharply and looked at me just as I raised my eyes to meet his.

"Bloody hell," he muttered, then snapped off his illuminator. "That changes everything."

Miss Stoker

~ *The Evening's Second Unsatisfactory Tete-a-Tete* ~

"EVALINE, I CANNOT *BELIEVE* YOU DID SUCH A THING!" Florence hissed as she settled next to me in Mr. Oligary's carriage. "I've never seen such vulgar, unladylike behavior in my *li*— Oh, thank you so much, Mr. Oligary, for seeing us home. What a tragic event! A terrible way for the evening to go."

"Think nothing of it," replied my suitor as he climbed into the vehicle, taking care not to step on our hems. "Of course I wouldn't leave you to your own devices, Mrs. Stoker. I can only imagine the nightmares you might incur."

"It was quite a frightening, startling experience," she replied. There was true sympathy in her voice. "But *poor* Lady Cosgrove-Pitt. How absolutely *horrifying* for her. All of it."

I brooded as Mr. Oligary and my sister-in-law chattered in the quiet tones people use when they're discussing a tragedy. As we drove away, the smooth, rumbling carriage took on the feeling of a swiftly shrinking cage. I was trapped, surrounded by two people who wanted to control me...while leaving at Cosgrove Terrace the life I *wanted* to leave.

And I wasn't being dramatic.

Mr. Oligary had made his intentions quite clear as we were waltzing. He mentioned calling on Bram—which meant only one thing: he was going to discuss marriage arrangements and get my brother's permission to propose.

Things were getting too serious, too fast. I was afraid that before I knew it, I'd find myself engaged or even married.

The lights blazed from every window at Cosgrove Terrace as we drove away. Mina was still inside. *She* hadn't been whisked away and bundled off to go home in order to protect her delicate sensibilities.

Nightmares my *eye*.

I glowered in the dim light. Florence was upset that I'd

saved a man's life by knocking him out of the way of danger (I was going to have bruises all down the side of my body)? If she only knew what else I'd seen and done…

And Mr. Oligary. To be fair, he'd not *said* anything. He hadn't needed to. The look he gave as he helped me to my feet after I threw myself at Lord Cunningham had been one of shock and dismay.

And I absolutely wasn't going to think about Pix. He didn't figure into any of it. He hadn't even seen fit to apologize for disappearing. And for not letting me know he was even alive.

The reprobate.

"And here we are."

I came out of my thoughts with a start. That had been a much faster trip home than to Cosgrove Terrace—or maybe I'd just been lost in thought.

Mr. Oligary moved to unlatch the door, then stepped out gracefully. One at a time, he handed us down: Florence and then myself.

I was still shaking out my skirt and petticoats and ensuring my cloak hadn't caught on the door when Florence exclaimed, "Oh! Those *dratted* chambermaids. Will they never learn? I can see from here that they— Excuse me, Mr. Oligary, but I'm going to have to see to them at *once*. Thank you again for a wonderful evening." She simpered up at our host, then hurried off toward the house at what *I* would consider a vulgar and unladylike pace.

And considering the fact that we didn't have chambermaids—plural—I knew exactly what she was up to.

Mr. Oligary seemed to understand as well, for he took my hand and tucked it into the crook of his arm as we made our way *slooowly* up the walk.

"Alone at last," he said with a smile, leaving a cloud of white air from his breath in the cold night. "Your sister-in-law is quite amusing and her company enjoyable, but you know of course that it's your company I prefer, Miss Stoker."

My heart was beating a little faster now, and I tried to increase our speed without appearing to do so. But my companion seemed in no hurry—despite the fact that the tip of my nose was getting cold.

"She was very grateful to be included tonight. That was a particular kindness you did, asking her to come," I said. "The Yule Fête was quite spectacular. Thank you for a wonderful evening."

I meant it. Mr. Oligary was a nice man—and almost handsome, and, of course, wealthy. I didn't have any strong objections to *him*. It was the idea of marriage itself that put me off.

"It's unfortunate the way it ended—for all involved," he replied. "I was looking forward to watching the yule log be lit. And to at least a few more waltzes with the most lovely woman in the room." He smiled down at me in the frosty moonlight.

"As was I. But I can't imagine what made Lord Cosgrove-Pitt do such a thing," I murmured. "Not only to himself, but he nearly killed Lord Cunningham as well. It was lucky I noticed in time to act."

That was not the right thing to say, for even through the layers of my glove and his overcoat and tailcoat, I felt Mr. Oligary's arm bunch up a bit.

"Quite. It was very near a double tragedy, to be sure. But my darling Evaline," he said in a far too calm voice, and using my familiar name for the first time, "it was a bit…out of char-acter…for you to become involved the way you did. That sort of heroic action is best left to the gentlemen of the world, don't you agree?"

A roar of tension rushed through me, and it took every bit of love for Florence and Bram to keep myself from retorting: *If I hadn't acted, Lord Cunningham would be* dead. *I saved his life.*

No one else had seen fit to act—or move quickly enough.

Instead of responding to Mr. Oligary's statement the way

I yearned to, I merely made a noncommittal sound. Almost like Mina's sniff.

We'd arrived at the front door, and just as I was about to reach for the latch, Mr. Oligary took both my gloved hands and turned me to face him. He tugged me closer so that my hem brushed over his shoes.

"Miss Stoker...Evaline," he added belatedly. "May I call you Evaline?"

"Of...of course," I replied. (I couldn't very well say no at that point, could I?) But that put a layer of intimacy between us that I wasn't ready for—or wasn't even certain I wanted.

"I think you are one of the most beautiful and charming women I've had the pleasure of knowing," he said, squeezing my fingers lightly. "I look forward to getting to know you even better. And I sincerely hope that tonight's event won't become a usual sort of thing."

"I certainly hope not either," I replied flatly. "Watching a man jump to his death in public was not a pleasant experience."

The smile curving his mustache faltered a bit. "That as well, but I was referring to that—er—display when you ran over and threw yourself at Lord Cunningham. You were *running,* and there were your ankles and petticoats showing when you *jumped* on him, and, well—Evaline, it's simply not done." His eyes crinkled at the corners as he looked down at me with a meaningful expression. "And I wouldn't want actions like that to...er...taint the Oligary name."

My throat dried up. My palms went damp and my insides fluttered in more of a discordant way than a happy one.

"I should have thought any person would put a man's life ahead of the reputation of his name," I countered quietly. "Mr. Oligary."

"Ned," he replied. "You may call me Ned, Evaline—and of course a man's life is more important than one's reputation. But the dignity and composure of a woman is also very important."

I wanted to demand to know *why*, especially when someone's life was at stake, but I was a coward. I thought of Bram and Florence, and how I held their future—and mine—in my hands (literally, as I was still holding Mr. Oligary's), and I remained silent.

Yes, I could face down a glowing-eyed, sharp-fanged demon with hardly a change in my pulse, but here my courage failed me.

"Evaline," he said, tilting his head a bit. His eyes grew warmer. "May I kiss you goodnight?"

I couldn't swallow. Nor could I say no—partly because I didn't have the courage to do so, and partly because, well, I thought I should at least give it a try. If there was any chance I was going to marry the man, I should at least—

He must have taken my silence as permission, for he leaned forward, drawing me closer so that we collided gently, and kissed me.

My first sensation was of the bristly prickles of his mustache, and the second was of the warmth of his lips on such a cold night. Third, I smelled him: the men's cologne he wore and whatever pomade was in his hair. And last: it was much warmer being that close to him.

It wasn't unpleasant, tasting him that way. Nor did it last very long. Our lips brushed together once, twice, settled for a longer moment, fitting together at the seams...and then it was over.

When he pulled away, Mr. Oligary—I supposed I could think of him as Ned now that he'd kissed me—looked at me with that very warm, sparkling gaze.

"Thank you, Evaline," he said. "I hope that will be the first of many kisses—and other moments—that we'll share. And now," he said, stepping back reluctantly, "I suppose I should relinquish you to your sister. I believe the curtain has twitched, indicating that she's watching us."

"Good night, Mr.—Ned," I replied.

"I am quite busy tomorrow, but I will call on you Monday. And I'll speak to your brother then as well."

"Right," I managed to say. *Oh drat!*

As Mr. Oligary—*Ned*, I mean—started down the walkway, I thought I saw something move at the edge of shadows just beyond the tree near my bedroom window.

I paused, my heart thumping, my hand on the door latch, and peered sharply into the darkness. My insides churned and fluttered, but I saw nothing else.

Nothing else to support my sense that someone had been watching.

Miss Holmes

~ Of Permissible Nomenclature and a Delayed Reaction ~

THE NEXT MORNING, I SAT AT THE KITCHEN TABLE utilizing my Profitt's Dandy Paper-Peruser to hold the papers open, and then to turn them, while I scanned the sheets and nibbled on my breakfast muffin at the same time. I'd discovered how necessary the Peruser was in keeping my news free of the inevitable tea stains and crumbs, and so I rarely read the news without it.

It was no surprise that all of the early editions carried the startling news that Lord Cosgrove-Pitt was dead.

MP Plunges to His Death, said one headline. *Lord C.P.'s Last Party*, was another. *A Terrifying Farewell*, screamed a third. *What Happens Now?* inquired yet a different take on the situation.

What did happen now? That was, indeed, my question. One that had frustrated me for several days—ever since the crow had tapped at my window and delivered a red cloisonné version of itself—but was becoming even more urgent.

It was well past one o'clock by the time Grayling and I left Cosgrove Terrace last night. Though he'd attempted several times to make arrangements for a vehicle to take me home while he handled the scene in his official capacity as a member of the Metropolitan Police, I'd declined.

There were far too many considerations for me to leave before it was strictly necessary, and although I'd hoped to have a private moment with Lady Isabella (for obvious reasons), that didn't materialize. She'd succumbed to the "vapors" and was taken solicitously to her bedchamber by an entire fleet of ladies and maids. I hadn't bothered to attempt to follow or otherwise intercept her.

Due to the late hour, there was a dearth of traffic, so the carriage ride back to my house was relatively brief. This gave Grayling and me only a short time to confer over the startling discovery we'd made on Lord Cosgrove-Pitt's body, as well as to agree that meeting at his office for me to try his hyper-magnifyer would need to be post-poned.

"Two puncture marks on the back of his neck," Grayling said as he eased into his seat across from me. Obviously, he'd been waiting for an opportunity to broach the subject in private. "Hardly noticeable unless one was looking for them —excellent thinking on that, Miss Holmes."

"Similar to the ones on the guard who was killed at the British Museum during the Betrovian visit," I pointed out, probably unnecessarily.

"And identical to the marks on the UnDead in the Ankh's underground laboratory," he added. "The vampires on which she appeared to have been experimenting."

I spared a moment to appreciate his proper grammatical usage (there's something about a misplaced preposition in speech that I find particularly annoying), then allowed my thoughts to move on to consider the situation.

We knew that the marks in question—the ones on the vampires, at least—had been made by two wires being inserted into the backs of their necks. These wires extended from the small metal devices that Pix had been known to deal in—something that Dylan had described as batteries. Apparently, they were a mechanism that stored power (electricity, in this case, or so we believed) and the wires allowed the power to be conducted into a machine or other device. That sort of device would be not only illegal (due to the electrical attachment), but also a unique and advantageous item.

What was hoped to be accomplished by this activity of poking two wires from a battery into the back of the UnDead was open to conjecture, but based on what we'd witnessed in the Ankh's lair—just before she electrofied Pix—I believed the purpose was some sort of attempt to control or tame the vampires.

While we hadn't actually seen wires poking into the back of the British Museum's guard's neck—or anywhere else—the placement was similar to that of the ones on the UnDead in the Ankh's lair, and also on the vampire on which I'd leaped in Pix's underground hideaway. (I chose not to mention this recent encounter to Grayling for obvious reasons.)

Most importantly—and quite horrifyingly—the placement and size of the punctures on the UnDead also matched a pair of marks I'd discovered on Lord Cosgrove-Pitt's neck.

"Clearly the Ankh is somehow behind this." Grayling sounded weary and frustrated as he ran his fingers around the brim of the top hat he held. "But I saw no indication that she was present at Cosgrove Terrace tonight. I'm certain you've already taken the opportunity to question as many bystanders as possible as to whether they'd seen the Ankh, or anyone who could be her. Did you learn anything helpful?"

I opened my mouth then snapped it shut. I couldn't inform Grayling that his distant aunt by marriage—not to mention one of the foremost members of Society—was, in fact, the evil villainess known as the Ankh. At least, not until I had some sort of irrefutable proof.

"There was a particular maidservant who caught my eye," Grayling continued. "One of the servers, perhaps having been brought in as extra help for the party. She seemed out of place, and somehow familiar. But I never was able to see her face—you know how busy they are—and once Lord Cosgrove-Pitt made his tragic move, I was otherwise occupied."

"Understandably so."

Fortunately, before Grayling could press the topic further —for I wasn't certain I'd be able to keep my knowledge of the Ankh's identity to myself if he pressed—we arrived at my home.

"This was not precisely how I anticipated the evening to end, Miss Holmes," Grayling said as he assisted me down from the carriage.

"Nor I," was my reply.

Obviously, neither of us made the jest about my affinity for attracting or discovering dead bodies. It would have been in poor taste, considering that the dead body in question was a distant relative of the inspector's.

"Nevertheless, I thank you very much for the invitation," I said as I withdrew my key for the door.

"I—er—particularly enjoyed our waltz tonight, Miss Holmes. Despite the fact that it was interrupted so unpleasantly."

"I concur; it *was* far more enjoyable than waltzes past— that is, until poor Lord Cosgrove-Pitt made his move." I shook my head sadly. "He was clearly not in his right mind, Inspector. And yet...at least he seemed jovial at the end."

"I suppose that is some small comfort," he replied, and the underlying sadness reminded me again that we were speaking of his family member—albeit a distant one.

"Good night, Inspector," I said, stepping up onto the threshold. As I turned to close the door, I saw that he was still standing there. He seemed to want to say something more, for he exhaled a cloud of frosty air.

"Is there something else, Inspector?" I asked, my hand on the door. As I was just inside the house, I placed a bit higher than normal, which, with my heeled shoes, raised my eyes to nearly the same level as his.

"Er...perhaps you might wish to— That is...Miss Holmes, I believe it would be perfectly proper for you to refer to me by my given name. Ambrose. Rather than Inspector. Particularly on—er—occasions such as tonight, when we are in a social environment. Rather than in an official capacity."

I blinked. "Oh. I see. Right. Yes, yes, I do believe that would indeed be permissible. Ambrose."

My face felt unaccountably hot, despite the December night air, and even now, as I thought about it sitting at my breakfast table the next morning, I felt my cheeks grow warm once more.

Ambrose. It was a nice, strong name that suited him well. I probably should have offered him the same token of famil-iarity—that he should call me Mina—but I'd been so taken by surprise by his suggestion that I hadn't thought about it until after he'd left.

And the fact that I was thinking about it again yet this

morning—when I should have been focused on other, more important matters—frustrated me. It was simply a *name*.

So I thrust away the warmth that had fluttered in my stomach when he made that request (and every time I thought about it afterward) and forced myself to review what I knew.

There was no doubt about it: a number of interesting and curious things had occurred over the last week. If they hadn't all happened within days of each other after me having a very dull two months, I might not have thought the incidents were connected.

But, as my uncle was inclined to repeat: there are no coincidences.

Beginning with the visit by the insistent crow and his delivery of the pendant, to the attack by UnDead—who had puncture marks in the back of the neck—at the supposedly *missing* Pix's hideaway…to the death of Lady Thistle, the closing of her shop, and the information that my mother had often disappeared (and probably used the now-missing door to The Carnelian Crow) in the back room for hours—to Grayling's coincidental knowledge of The Carnelian Crow (which must mean he was investigating something about that elusive establishment that he hadn't seen fit to share)…to the strange and sudden death of Lord Cosgrove-Pitt in a very public forum…

No. There was no one who could convince me that all of those events and their close timing were mere coincidence.

And, though I wasn't certain why, I was also inclined to include on that list of non-coincidences the sudden and desperate necessity for Evaline Stoker to get married.

But how the pieces all fit together, what they portended and what threat—for surely there was some sort of threat underlying them all if the Ankh was involved—I couldn't yet deduce.

And I'd forgotten one other thing in my list of not-coincidences: the inexplicable resignation of Irene Adler from her position at the British Museum.

That, I decided, was something that bore more investigation. Particularly since I had left a very special and unique object in her safekeeping at the museum.

I FOUND MISS ADLER'S OFFICE QUITE UNDISTURBED WHEN I entered it at the British Museum a short while later. That alone was curious, for if she'd tendered her resignation and had no intention of returning, surely her personal objects would have been removed—or at least packed up.

But everything was still intact: her cogwork teapot, the neat stacks of books, the Tome-Selector and its skeletal fingers reaching for a book by Edgar Allan Poe, the mechanized privacy shields over the windows that looked out onto the grounds. The room even smelled like Darjeeling tea, Miss Adler's preferred beverage, and her favorite gardenia *eau de parfum*.

There was a soft layer of dust over everything—something that would never have dared occur when Miss Adler was in residence—and it was that fact which made my curiosity sharpen into worry.

I'm mildly ashamed to admit that I'd been so put off by the debacle of the chess queen affair that I'd been—well, not precisely *hiding* from Miss Adler (a Holmes is never a coward), but staying out of her way, so to speak. And the fact that she hadn't been in contact with me merely added to the belief that she shared my feelings.

Thus, when Grayling informed me she'd resigned from the British Museum without notifying me, I confess I'd construed the non-communication and lack of a new address as an indication that Miss Adler no longer had any interest in acting as my mentor. If I *had* had a niggling suspicion that her disappearance might have been something more sinister than a mere change of occupation, I'd not allowed myself to dwell on it—for fear I was merely attempting to placate my bruised feelings.

But now, as I looked around the office, I realized my niggling suspicions might have been more valid than I'd allowed them to be. There was no indication in this chamber that Miss Adler had planned to vacate it; in fact, all evidence was that she had been in the middle of her normal daily tasks when she left. There was a bit of dried dregs of tea at the bottom of a white bone-china cup. A stack of books sat at the edge of her desk, her mechanized ink pen lay next to them, and the ledger that listed the latest items to have been unearthed from the hundreds of crates in the museum cellar was closed and set aside.

A horrible thought struck me, and I rushed across the room to the bookshelf where I snatched the copy of *A Connecticut Yankee in King Arthur's Court* from the shelf. Mark Twain's story about a man time-traveling from late nineteenth-century America to medieval England had been a whimsical choice as the hiding place for the device Dylan had given me when he'd gone back to his own time.

In my haste, I nearly dropped the slim, leather-bound volume, but managed to keep hold of it at the last minute. This book had an unusual feature in that there was a leather piece that flipped from the back cover over the outside edges of the pages onto the front, and was latched into place—thus keeping the book closed. When the small latch was unhooked, the book opened, and what had previously been a stack of pages of the story—as well as some short humorous pieces also written by Twain—now had a small rectangular shape cut out of the papers, which—to my dismay—*had* contained the slender device Dylan called a smartphone.

I glared furiously at the empty spot. There was only one other person aware of what had been secreted inside the book: Irene Adler.

She'd taken the smartphone with her, wherever she'd gone. And without a word to me.

I'd trusted her, which was why I'd left the very unique and special object here at the museum. She and I had agreed it would be best kept in the building because it was the only place Dylan had ever experienced the smartphone doing what he called "connecting" to wherever it connected to. Something called Wie-Fie, something that enabled him to interact or communicate with his time.

The smartphone had been his lifeline while he was trapped here in 1889 London, and he'd left it with me on his return home so that if there was ever the chance we might need each other—or want to communicate—we could attempt to use the strange, sleek device.

And now it was gone. And so was Irene Adler.

What did that mean? Why would she have taken it? For safekeeping?

Surely she hadn't been using it to attempt to contact Dylan…had she? If so, why?

And why would she have done without a word to me?

I glared around the chamber, now irritated with myself as much as with my former mentor. Perhaps if I hadn't been so reluctant to contact her, I would have realized her disappearance weeks ago. I swiped my finger through the thin layer of dust. Yes, weeks. Three, by my estimation.

(Hmm. There was an idea for a new device that might come in handy for an investigator: a mechanism that measured the amount of dust and calculated the time lapse based on the environment and the layer of debris collected.)

I looked around the chamber with different eyes. Where had Miss Adler gone, and why? Now I had yet another puzzle to solve, and where there was a problem, there would always be clues that led to a solution.

I began by sitting at her desk and studying the papers, books, and other items arranged thereon. Then I settled back in her chair and looked around the room carefully and slowly. When my attention rested on the Tome-Selector, I paused then bolted out of the chair, bumping my knee painfully on the underside of the desk.

Muffling an unladylike curse while rubbing the top of my screaming knee, I limped over to the shelf. Then I moved the Tome-Selector's metal digits out of the way so I could pull the Poe book from its place on the shelf.

Ah.

No, I must agree with Uncle Sherlock. There were no coincidences.

Of course the collection included "The Raven," and upon my examination of the volume—that is, allowing it to fall open naturally—I made a sound of satisfaction.

On the page where the book opened, near the beginning of the contents, there was a deep impression made in the pages—as if something had been wedged inside and left its mark after the book was closed and perhaps even weighted down. The indentation wasn't very large; hardly the size of my littlest finger. But its shape was distinctive, and familiar to me.

I removed the pendant I had pinned to my collar earlier today. I was not the least bit surprised when its shape fit perfectly in the depression of the pages.

Someone—likely Miss Adler—had hidden a carnelian crow pendant inside this book, right at the beginning of "The Purloined Letter."

Miss Stoker

~ Of Ales, Pickles, and Carnelian Adornment ~

"Why, Miss Evaline," Pepper said the morning after the tragic Yule Fête.

My maid had just risen from bending over near the wall behind my dressing table. "Wherever did you get this?"

"What is it?" I asked listlessly. I hadn't slept well last night after Ned had kissed me and left.

I'd half expected *someone* to climb through my window, or to at least throw a stone at the glass to get my attention.

But no one had.

Not that it mattered.

Pepper opened her hand to reveal the tiny crow pendant Mina had given me and ordered me to wear—which I had thus far neglected to do. It must have fallen out when my jewel box was upended the other day, and had been missed during the cleanup.

Despite my glumness, I felt a spike of interest. "Have you seen something like it somewhere else?" I asked Pepper.

"Yes, that's why it caught my eye. Kitty—she used to work at Varrel House, for Lady Firgate—she was wearing one just like it, pinned to her blouse."

I sat up straight. "A lady's maid was wearing a carnelian crow pin—like this?"

"That's right."

"I need to speak to her. As soon as possible." I surged up from my seat, at once excited about the prospect of the day. "Let's go to Varrel House and talk to her now. I'll think of some excuse—"

"No, miss, that won't do, 'cause she ain't working there no more."

"Well, where is she working? We have to find her." I was already digging through my wardrobe to locate something to

187

wear. It was a relief not to have to choose something that "matched my eyes," or "brought out the color in my cheeks."

"That's just it, miss. She got another position. I don't know where she's working now."

"I need to find out where she got that pin. It's very important. Can you help me?"

"Right, miss. I can ask around with the other 'elp at Varrel House. She used to go walking with one of the footmen there. He might know, or Bessie from Sir 'emington's 'ouse."

"We need to find her, and find out what she knows about it." I dragged out a bodice and simple skirt ensemble in light blue wool with navy French knots embroidered along the hem and cuffs. "I think it's time for you and I to go to the market in Smithfield. That's where you might see the others, correct? Bessie and anyone else who might know Kitty?"

"Yes, miss. Even though it's Sunday, they'll be there." Now that we had a solution, Pepper's expression changed from concerned to bright with interest.

I considered sending word to Mina, but decided not to. I might be getting out of the house without being on the arm of a beau—or without my sister-in-law—but that didn't mean I wanted to be lectured or otherwise have my ears talked off.

"What about Mrs. Stoker?" Pepper said hesitantly.

I straightened from doing up the tiny buttons on my shoes with a hook. I never could understand why, with all the gadgets and devices and machinery that had been created to make our lives easier, no one had designed a better way to wear—and fasten—shoes than a row of tiny, tight buttons that required a *tool* to open and close them. "I'll handle it with Florence."

To my relief, I didn't have to handle anything. Mrs. Gernum informed me that my sister-in-law had left the house not ten minutes earlier. She was heading out to make calls on her friends.

I grimaced a little. I hoped Florence wasn't going to be spreading too much gossip about me and Ned (I still had to remind myself not to think of him as Mr. Oligary). She might believe an engagement between the two of us was a foregone conclusion, but I certainly didn't.

Although…tomorrow was Monday. The day Ned said he meant to speak with Bram.

But probably Florence was mostly going to gossip about what had happened with Lord Cosgrove-Pitt last night. Having been an eyewitness to the most shocking thing to happen in Society would put her on center stage, as Bram would say. And Florence would love every minute of it.

I put it all from my mind as Pepper and I set out on foot to the market. It was a brisk day, normal for London with its cloud-laden sky and a constant drizzle in the air, but cold enough that my breath came out in a frosty gust. At least it wasn't snowing.

"Miss," Pepper said as we approached the dead-end street in Smithfield where all of the grocery and household merchants set up their wares. "Begging your pardon, but it's best if you let me do the talking. Sometimes the upstairs people—well, they make those of us downstairs ones a bit shy when it comes to talking."

"Right," I said.

Even though I'd made a point of dressing in plain clothing and wore my hair in a simple braid wrapped around the back of my head, I wasn't certain whether I could be mistaken for a housemaid.

Unlike Pix, who'd obviously gotten away with it for hours.

The thought of him soured my enthusiasm, and that just made me angry again. *Drat* him.

"I'll just sit over here, Pepper." I gestured to a semicircular bench positioned next to a large metal fire bowl. The roaring blaze gave off some welcome heat, and several people— judging from their clothing and accents, they were of the downstairs type—stood around it talking and warming their hands.

At the last minute, before I'd left my bedchamber, I'd affixed the small carnelian crow to the stiff, high collar of my bodice. Now, as I waited (wishing I'd thought to bring the sable muff I'd used at New Vauxhall Gardens three nights ago), I adjusted my cloak so it was open at the throat and the pendant could be seen.

Mina had told me to wear it, and Pepper had seen Kitty with one. Maybe someone would seek me out if they noticed. I sat idly, tracing a pattern in the dirty snow with the stubby heel of my shoe, and then with the pointed toe. Occasionally I looked up to watch what Pepper was doing, all the while trying not to feel bored. This was far better than sitting at home being fussed over or waiting for gentleman callers.

As I bided time, my attention skimmed over the shoppers. Everyone moved in and out and around like an infinite number of cogwheels, balancing baskets and bags and packages.

One of those human cogwheels caught my attention. There was something familiar about the way he— My heart stopped, then began ramming again. I was on my feet in an instant, pushing through the people, keeping my attention focused on the smooth movements of one quicksilver, graceful figure as he made his way through the crowd. Slippery as a snake.

Pix.

If I was actually paying attention (unlike last night, when I'd nearly knocked him over), I'd know that man anywhere— his movements, the way he nearly oozed around and between people like a cat.

I didn't even think about why I was following him when I didn't have anything more to say to the man—but there I was, off on his tail.

Unfortunately, I'm not particularly tall, so it was difficult for me to keep him in sight as I wove through the shoppers. Today, he was wearing the dark gray cap of a young man and a battered overcoat that was too big for him and therefore hid the size and shape of his body. That was part of his disguise —along with the large ears that protruded through his hair and beneath the cap.

I caught Pepper's eye as I pushed through, and she nodded in acknowledgment that she saw me going off on a trail.

One of the many things I appreciated about my lady's maid was her knowledge of my secret life. Any other maid would be in hysterics at the thought of her charge—a young, unmarried, wealthy (or, at least, presumably wealthy) woman —going off by herself in Smithfield. But Pepper was aware she had no reason to worry. And I knew I could count on her to make up explanations to Mrs. Gernum or Florence if I was delayed and didn't return with her.

By the time I pushed through a particularly thick mass of people—they were crowded around a merchant selling lemons—I'd lost sight of Pix.

Drat.

I stood at the T-intersection of two streets and looked both ways. There was no sign of my quarry.

Unwilling to go back and sit like a toad on that bench, I turned left and began walking. I'd gone two blocks from the T-intersection when I realized the street was vaguely familiar.

When I saw the sign for The Pickled Nurse, I knew I was back in the same area I'd been while investigating the spirit-glass case. The tavern's windows were still dusty with coal smoke, but they gave a much better view—whether you were looking in or out—than anything in Whitechapel. Including Fenman's End.

I strode up to the door of The Pickled Nurse in a brash, unladylike manner that would have made Florence wince. Without hesitation, I opened it and walked inside.

Though far cleaner than Pix's favorite haunt, this pub was still dim and layered with shabbiness. The floor was made from broad, worn planks, and solid wooden tables were arranged throughout. As it was early afternoon on a Sunday, however, the tables were occupied by only a handful of patrons.

At the back of the small, square room was the imposing serving counter that had given it its name. The bar stretched from wall to wall across the rear of the place, and there was currently only one patron sitting on the stools that lined up in front of it. He was hunched over a tall glass and seemed uninterested in anything going on around him.

High above the bar, a row of large jars was suspended by a complicated copper and brass rack. The glass jars were filled with huge, flavored pickles—each about the width of two fingers. Beneath each container was a small sign with the flavor written on it. The last time I was here, the signs had been chalk written on slate. But apparently The Pickled Nurse had invested in an improvement, for now the description of each jar's pickle flavor was engraved on a copper plaque in bold script.

There were, among others, signs for Honey-Ginger, Spicy Anise, Zook Spears, Sweet, Fancy-Hot and Orange-Clove.

The same pubmaster was behind the counter, and he was doing something I couldn't imagine Bilbo ever doing: he was polishing the gleaming wooden counter with a rag. As if he *cared* that it should be clean and shiny. Or, at least, not sticky.

I pulled up a stool for myself and sat at the opposite end of the bar from the other customer. Because it was warm inside, I unfastened my cloak and draped it over the seat next to me.

The pubmaster glanced up from applying his elbow grease to a patch of the counter. "Sweet, right? And ye were light on the ale. Jes' wanted mostly the pickle."

"But only one pickle—unless I want to pay extra for more," I replied with a grin.

He smiled back—something else I couldn't imagine Bilbo doing—and exposed a missing tooth near the left corner of his mouth. "'at's right, miss. Shall I pull a full one for ye, or ye jes' want the pickle?"

Pull a full one for me? I wasn't certain what that meant, but I replied, "I'll take a small ale with a...oh, pull the lever on the tap to fill my glass. Right." I considered briefly, then decided, "I'll have a full ale today, sir. And put an orange-clove one in it for me this time."

He winked at me then turned to do as requested. I watched with the same fascination as before as he selected the proper pickle flavor by pulling a lever beneath the corresponding jar. A set of metal contraptions clattered along the brass fittings, one part above and one part beneath the line of jars until the mechanism came to an abrupt halt beneath the orange-clove pickle jar.

A large metal claw reached down to grasp then lift the glass top of the jar. Then a set of brass fingers from the bottom portion of the rack extended up and over the container, reaching inside to pluck out a single pickle.

In the meantime, the pubmaster had filled a tall glass with an amber-colored beverage topped with two inches of white foam. Even from down the counter a ways, I could smell the pungency of the ale. That told me it was at least slightly better in quality than the bile-colored stuff they served at Fenman's End. That didn't mean I was going to drink it. But if I did, it probably wouldn't poison me.

The pubmaster used the pickle to give the ale a stir before dropping the spear into the glass and setting the whole thing in front of me.

I eyed the infused ale. The pungent, spicy odor from the pickle was surprisingly appetizing.

"You ever find that lady with the pet spider?" he asked, surprising me. He really did remember me. "She warn't looking like a very nice lady."

"She wasn't a very nice lady at all." That was an understatement. The lady with the pet spider had been involved in *La société de la perdition*, a secret group of normal people who enjoyed being around—and fed on by—the UnDead. If you could call them normal.

I'd later learned from Miss Adler that this place, The Pickled Nurse, had been a location where members of *La société* sometimes congregated or left communications for each other. I looked around with more interest, swiveling slightly on my stool. Only five other people in here, including the brooder at the end of the counter. There was a pair of patrons at two different tables—two men, and a man and a woman. None of them gave me any sense of danger or even interest. The back of my neck wasn't chilled from the proximity of the UnDead, either.

I sighed and looked down into my ale. The juice from the pickle had given the foam an orangey tint. I had a feeling this was an indication of how my life was going to be once I got married (ugh!): something that seemed interesting or exciting turning out to be nothing but boring.

Then it came to me once again with a horrible, sinking feeling: after I got married, I wouldn't be able to visit places like Smithfield or Whitechapel—or, at least, very easily.

I wondered again how my great-grandmother Victoria Gardella had handled it. She'd been married, hadn't she?

Had her husband been worried about vulgar, unladylike behavior *tainting* his family name?

"Go on. Take a sip." The pubmaster leaned his elbows on the counter and edged closer to me. He cast a glance toward the man at the other end of the bar, then returned his attention to me. I got the impression he wanted to say something without being heard.

Turned out I was right, for the pubmaster angled himself slightly away from the other end of the counter and said in a lower voice, "So you got one o' them too, do ye?"

I looked down, then I saw what had caught his attention: the red crow pin on my collar.

Ah. Finally. *Something.* "Have you seen another one like it?" I asked.

"Last time I seen it, was on a girl like you, she had it on. Kitty said she got herself a new position." He gestured to the pin. "Working that place."

"Kitty? Her name was Kitty, and she had a pin like this—and said she had a new position, working there? At the Crow?"

He slapped his hands on the counter. The hair around his

ears seemed to bristle. But he still kept his voice low. "Now, ain't that what I jus' said? That Kitty's a nice girl. Nice all around. She always got a smile when she come in here. Don't tell me you gotta job there now too, miss."

I didn't even blink. "Why, yes, I do. As a matter of fact. I just…I don't remember where the place is. How to get there." I tried to look both innocent and determined. "I don't want to be late for my first day."

"Well, setting there and drinking a pickle-spiked ale before you goin' in t'work ain't really a smart idea."

Now I was going for bashful and confused. "I know. I just don't remember how to get there. It's kind of a hidden place, isn't it?"

He looked at me like he didn't believe a word I said, so I began to layer on more to convince him. "Kitty used to work for Varrel House, and now she's got this new position. I heard about it from her. Can't you tell me how to find it—The Carnelian Crow?"

"You think I know?" He gave me a baleful look.

"Don't you?" It wasn't difficult for me to look disappointed. Here was my first real lead on The Carnelian Crow, and I was at a dead end already. "I thought you knew everything. You're a pubmaster."

He picked up the rag and began to vigorously rub the counter again. As far as I could tell, there wasn't a single spot anywhere that needed cleaning. You could almost see your reflection in the shined-up walnut surface, except where people had stabbed it with their knives and carved names or initials into it.

"Maybe you want to wash up, there, miss, before you pull that pickle outta the glass." He jerked his head to the right. "Back 'ere."

"My hands are perfectly clea— Oh. *Oh.*" I slid off the stool so quickly that I almost knocked it over. "Thank you," I whispered.

"You owe me," he said, leaning forward.

"Right. I'll remember this, I promise—"

"For the ale, missy. Threepence."

"Oh, right." I dug in the small pouch pocket tucked inside my skirt and laid the money on the bar.

Remembering the situation at Lady Thistle's where Mina had found a door marked with the double-C symbol that looked like an infinity sign, I took my time once I got through the small door he'd indicated. The door led to a narrow corridor that seemed to have been tacked onto the back of the building. The passageway was hardly more than a lean-to that would blow over in a strong wind. The corridor, I learned a few steps later, led to an alley.

Once I found myself there, outside, I stopped and looked around in confusion. I'd forgotten my warm, dark blue cloak on the stool in the pub, so now I was cold as well. There was no chance of any warmth from the sunshine (if there even was any today) back here, for the layers of the buildings were stacked on top of each other so haphazardly that they nearly met across the narrow alley.

Surely the pubmaster hadn't sent me out here on a wild goose chase.

I walked a little way down the alley, becoming more and more annoyed once I realized how far I was from Lady Thistle's—which was many streets and blocks away. If The Carnelian Crow had been accessed through the back of Lady Thistle's—on the third street level— it certainly couldn't be located in the heart of a Smithfield alley.

Drat. And *blast.*

I kicked at a pile of garbage and was rewarded by getting my shoe covered in rotting potatoes. The smell was disgusting, but I supposed there were worse things I could have stepped in.

Just as I turned to go back to the pub, I saw it. A rickety wooden door, set low in the side of a building four doors from the pub. It looked like it led down to a cellar.

And it had a symbol carved on it: the sign of The Carnelian Crow.

Miss Stoker

~ In Which Evaline Acquires a New Position ~

I LOOKED AROUND TO MAKE SURE NO ONE WAS WATCHING, but the alley was littered with refuse and a single cat—and no one else that I could tell. Even the few windows that faced the alley were boarded up or dark and dirty.

I took a moment to be glad Mina wasn't here to point out that I had neglected to bring a stake or any sort of weapon to defend myself against mortals. Even though I had brought a stake last night—and I certainly hadn't expected to run into a vampire today, in *broad daylight*—I doubted that would have kept her from lecturing me.

I reached for the latch on the door. It opened easily and I looked down inside. Six stone steps that led into a tunnel or passageway. Even from above, I could tell there was some sort of illumination beyond, so I wouldn't be feeling my way through the dark.

I stepped in and down, pulling the door closed after me. It was dark, narrow, and dim—although there was a single gasping light some distance away, so I could at least see where I was going. Mina would have been digging into my arm with her fingers if she'd been with me, and probably have her eyes closed, but the dim light didn't bother me in the least. Nor did the close space and the low ceiling.

There was only one direction to go, but the passage turned at sharp angles several times. I estimated I walked for at least thirty minutes. There were no other doors or entrances the entire way.

If Mina had been with me (and if she'd actually opened her eyes), she probably would have been able to tell exactly where the tunnel led. She claims she has a map of London—including each alley and mews, as well as every railroad and omnibus schedule—printed on her brain.

I didn't know where I was going, but I had no concerns. By now I'd concluded (or should I say *deduced?*) that Pepper's friend Kitty had not only gotten a job working at the Crow—which made some sort of sense, for servants were needed for everything, even underground meeting places—and that she'd accessed it from the back of The Pickled Nurse. If this was the servants' entrance, it made even more sense that it wasn't convenient to get to.

When had servants' entrances ever been convenient? Or comfortable, well lit, or clean?

At last, I came to an entrance. There was a high, small door the size of a cigar box inside the bigger one, obviously so whoever was on the other side could peek through.

First I tried the latch. The door was locked, as I'd expected it to be. I knocked briskly, hoping the sound would be heard through the thick wood.

After a long wait, I knocked again. Still no one answered. *Drat.* Here I was, so close—closer than even Mina had gotten—and I couldn't go any further.

Then I saw the slender chain hanging next to the door. It went up and through a hole in the wall and resembled a bellpull. I gave it a good tug, and I was certain I heard a distant jangling sound.

I must have, for a moment later, the small peephole door opened. Two eyes peered out at me; I couldn't tell if they belonged to a man or a woman, young or old.

"Who're you?" It was an irritated-sounding man.

"Kitty told me I could get a job here."

The eyes squinted, glaring at me. "Kitty, huh? She give you that too?"

"That's right," I said quickly, realizing he must be talking about the crow pin still on my collar. "She said the position here is much better than at Varrel House. I can work hard."

The peephole slammed shut. Was that it? Had I said something that tipped them off—

No, the door was shuddering in its place, then there was a scraping noise as it opened.

"Well, come inside. Let's see what we got 'ere."

Without hesitation, I stepped over the threshold. I nearly gasped when the back of my neck immediately iced over. There were UnDead in the vicinity. At least a few of them. Why hadn't I felt their presence before now?

I didn't have time to wonder more about that, for he was looking me over as if I were a farm horse. I gave him a good once-over too. No, not a vampire himself, I decided. But there was a flicker of intelligence in his eyes, so he wouldn't be fooled very easily.

My prospective employer was short and burly and dressed like a royal servant. He wore black trousers and a black uniform jacket that buttoned up along one side with shiny jet beads each the size of a silver piece. The uniform coat was trimmed with looping red braid, and a cobalt-blue shirt peeped out from beneath at the cuffs and neckline.

On each cuff, and also on one lapel, was a small bird embroidered in red. The man's hair—thinning and black—was slicked back on an oblong head that seemed too long for his short, stubby body. He wore a large mustache that curled up at the ends, and was tipped in the same vibrant red that trimmed his coat. A tiny scarlet (or maybe I should say "carnelian") crow had been affixed to the front of one side of his mustache.

That little detail might sound odd, but actually, it looked almost dashing, for his mustache was thick and tall. The little crow sticker reminded me of the beauty patches worn by Marie Antoinette and the French royalty in the late eighteenth century. I wondered if that sort of mustache adornment would ever catch on in London Society, and if Ned Oligary would wear one.

"Ya don't look too strong," he said, frowning as he glared at me. "Gotta carry heavy trays. Can't be dropping them on the clien*tele*." He emphasized the last syllable as if that made him sound fancy or something.

"I'm stronger than I look." That was an understatement.

His eyes swept over me with blatant disdain. "Well, I ain't got no choice, do I? Got the pin, Kitty sent ya, gotta let ya work. Short o' staff right now anyways—first time in four years 'at's happened. Bettilda done somethin' to her blasted arm. Can't be carrying a tray like that."

I reached up to finger the little crow pin as if to thank it for being my entree to the place.

"Ya gotta name?"

"Uh, yeah." My mind went utterly blank. I blinked. My mouth wanted to move, but nothing came out.

"Well, what is it?" he demanded. His mustache bristled and the crow shivered.

Still nothing. "Uh...what's your name?" I countered. "Sir."

"Gillies. An' that's *Mr.* Gillies t'*you*." He pointed and glowered. "Well? You forgot your name?"

My brain had unfrozen by now. "It's Pepper. My name is Pepper." That might work. If someone asked Kitty about her friend Pepper, at least there was a chance she'd play along.

"Awright. You get yer uny-form and report back here tomorrow night at eight o'clock sharp. Not before. I ain't gonna have you sitting around waiting for the clien*tele* to arrive, getting in the way. And I got stuff to do before *She* gets here anyway."

"What about tonight?" I asked.

"Ain't no one gonna be here tonight. It's *Sunday*, ain't it? *Tomorrow*, I said. Didn't you hear me?"

"Uh...right. Where do I find a uniform?" There was no way I was going to leave without snooping around first.

An actual plan—with preparation and contingencies—was already beginning to form in my mind (Mina would be so proud). But I needed more information before I left. I'd have to shake off Mr. Gillies and check things out on my own. At the very least, I wanted to determine how many vampires were here. And what they were doing.

A little shiver danced over the back of my neck. Whatever they were doing wasn't going to be pretty. It never was with the UnDead.

Mr. Gillies was still irate. "Right. Bloody damned unyforms. Always gotta be something. Ain't like I don't got enough bloody things to do, now I gotta play lady's maid too. Don't know why Bettilda had to go break her bloody arm." He was mumbling and cursing, and clearly didn't think of me as the genteel Society lady I was supposed to be if he was using words like "bloody."

That was completely fine with me.

"Just show me where to find them, and I'll take care of it, Mr. Gillies," I said in the most helpful tone I could muster. "You've got work to do."

"Fine, fine, this way."

I followed him up a short flight of stairs and then past several doors—none of them marked, all of them closed. There were no other signs of life, though I thought I heard the sounds of piano in the distance. And the more he grumbled and talked, the more it became obvious to me that The Carnelian Crow was some sort of club. And it was closed to client*ele* on Sundays.

And from what I could figure out, I was going to be waiting on tables and serving food and drink.

Well, there went my plan to have Mina come with me tomorrow as another waiter.

There was no possible way Mina Holmes could pass as a servant. Even if she could manage to hide her imperious attitude, she'd dump the tray on her first customer. Then she'd trip over the second one—probably land in his or her lap. And then she'd lecture the third about whether he (or she) had ordered properly and efficiently, and if anyone dared ask any questions about the food, she'd lecture *them* that they hadn't *observed* enough about the menu.

No, that idea was not going to work.

So much for me planning ahead.

"In there." Gillies jabbed at a door. "Don't bother me unless it's important—like the place is burning down or something. Be back here at eight o'clock tomorrow. Sharp." He spun and stalked off in the opposite direction from which we'd come.

I could hardly believe my luck. Gillies was going to leave me to my own devices. I could do all the snooping I wanted.

I supposed I better look through the uniforms first, then afterward I could pretend I got lost on my way out. (Blooming Pete. Here I was, making a plan again.)

The wardrobe chamber was neat and organized, and it didn't take me long to find what I needed. The female uniform was similar to that of Mr. Gillies, complete with tiny red crow insignias. I bundled everything up and shoved it into a canvas sack I found. Then, slinging the bag over my shoulder, I peeked out the door. No one seemed to be around.

I followed the sensation on the back of my neck, wishing I had a stake with me. Or that I was wearing a silver cross. (Who'd have thought I'd find an UnDead on my way to the market on a Sunday morning?) But then I realized even if I had the stake with me and found the vampires, I couldn't do anything about them. The smell and residue of UnDead ash would be a definite giveaway, not to mention the fact that one or more of the vampires would have disappeared. And I supposed the noise from the actual staking would probably alert anyone else who was around.

The sound of piano had become more distinct. I followed it, reasoning that wherever the instrument was would also be where the entertainment happened—that is, in the main room of the club.

I was correct (Mina would be so proud). There was an opening that led from this backroom area to another chamber from where the music—and now a female voice—was coming. Instead of an actual door, there was a swath of translucent black fabric acting as a barrier. I could see a faint shimmer of light through it.

When I carefully moved the curtain-like door enough to peek through, I saw that on the other side of the silky door was a waterfall of glittering red beads that hung in front of it.

And, finally, I got my first glimpse of The Carnelian Crow.

The club was several levels above The Pickled Nurse when it came to decor, cleanliness, style—and technology. I couldn't help but gawk when I realized the ceiling of the place was a square-shaped dome made from glass, which revealed the foggy winter sky above. Through the sides of the dome, I could see the edges of the buildings that rose above the club's walls, bordering closely.

From what I could tell, The Carnelian Crow was in either a courtyard or alley, completely hidden by buildings on all sides. It was no wonder no one knew how to get here. The place was completely out of sight from the street, and could probably only be accessed via underground tunnel or by going through a storefront to the rear.

Like Lady Thistle's.

Or through any other storefront that bordered the same alley as The Pickled Nurse. Who knew how many other secret entrances there were.

I glanced toward the small, low stage near one end of the room where the piano player and a female singer were practicing their act. Neither seemed to notice me. She continued to croon in a dusky voice about wanting to give all of herself to all of me, or something like that. The piano followed along without a hitch.

I didn't want to take any chance of being seen, so I was careful to barely move the silk-and-bead curtain, and didn't poke my head through too far. Even so, I could still see quite a bit of the room. And though there wasn't any lighting except two lamps near the piano, enough illumination spilled through the glass ceiling to enable me to see how the place was furnished.

Four fireplaces studded the room, two on each of the side

walls—including the one through which I was peeking. I could smell a tinge of wood smoke and knew they'd been in use recently and, as there was a definite chill in the air, probably would be as well tomorrow night. I wondered if setting and managing the fires was one of Mr. Gillies' tasks.

Scattered through the center of the room were five round tables, each with four upholstered, high-backed chairs around them: two black, one red, one cobalt. The tables were covered by a luxurious fabric of red paisley on cobalt brocade. Matching blue crystal glasses and a decanter sat in the center of each round.

Along the edge of the room were four more round tables, each cupped by the semicircle of a privacy wall around the back and sides. Instead of chairs, a curved bench seat built into the privacy wall offered seating.

Large, ornate birdcages of brass, each base half the diameter of a carriage wheel, added to the decor. Three hung suspended from the ceiling on chains of varying lengths, and there were another three on black pedestals throughout the room. As far as I could see, the cages were empty of crows—carnelian or otherwise—but each contained a cluster of black pillar candles of different heights and sizes. They would look like small bouquets of flame when they were lit.

At the back of the room, directly opposite the stage with the piano and musicians, was a massive tapestry that shivered silkily from ceiling to floor. The background was the signature cobalt blue, and on it was a crow: black with carnelian accents on the top of its visible wing, and brilliant blue eyes. A smaller version of the same silken banner hung behind the stage.

Besides the faint aroma of wood smoke, other scents hung in the air. There was an unidentifiable essence that was faintly sweet and pungent, and not altogether unpleasing, and reminded me a little of the night in the opium den.

But, most unsettling of all, there was also the underlying scent of blood: deep, rich, as if ingrained in the very furnishings. I subdued a little shiver. I have a problem with lots of blood and gore and spilling guts...

I swallowed hard and pushed it away. I was a Venator. I had no time for weakness.

Then I finally saw what I was looking for: another door.

If I was standing at the servants' entrance, then that other one must be where the clien*tele* came in. If I wanted to find out where it led, I was going to have to be very careful.

After glancing once more at the musicians (the singer was still crooning something about all of me), I adjusted the bag with my "uny-form" over my shoulder, then carefully slipped beneath the curtain and its beaded attachment. I did my best not to make the fabric ripple or the hanging beads click against each other.

Once inside the main room of the club, I crawled along the wall toward the other door, using the tables as cover between me and the stage. Crawling wasn't the easiest thing to manage in skirts and petticoats, so I bunched up as much of the fabric as possible and held it gathered against me as I inched along.

Because it was me, and not Mina, I reached the other door without falling on my face, bumping into a table, or knocking over a pedestal. Like the other, this entrance was hung with shimmering black fabric and long strings of shiny, coin-sized beads—cobalt and black this time. I peeked around the edge of the curtain and confirmed that no one seemed to be around, then slipped through and pulled to my feet.

Another corridor that led somewhere beneath the streets of London. Unlike the other, this one was well maintained and lit. It was even whitewashed, and there wasn't any sign of rats or their leavings. I could stand up straight and hold my arms out to either side without brushing the walls. Still there was no sign of anyone else around.

Obviously, the club had specific business hours, and at this time (and probably because it was Sunday) few people were about. This *deduction* encouraged me, and I hurried along the tunnel with less caution than before.

I'd nearly forgotten about the ever-present chill at the back of my neck and what it portended until I rounded a corner and nearly collided with a man standing there.

In that instant, I realized not only was he a sort of guard, but he was also an UnDead.

Miss Holmes

~ Wherein Evaline Divulges a Plan ~

"GOOD HEAVENS, EVALINE! HOW MANY TIMES HAVE I warned you not to be so careless? Especially when you're snooping around," I exclaimed. "You came face to face with a vampire—what did you do?"

It was Monday, just two days after Lord Cosgrove-Pitt's untimely death, and I'd arrived at Grantworth House shortly before noon. Fortunately, Evaline's maid Pepper was under no misconception that I merely made random social calls, so she brought me up to Evaline's bedchamber. I found my so-called colleague finishing up her morning toilette.

"I've come face to face with the Undead more than a few times in the past." Evaline responded to my shocked exclamation in her characteristically tart manner. "It's not anything new—"

"Yes, but you weren't supposed to be snooping around, and you—"

"Actually, I was. I'd been hired to work there, remember? I just acted confused and lost. *He* didn't know I knew he was a vampire. What I mean to say is, his fangs weren't out and he wasn't acting UnDead-ish."

"And he just let you walk by?"

She shrugged. "I showed him my uniform in the bag I was carrying, and told him I got turned around, and he let me leave. Maybe he's not allowed to attack the help," she said with a giggle.

I glared at her, which had no marked effect on her giddiness. "And...?"

"So now you know there's another way to get into The Carnelian Crow. The way for the customers, not staff. And that's the way *you're* going to go in."

She muttered something about dropping trays and observing menus, but I ignored her under-the-breath ranting.

That was the least of my concerns. More importantly, she'd encountered a vampire—and, for once, not in a combative situation. "I don't suppose you—"

"No, I didn't take the time to interview him about being a vampire," she snapped. "Maybe you'll have the chance when you go. Ask him what sort of blood he prefers, or why he decided to become a half-demon immortal—"

"Really, Evaline, your lack of imagination and fore-thought is quite—"

"—but I did question him about The Carnelian Crow," she added in a rather loud tone from behind clenched teeth. She paused, then gave me an arch look I find particularly annoying. "And I got quite a bit of useful information."

I settled back in my seat. "Why, how—"

"Forward thinking of me?" she replied smugly. "Yes, I thought so."

"Well, what did you learn? And how did you go about getting information without raising his suspicions?"

Evaline's eyelashes fluttered. "Mina, you've said it yourself —it's something I do very well. Though he didn't even try it, he wanted nothing more than to sink his fangs into my wrist, I'm quite certain. So I was able to use that distraction to my advantage."

I nodded. "Excellent."

"Apparently, in order to gain access to The Carnelian Crow, one must have the pin if one is a staff member. However, I think it would be best if you didn't even attempt to—er—take orders from anyone. You should come in as a customer. And all you need for that is an invitation ticket."

I opened my mouth to speak, then closed it when Evaline whipped a small placard from atop her dressing table and handed it to me. It was simple and unassuming. One side had an image of a crow with red ornamentation on its wing and a bright blue eye. The reverse simply said:

The Carnelian Crow

NO ADDRESS OR OTHER INFORMATION, NOR ANY INDICATION that the ticket had been previously used. I smiled.

"How did you get this?"

"There was a stack of them on the floor near his feet. He —or whoever is there—must collect them at the door. I knocked them over and was extremely helpful in picking them up." Evaline beamed at me.

"Excellent, Miss Stoker. Did you learn anything else of note?"

"I got him talking—which was quite easy, because he kept looking at my throat and then my wrist, as if he were ready to lunge at me. I thought about letting him lure me into a corner and letting him have a taste, then I'd stake him—but that would leave a trail of dust, and someone might notice." She seemed to be enjoying herself. "But what I learned was many of the customers are female, and they *don't* bring their husbands."

"Fascinating," I replied. "It's like a women's club, then. Instead of a men's club. That explains the secrecy."

"Except at a men's club, there are no women allowed," Evaline pointed out—extremely unnecessarily, considering the fact that one of our most recent adventures included a sojourn into the male-only club Bridge & Stokes. "The customers—well, they are often accompanied by an escort. Or they meet one there."

I raised my eyebrows. "Indeed. You mean, of course, escorts of the male variety."

"Yes."

"Possibly romantic interests?" I pressed. "Or chaperones or guards—like a footman?"

Evaline shrugged. "He didn't say."

"Hmm." I considered that carefully.

"There was one more thing you might find interest-ing," she said after a moment, then paused, as if to create suspense. "It could be part of the reason he didn't actually attack me—besides that I'm of the 'downstairs' variety."

She giggled again. Apparently the idea of being employed was quite amusing to her. I wondered how she'd feel if the Stokers did get removed from Grantworth House and she had to return to Ireland—possibly finding real employment as a lady's maid. I resisted the urge to point this out to her.

"The vampire had two wires sticking into the back of his neck," Evaline continued. "They went down behind his collar —just like in the Ankh's laboratory. I believe she's still using those devices to try and control the UnDead and their urges!" she finished with a dramatic flourish.

When I didn't react in the manner she apparently expected, my companion glared at me. "You aren't the least bit surprised."

"Of course not," I replied modestly.

"Why?"

That was my opportunity to tell her that I'd discovered two similar marks on Lord Cosgrove-Pitt's neck. I went on to remind her of all the non-coincidences that had happened in the last few weeks (although I didn't mention the curious timing of her need to choose a husband, for I wasn't certain that particular point was relevant. It might just be bad luck).

I ended with an explanation of what I'd observed in Miss Adler's office yesterday, then summed up by stating the obvious, in case she had missed it: "Clearly, our mentor has some knowledge of The Carnelian Crow. It was no accident she'd hidden the crow pendant inside 'The Purloined Letter.' Likely for me to find."

When Miss Stoker gave me a blank look, I sighed. "Really, Evaline, your lack of literary knowledge is quite off-putting. 'The Purloined Letter' is a story by Edgar Allan Poe, the American writer—"

"I know *that*," she said snippily. "He wrote 'The Murders in the Rue Morgue' too—"

"As well as 'The Raven.'" I lifted a brow archly. "I'm certain you know why that's also no coincidence in this particular case."

"I suppose someone might *think* it's relevant, but it's The Carnelian Crow, not The Carnelian *Raven*," she continued in that snippy voice. "Even *I* know there's a difference between the two birds."

"Indeed," I replied frostily. I had been looking forward to educating her on how to differentiate between the two Corvi. "And what, my dear Miss Stoker, would the difference be?"

"Well, crows have a different shape to their tails, first of all. The edge is straight, almost like a fan. The center feathers of a raven's tail are longer, so when it's open and they're flying, it looks like an arrow. And crows make that annoying cawing sound, and ravens don't. Their call is lower and not as annoying. They're more quiet."

"They're quieter," I said, gently correcting her grammar. "Yes, that's generally true. And ravens are larger——"

"But it's difficult to tell that, if they aren't next to each other to compare their sizes," my companion replied primly.

"Naturally." I lifted my nose a trifle. "Well, then, apparently I don't need to point out the pertinence of the choice of book in which to hide the crow pendant. Ravens and crows are similar enough that Miss Adler's point was made.

"And even though the pin was no longer in the book, the impression it made in the pages was distinct. And an obvious clue for us." I frowned. "If only I'd come upon it sooner, we might be further along in solving this case."

Evaline frowned and settled back in her dressing table chair, crossing her arms like a barrier. "What case? What is there to solve? That Pix is missing? Well, he's not really missing anymore—at least, he's not dead. He seems to be perfectly well in fact," she added testily.

"You've seen Pix?"

Her expression was not a flattering one, but I refrained from pointing out that making a moue with one's lips made one look as wrinkled as a prune—and, according to Mrs. Raskill, left little lines radiating from one's mouth as one grew older.

"I saw him at the Yule Fête. He was dressed as a *maid*."

"A *maid*? How extraordinarily clever. What did he tell you? Did he share anything relevant? Anything about The Carnelian Crow?"

"Not at all," she replied, still prune-lipped. "He had nothing to say. He was just his normal sly, mysterious, untrustworthy Pix-ish self."

I raised my eyebrows mentally, but chose not to pursue the topic. It was a rare occasion when Evaline was so uncomplimentary to the slippery rogue. Perhaps she had finally come to her senses in regards to consorting with him.

Speaking of which…I decided to broach another touchy subject. "You and Mr. Oligary seemed quite companionable on Saturday night. Many people noticed, and there were whispers everywhere. There was even a sketch of the two of you in the *Times*, looking quite tête-à-tête at the ball, with the obvious captions and leading questions. People are talking, and the expectation for an engagement announcement is there. Have you made a decision?"

To my consternation, Evaline's face crumpled into a distressing combination of frustration and sorrow. "Mr. Oligary is coming here this afternoon to call on me—but more importantly, to speak to Bram. He's going to ask for permission to propose."

"And what will your response be?" I realized, suddenly and quite shockingly, that her answer mattered to me—for a number of reasons.

First, because of course I wouldn't wish the necessity to wed on anyone who didn't want to embark on such an enterprise. Matrimony was a heavy and unwelcome burden that many women bore, and that was the one thing on which the Ankh and I agreed: women should not be shackled to a man unless they chose it.

Second, I could see how devastated Evaline was about making such a decision. She had not been herself for over a week, and I feared the matter wouldn't improve if she agreed to wedlock.

And third—the most striking and unsettling realization—was that Evaline's marriage would, of necessity, put a significant damper on—if not an outright halt to—our volatile partnership.

I would be without a valuable companion and counterpart for my adventures, and I discovered, to my surprise, that that realization did not sit well with me at all. For all her weaknesses, Evaline Stoker was also a significant force to be reckoned with in her own way. We did complement each other, and I would miss having her by my side on any future endeavors.

"I haven't thought that far yet," Evaline replied soberly. "To be honest, I've rather avoided thinking about it."

Was that a glisten of tear in her eye? In the brave, bold, and enthusiastic Evaline Stoker? I felt a stirring of sympathy for my partner.

"But if I have to wed," she continued, "I suppose Mr. Oligary—Ned, I mean—is as good a choice as any. He's nice, and we get on well. As long as I don't *taint* his family name," she added with an uncharacteristic sneer.

I lifted my brow. Apparently there was some other story there. When I probed further, Evaline explained about the conversation—or, more accurately, the set-down her suitor had given her on her front porch.

"Vulgar?" was my outraged response. "Your ankles showed? And a bit of petticoat? *Truly?* You were supposed to stand back and watch while a man died when you could have prevented it *because your ankles might be exposed?* Good *gad*," I huffed.

Through angry tears, Evaline smiled, and I felt a trifle better having coaxed such a response from her. "I knew you'd understand. That man who was standing over you while you were examining Lord Cosgrove-Pitt's body was just as offended by your actions."

"He *was* terribly insulting." I drew in my breath and exhaled. "Well, Evaline...as tonight could possibly be one of our last adventures before your life changes, I suppose we'd better make it a good one."

She grinned. Her eyes lit up and her expression eased, and I could see once again why Evaline Stoker had attracted the attention of so many potential husbands—including one of the wealthiest bachelors in London. "Right. I'm not going to worry about the future tonight. I'll see Ned today, and—and if he proposes, then I shall have to put him off."

"A modest young woman would be in her rights to do so," I said with a coy smile. "It wouldn't do to appear *too* eager."

Her eyes danced, and I was relieved that she seemed to have recovered her sense of enthusiasm. "Exactly. Even Florence couldn't argue with that. And then tonight, at eight o'clock sharp, I'm going to go to my new job at The Carnelian Crow. Who knows—maybe it will pay well enough to help me settle Bram's debts and I won't have to get married after all!"

Although under normal circumstances, I would have shaken my head sadly in light of Evaline's impetuosity and fancy, this was different.

Not only was I good enough to make the plans for both of us, but it seemed inevitable that tonight's visit to The Carnelian Crow would be the final curtain call of the partnership of Holmes and Stoker.

Miss Stoker

~ In Which Our Heroine is Catapulted Over the Waterfall ~

WHEN SHE LEFT MY HOUSE, MINA WAS HAPPILY PLANNING for all contingencies during her evening at The Carnelian Crow.

However, I was dreading the afternoon to come before I could slip out of the house and don my "uny-form" for my new "position."

Pepper seemed to understand my mood, for she was particularly quiet as she helped me to organize my attire for the evening.

"It can't be all bad," she said, sliding a stake inside a hidden loop she'd sewn into my maid uniform. "Being married to a rich man."

I glared at her, and Pepper being Pepper, she just looked at me with her big eyes beneath puffs of carroty hair and shook her head. "There's ways," she said. "My Granny Verbena used to always say where there's a will, there's a way."

I just shook my head. I'd heard plenty about Granny Verbena over the years—oftentimes quite amusing anecdotes—but I wasn't in the mood to enjoy the dead woman's wisdom. I felt as if I were waiting in the Tower of London to be taken to my execution.

Shortly after Pepper left to go press the petticoats I was supposed to wear under my afternoon dress, I heard the sound of a carriage door slamming out front.

Heart in my throat, I rushed to the window to see whether it was Mr. Oligary. It was indeed his sleek black horseless motor vehicle sitting in front of the house.

I sank down onto the chair in front of my dressing table and waited. It was one of the rare times when I felt completely helpless.

Less than an hour later, Florence knocked on my door. She didn't even need to speak; her expression said it all.

"Come downstairs now, Evaline, dear. Mr. Oligary has come to call." She was fairly dancing on the threshold of my chamber, and her eyes were sparkling with more happiness than I'd ever seen in them. "He and Bram have just finished speaking in the study, and he's asked to meet you in the parlor."

I managed to paste on a smile and followed my pirouetting sister-in-law down the stairs and into the parlor. Bram and Mr. Oligary—I supposed I really should start to think of him as Ned—were standing there. They appeared to be having a jovial conversation.

"Miss Stoker," said my suitor as I came in. "You look lovely, as always."

My knees were shaking, and something in my belly was doing such wild flip-flops that I felt nauseated. I hoped I didn't puke on his shoes.

"Bram, I believe there's something Mrs. Gernum wishes to speak with us about," said Florence, making little attempt to be casual about their exit.

Everyone in the parlor knew exactly what was going on. It was like our own little stage play.

I only wished I didn't know my lines.

The door closed behind Florence and Bram.

"Miss Stoker. Evaline," said Ned in a warm voice as he sat next to me on the divan. "I've met with your brother, and he's agreed to allow me to speak with you privately for a moment."

I nodded, trying to swallow the lump in my throat and, at the same time, not appear ill. My fingers, ungloved and freezing, were enfolded in his warm hands as he looked earnestly at me.

"Evaline, you must have noticed that I hold you in the highest regard," he said. "I've long admired you—unfortunately, from a distance until recently, but that lessened my admiration not at all.

"In fact, getting to know you better has only confirmed my esteemed opinion of you. You are lovely and charming and well bred, and would honor any man by being on his arm or wearing his ring." He squeezed my hands a little. "I am very hopeful that you might make me the happiest of men and agree to be my wife."

———

Everything after that was a blur. I don't really remember what I said. I must have given some sort of acceptable response, because moments later, Florence and Bram surged into the parlor—just as Ned was pulling back from giving me another soft kiss on the lips.

He left soon after with a promise to call the next day at two o'clock.

No sooner had the front door closed behind him than Bram and Florence returned to the parlor and rounded on me, giddy with excitement.

"We did it," Florence said, taking my hands and pulling me up from the divan, forcing me to join her in a dance around the room. Fortunately, Mr. Oligary's carriage was facing the opposite direction and he wouldn't see us through the window. "We did it!"

"Nicely done, Evaline," said Bram. This was actually the first time he'd even acknowledged the situation, let alone spoken to me about it. I supposed he thought it was best for Florence to handle it, though his avoidance struck me as being a little cowardly. "Congratulations," he said.

"But…I haven't done anything yet," I said, pulling away from Florence's grip. "I mean, I didn't give him an answer."

"Of course you didn't—and he didn't expect you to. After all, a proper, demure young woman doesn't just *rush* into marriage," Florence said. (Could she have any idea how ridiculous her statement was in light of the current situation?) "You don't need to seem too eager. Tomorrow when he comes to call, you'll accept, and we'll get the announcements published immediately—that ought to hold off the bank, knowing you're going to marry an *Oligary*!"

"But…I'm not sure I *am* going to accept," I said.

Neither of them seemed to hear me, for they were talking excitedly about paying off banknotes and upgrading the Lyceum Theater's lighting system, and even taking a trip to Paris. They seemed to expect—or perhaps it had been discussed specifically—that Mr. Oligary—Ned—would help to settle their debts and would provide a generous dowry for my hand. After all, it wouldn't do to *taint* the family name if the wife of Ned Oligary's family was on the street or had bill collectors calling.

I also learned, to my dismay, that Florence had already drafted the announcement for the *Times*—and that Bram was eager to read it.

I said it again, more forcefully this time, and Bram must have heard me. He stopped abruptly, holding up a hand to Florence's rattling speech, and turned to look at me.

"What did you say, Evvie, dear?"

"I said, I don't know that I *am* going to accept the proposal."

They stared at me as if I'd announced I was from the center of the earth.

"Of course you're going to accept it," Florence said briskly. "It's one thing to be coy with Mr. Oligary, but there's no need to play that game with us."

"Come now, Evaline. You'll not get a better offer," said Bram. "Oligary's a good man, and just *think* how your liaison with his family will help the theater! We'll be sold out weeks in advance." He pulled out a cigar and made to light it—and Florence didn't even reprimand him for smoking outside his study, as she normally would.

I stared back at them. It felt as if the ground was falling away beneath my feet. Didn't they understand? Didn't they *see*?

Didn't they care about me?

"But...I don't really want to get married," I managed to say.

"Evaline," Bram said, holding his unlit cigar and mechanical lighter suspended in midair. "I don't believe you understand how important it is for you to make this match. For us. For your family. It's your *duty*. Ned Oligary is besotted with you, and he'll give you a very comfortable life—and help us to keep Grantworth House as well as being able to stay in London. Everything else," he added, giving me a meaningful look that I took to mean he was referring to my vampire-hunting vocation, "will work out."

Didn't he understand? It wasn't just going to "work out."

"Now, we'll have no more of this nonsense," Florence said when I merely stared back at my brother through the tears welling in my eyes. "I know you're going to do the right thing, Evaline. Think of your family."

I shook my head mutely.

My entire life was going to change. I was going to be living with a man who, though kind and far too proper, was basically a stranger. I was going to be a wife, and probably a mother, and I'd be responsible for running a household *and* I'd be forced into attending balls and fêtes and dinners and teas, and I'd have to make social calls and host them as well...

My lungs felt tight, and I felt myself swaying a bit. I grabbed blindly for the back of the nearby armchair.

"I'm not feeling well," I said. "I'm going to go lie down for a bit."

I heard Florence laugh lightly behind me as I fled the parlor. "Too much excitement, I suppose, over her good fortune. She can hardly believe it, I'm certain. Maybe a bit of cold feet, too—of course she's nervous. Who wouldn't be? Mr. Oligary is quite the gentleman. I believe I'll go ahead and send off the announcements today, so they can be in the *Times* and *Herald* tomorrow. I just *knew* Evaline would make a good match one day—when she finally got around to it, Bram. I just knew it. She's such a lovely girl…"

That was the last I heard as I dashed up the stairs to my bedchamber.

SEVERAL HOURS AND MANY BUCKETS OF ANGRY TEARS later, I found myself in the alley behind The Pickled Nurse. It was only half past seven, but since it was December, it was cold and dark.

No one noticed me picking my way through the garbage in the alley—but I was rather hoping someone would challenge me. Because I was raring for a fight.

I was armed to the teeth, with several stakes and other anti-vampire weapons secreted beneath my uniform—as well as a dagger. I left the gun-like weapons to Mina; I preferred hand-to-hand fighting.

And I was really hoping I'd have the chance to do some tonight.

As I made my way down the tunnel to the servants' entrance of The Carnelian Crow, I realized there was another figure making its way just ahead of me. Possibly Kitty, formerly of Varrel House—or any one of the other servants that worked for the ladies' club.

I took my time, and when I got to the door where Mr. Gillies had let me in the first time, I found the other girl waiting there as well.

"I'm Pepper," I said before I really thought about it. I hoped this other female wasn't Kitty, because obviously she'd know I wasn't Pepper. "It's my first night here."

"Matilda," she said. "It's not bad. Done worse. Been here goin' on three years. Better'n my last position, dressing up fancy ladies. *She's* quite brilliant, you know. And Gillies is a bit of a pain, but there's a handsome footman who makes up for it. I keep hoping he'll pull me into a dark corner when no one's watching." She giggled.

The door opened and Gillies was there, complete with a red crow sticker on his red-tipped mustache and a neatly pressed uniform.

After that, I didn't have much time to think, let alone to talk, for I was very busy. The list of things that needed to be done before the clien*tele* arrived seemed endless: making sure all the tablecloths were smooth, all the glasses arranged just so, the fires built, the candles lit, the floor swept, the dishes clean, the napkins pressed, the food cut and chopped for the cook… Thus, I didn't have the chance to snoop around much, but I could hear the musicians warming up in the main club area. And I could sense the presence of UnDead as well.

My stomach wanted to growl because I'd been so unsettled that I hadn't eaten anything since breakfast. The food smelled really good. I wondered if there would be the chance to snatch up a bit of a snack—something that had never worried me in the past, having never been a servant before. I was used to being able to go into the kitchen and find something to eat any time I wanted.

Matilda and I were carrying huge trays loaded with plates, cups, and silver when we passed a young man in the corridor that ran between the servants' entrance to the main club chamber and the warren of back rooms. He was dressed in the same livery as Gillies, and he stopped, blocking our way.

"'lo there, Matildy," he said with a charming grin. He was carrying several logs for the fire, and his muscles bulged beneath his coat. "Where ya going with that big load?"

She giggled and simpered, and I rolled my eyes as she replied, "I might be getting lost and needin' some help to find my way back."

"I'll surely help ye," he replied. "Let me drop these logs off and I'll come right back an' give y' a hand, Tildy."

"See? Isn't he divine?" she whispered as he went off. "There's another one, but he ain't so fine. Got big ears and a big nose, though his eyes are nice."

I had an idea. "How about you give me your tray and I'll take all this up, and then you and—whatever his name is— can get lost together." That would give me the chance to slip away for a few minutes and see if I could find out anything interesting.

"Really?" Matilda's eyes sparkled. "But can you carry all this? It'll be pretty heavy—"

"It's not that bad. Help me stack it all up on one tray…"

Moments later I was hurrying along the corridor, alone for the first time since arriving here. The tray was much heavier now, but nothing to an unusually strong vampire hunter. I planned to drop the dishes off in the serving room next to the kitchen as directed, then I'd get "lost" on my return, following the chill on the back of my neck to locate the UnDead and see what—

Someone was coming, drat it. I heard voices and footsteps.

I quickly put the laden tray where it belonged, then ducked behind a door until they passed—it was Gillies and some other person I hadn't met, who was receiving a litany of orders from our boss.

I slipped out and went in the opposite direction, which took me toward the front of the hall where the stage and musicians were, but still in the side corridor.

The chill on the back of my neck was growing strong, and I wasn't paying attention to much other than that sensation— measuring it and trying to follow it—so I didn't realize someone was coming up behind me until it was too late.

The soft scuff of a shoe had me spinning just as a strong hand grabbed my arm and thrust me into a dimly lit side room.

Startled, I yanked away. In the drassy light, I saw a pair of large, protruding ears and a blade-like nose to rival Mina's, and then I looked up. Into Pix's dark, stormy eyes.

I opened my mouth to speak, but I didn't have a chance. The next thing I knew, he'd eased me up against the wall and was kissing me.

Miss Holmes

~ The Princess of Vovinga Arrives ~

"THIS IS QUITE IRREGULAR, MISS HOLMES," GRAYLING said. "But I suspect you wouldn't want it any other way."

"Naturally," I replied with a smile.

Moments ago, I had alighted from a hired hackney cab, and met him at the corner of the tiny, unassuming Proud-street and Carry-street as planned. We stood just outside the pool of light from a gas lamp. Big Ben and the Oligary Tower clocks had just struck nine. Although we weren't alone on the street by any stretch of the imagination, we certainly drew no undue attention.

He was wearing an old-fashioned cloak of midnight purple that swung about his knees and had a sort of attached capelet that flowed over broad shoulders like large woolen epaulets. Though his head was covered by a satin aubergine top hat that rode low over his brows, I could see a bit of dark hair peeping from beneath the brim. When he turned slightly, I noticed the wig actually sported a long braided queue that put me in mind of the style of Chinese men. Grayling also wore round spectacles tinted with the same purplish hue as his hat, and there were tiny magnifyer lenses of yellow and blue affixed to the rim of the glasses. They were quite cunning, for they could be flipped into place in front of the larger lenses.

He'd also included in his costume a trim black mustache and a triangular beard reminiscent of Walter Raleigh, but Grayling's false beard extended several inches past his chin and was tied into a tiny queue with a copper wire entwined with opaque blue and copper beads. He wore smooth, light gloves of some shiny bronze material and knee-high boots of buffed black leather, with copper bracings on the heel and toe.

Aside from the obvious physical and apparel attributes, he

finished off the details of his new persona by changing the way he held his body and moved: a bit more angular and measured than his normally smooth and sure movements.

"Your disguise is quite good, Inspector Grayling. I doubt I would have immediately recognized you had I not been specific with my instructions about where and how to meet." I realized belatedly that perhaps I should have addressed him as Ambrose—but I wasn't certain this evening would qualify as a social event.

"As is yours, Miss Holmes. I see you've taken care not only to cover your hands, but to alter the shape of your ears and jaw line. The bright blond wig appears extraordinarily real, and the veil is a nice touch as well."

"Thank you," I replied modestly from behind said veil, which covered the top two-thirds of my face. Thanks to well-placed snips in the fabric at the proper locations, I could see through the black fabric, but my features were hardly discernible to the viewer. "And thank you for agreeing to accompany me at the last minute. I would like to point out that I am keeping my word to not investigate The Carnelian Crow on my own."

"Duly noted, Miss Holmes," he replied gravely. "Am I to understand that tonight I am your guest at what amounts to a female dining club? I confess, I'd expected something more sinister."

"Time will tell that, Inspector. According to Miss Stoker, we are to walk another block here on Proud-street, and then there is a wrought iron gate that appears to lead to nowhere. Just inside that gate is a latch that will open a side door adjacent to the gate."

Everything was just as Evaline had described, and as we reached the wrought iron gate, a distinct shadow crossed above us.

I looked up, a bit of prickling settling eerily over my neck when I saw the crow. He had settled on the top of an aged iron signpost, extruding from the building.

"*Caw!*" it announced, and looked down at us with its beady blue-black eye.

"Well, then," I said, looking at Grayling. "I suppose we are, indeed, in the right place."

It was with mounting excitement that I unlatched the gate, then, moments later, went through the hidden side door with my companion (I led the way, of course).

Once inside, I was startled to discover that instead of walking through the tunnel as Evaline had described, even that inconvenience was eliminated—for the floor *moved*. (Presumably it had been turned on for the clients this evening, and she hadn't noticed it previously.)

Grayling and I had only to stand there as what I could only surmise was a large, long, belt-like conveyance trundled along, delivering us to our destination. It reminded me of the moving walkways I'd utilized during my visit to Princess Alexandra at Marlborough House with Dylan and Miss Stoker.

Along the way, the belt would end, we would walk several feet, and then step onto a new stretch of conveyor. During one of these such transfers, we caught sight of a trio of people slightly ahead of us—two women and a man. They too were veiled and otherwise discreetly covered.

Perhaps a quarter of an hour after we first stepped into the tunnel, we arrived at our final destination. I pulled the small invitation card Evaline had snitched for me and prepared to offer it to the two guards who greeted us at a sleek black door that I assumed led into The Carnelian Crow.

Presumably, the two guards were UnDead—although not being a vampire hunter, I had no way of knowing for certain. Neither of them showed any fangs, nor were their eyes glowing. However, I took solace in the fact that tucked beneath my cloak, nestled in my bodice, was a very large silver cross, and shoved deep inside one of the knee-high laced boots I wore was a slender but lethal stake. I'd dipped it in holy water earlier today.

"Name," grunted the taller man at the door, whilst the other one took my card. He barely glanced at it, then held out his hand to Grayling as if expecting him to proffer one as well.

When my companion merely looked at him silently from behind his amethyst lenses, the shorter guard said, "You need a voucher to enter." He made a move to block Grayling and me from going any further.

I had feared something like this might happen, but I was prepared, for I had interrogated Evaline about every minute detail of her experience at the club: every conversation, every room she'd seen or entered, every detail of the decor and layout.

I drew myself up and fixed my most arrogant Holmesian glare upon the guard—the stare my father had perfected during his work at the Home Office. The one that made even the boldest of generals and the most regal of royals flinch.

"Ze gentleman is with me. He needs no voucher. Make your bow to Baron von Vennsteinkopf. He speaks no English, and zerefore will have taken no offense by your ignorance. Yet." I spoke with a slight accent that could have been inter-preted as Russian or Betrovian. "As you have seen, *I* have ze card. We will both enter, or I shall make a complaint to *Her.*" I looked at both of them through my veil as if they were no more than six-legged creatures, scuttling about at my feet.

They exchanged glances. If they were indeed vampires and were going to attempt to call my bluff, this would likely be the moment their fangs would erupt and their eyes would begin to glow. I was also prepared for that, as my hand hovered near the throat of my cloak, ready to toss it away at a moment's notice to reveal the silver cross. I felt Grayling tense next to me, and I suspected the walking stick he carried concealed some sort of appropriate weapon as well.

The taller guard appeared ready to acquiesce. "Your name?"

I drew myself up again as if mightily insulted. "Pardon

me?" My voice was icy as the Arctic and still inflected with an accent.

"Your name, madam, for our records." This time, he sounded marginally apologetic.

"You *dare* ask my name? Do you not have ze eyes in your head? Do you not recognize ze royalty ven it stands before you? *I* am ze Princess of Vovinga, and you have delayed me long enough."

I gathered up my skirts, offered my arm to Grayling, then swept toward the door (which remained closed).

I must have made my point clear, for the guard rushed to open the door before I was required to even slow my pace.

"That was magnificently done," Grayling murmured in my ear as we at last stepped inside.

"Thank you," I responded in a similarly low tone. "Ambrose."

Though it was obscured by his tinted spectacles, I caught the look of surprise and pleasure that flashed across his face at my use of his given name. That, in turn, sent a little prickle of delight through me.

As we made our way to a table, I admired the arrangement of the club now that I was seeing it firsthand. Evaline had not stinted in her description of the place, and it was every bit as dramatic and luxurious as she'd described.

The arched glass ceiling exposed a beautiful starlit sky. In an obvious effort to keep that a focal point, all man-made illumination in the form of lamps and candles was set no higher than halfway up the sides of the walls. Black candles flickered in small forests of flame inside ornate bronze birdcages, and four roaring fires ensured the below-ground room was comfortably warm.

I intended to sit at one of the side tables Evaline had told me about, with the high privacy wall around two-thirds of it, and thus led my companion to the nearest unoccupied one. The table and its semicircular built-in bench were rather close together, and I hesitated before gathering up the layers of fabric of my clothing to bundle myself into a seat. It would be difficult and awkward to slide in.

But before I could make a move, a very proper man, dressed in a masculine version of the red, black, and cobalt uniform Evaline had shown me, approached in a rush of horror.

"Please, no, madam," he said, halting my attempt. "Allow me."

At first I thought he meant to keep me from sitting there, but when he shifted a lever at the back of the booth, the table began to move. It pivoted out and to the left, away from the bench seat, sliding smoothly and silently on some invisible arm. This completely exposed the half-moon seat, which was upholstered in lush blue velvet studded with jet-black buttons. Grayling and I removed our respective cloaks—giving them to our host—then stepped up onto the low platform on which the booth was moored. We thus settled easily into our seats.

The man, whom I identified as Mr. Gillies due to the red crow emblem stuck to his mustache, moved the lever once more, and the table returned to its proper position. During this entire time, the scarlet-on-cobalt paisley tablecloth barely fluttered, and the blue glass decanter and tiny tulip glasses didn't so much as clink.

I didn't deign to thank Mr. Gillies, as I believed Princess Vovinga would never stoop to acknowledging mere servants. Instead, I lifted my nose and turned to Grayling, who'd removed his hat and set it on the attached rack for such purposes.

"Permit me to demonstrate the privacy screen, madam," said Mr. Gillies.

When I nodded regally, he pointed out the mechanism that engaged a barrier which extended from the back of the booth's wall and curved around the front to the opposite side. The lower half was solid, but the upper half was made from some translucent material that offered some obscurity, but still allowed us to see a mottled version of the club. A small gas lamp glowed above our heads.

"Momentarily, you will be provided with a...ahem... menu of tonight's offerings," our host informed us with a very correct bow.

After Gillies had left, muttering something about missing servants, I looked at Grayling. "Now we wait for Miss Stoker to find us, and we will determine our next move from there."

"The music is quite nice," he replied, referring to the piano and crooning vocals coming from the stage. The woman was singing a song about how all her troubles seemed so far away, yesterday. "And I must say, this is a very comfortable arrangement."

My companion was sitting quite close to me, and I cannot say that I minded in the least. The privacy screen remained in place and it all felt wonderfully cozy. I almost forgot I was on an investigation. It was also becoming a trifle warm, and so I took advantage of our obscurity and carefully removed my veiled hat.

Grayling, whose appearance was strikingly different (and not quite as handsome, if one took note of such things) now that a sleek black wig covered his mop of gingery hair, followed suit. He pulled off his gloves and the purple-tinted spectacles, tucking both accessories into a large pocket of his jacket.

"Perhaps a bit of refreshment," I suggested, gesturing to the blue carafe.

Grayling poured for us, and it turned out the contents of the carafe consisted of a pale pink beverage that fizzed and foamed. I sniffed it and was rewarded with a noseful of strawberry, mint, and basil. It tasted just as refreshing as it sounds.

My companion sipped from his drink, then settled back in his seat and half turned to look at me. "Well, Miss Holmes, here we are at The Carnelian Crow. While I've seen no evidence of criminal activity, I've also no doubt there is something sinister underlying the veneer of this very excellent ladies' club. What do you propose for our next step?"

"If Evaline doesn't appear soon, or nothing untoward

occurs, we should take matters into our own hands and begin to—as she puts it—snoop around."

He grinned behind his false mustache and beard. "That is precisely what I expected you to say."

But I hardly heard him, for I had noticed something familiar about the woman singing on the stage. She'd had her profile to us most of the time, and the little bit of her face I could see had been in shadow. But now she leaned toward the pianist, resting her elbows on the instrument, and a swath of light filtered over her features. I didn't recognize them, but there was something very familiar about the way she moved, and tilted her head…

It took me a moment, then I recognized her beneath the layers of disguise. Without thinking, I grabbed Grayling's arm sharply and nodded toward the dais. "The singer."

He took a only a moment to scrutinize her before he nodded and murmured, "Irene Adler. How curious."

"Indeed."

That raised more questions, but also answered a few. I mulled for a bit, considering a variety of actions and scenarios, and was confident Grayling was doing the same.

We listened to Miss Adler sing about how she would always love you—though I have no idea to whom she was singing in a club mostly filled with females.

Predictably, there was no sign of Evaline. Clearly, she'd been delayed or detoured—as usual.

And just as clearly, there was something else about The Carnelian Crow other than the seemingly innocent dinner club—although I had noticed a woman who looked remarkably like Lady Hortense Kinney-Dell sitting very close to a man who was most definitely not Lord Kinney-Dell, a highly placed parliamentarian who was far broader and heavier than the man currently keeping company with his wife.

And there was another couple who appeared to be *kissing.* On the mouth. In *public.* (The couple in question was sitting in a privacy-shrouded booth like ours, so I couldn't identify the culprits. But I suspected they were not meant to be seen together.) The very sight of them was enough to make my cheeks heat uncomfortably.

I hoped Grayling hadn't noticed the other couple's activity.

It was then I noticed a very distinct odor—an essence that was rusty and pungent and rich. I felt my heart kick up a beat as I realized what it was, and was just about to turn to my companion when he leaned closer to me.

"Miss Holmes, do you smell—"

"Blood," I whispered. "Fresh blood." I swallowed hard, for now that the aroma had come to my attention, it was almost cloying in its thickness in the air.

"Look there," he said in a low, tense voice, "at the booth just to our left."

My heart stopped. "Good gad."

Whoever was at that table had neglected to position the shield for privacy purposes, for I could see quite well what was happening. Perhaps the woman who sat therein, sagging languidly back against the curved wall of the booth, didn't mind that the rest of us in the establishment could see that a vampire was feeding on her wrist. She tipped her head back, resting it against the plush velvet behind her, and seemed to be…*enjoying* the moment.

"Should we intervene?" I murmured once I'd caught my breath.

Grayling was very still next to me. "She doesn't appear to be in any…er…distress. In fact, I believe she is—"

"She's enjoying it," I finished, unable to take my eyes from a view that seemed both intimate and violent at the same time. The expression on the woman's face was most definitely one of pleasure rather than fear. I couldn't stop staring, watching in both horror and fascination.

"It appears that way."

Finally, I tore my eyes from the sordid scene, and as I did

so, my attention skittered over the rest of the chamber—including the other booth where the couple had been kissing.

That was when I realized with a shock that they were now doing more than merely kissing. The pair of glowing red eyes told me what I'd missed. "There, too," I managed to choke out, prodding Grayling's arm so that he looked as well. "He's biting her *neck*."

My companion muttered something, and what I could see of his features were dark and taut. "A very special, dark sort of establishment," he murmured. "It's no wonder it's been kept such a close secret for years."

Just then, a young woman dressed in the same uniform that Evaline had shown me—though it wasn't her—approached. She was accompanied by two very handsome, well-dressed men—one blond and one dark-haired, each perhaps a few years older than Grayling—and a beautiful, exotic-looking woman with unnaturally red hair. They weren't wearing servants' livery like their companion or Mr. Gillies; instead, the trio was garbed in well-appointed evening wear.

"Would you care for some refreshment?" The maidservant held up a small placard.

Grayling pushed a button, and a small panel flipped open in the privacy screen, creating a sort of table or tray through the opening. She slipped the card, which I immediately recognized as a menu, through the hole.

"And if you are interested in other sorts of…entertainment," she said with a smile, and gestured to the two men and woman, "you may make your selection."

It was all I could do to keep from gasping in shock and horror when I realized her three companions were vampires, *and she was offering us to select from one of them.*

Grayling's strong fingers on my arm were the only reason I didn't betray myself, and that gave me the moment to remember who I was—or, at least, who I was supposed to be.

Thus, as Princess Vovinga, I managed to give each of the UnDead an assessing look. I pretended to myself that I was merely choosing a footman or groom, and took my time considering the so-called options. Each of the three not only showed the tips of their fangs as I looked them over, but they also allowed their eyes to flare with the telltale red glow.

I had to admit, the dark-haired one would have been quite attractive if he hadn't been an immortal demon. Apparently, there were some women—and likely men as well—who truly did enjoy the feel of an UnDead drinking their blood.

After a moment, I shook my head and gave a haughty sniff. "Do you not have anyzing better zan zis? I expected...somezing *more*."

The young woman drew back a trifle as if surprised, but recovered herself quickly. "Of course, madame—"

"Your *Highness*," I said, snapping my body into full attention and giving her the Holmesian glare of my father.

"Of course. Your Highness," stammered the waitress. "I'll see if—if there are any other options." She turned to leave, then belatedly remembered her vampire companions and gestured to them.

The dark-haired vampire gave me a long, bold look and allowed his eyes to glow even brighter with challenge before he turned to follow the serving woman.

No sooner had they gone than I felt Grayling's hand shift from my arm to close over my fingers. He murmured something that sounded like a curse, but I didn't care. It was clear he was as astounded—and horrified—as I was.

"A vampire den. Instead of an opium den," he murmured. "And yet...I don't suppose that it's strictly illegal. I can think of no laws they are violating—at least in that manner." He sounded grim and rather worn out. "Do you believe me now, Miss Holmes, that this isn't the place for a gently bred young woman like yourself?"

"When investigating cases, one must make sacrifices," I said.

Grayling seemed just about to say something else when we saw Mr. Gillies and his mustache with the red crow ornamentation approaching our table. He was accompanied by two individuals that were so stone-faced and broad-shouldered they could only be guards of some sort. I got the distinct impression they were not another choice of vampire "entertainment."

I reached for Grayling's hand on the seat next to me, and he squeezed back gently. I had a feeling things were about to get even more interesting.

"Pardon me, madame. Your presence has been requested in a private meeting," said Mr. Gillies.

"And who, pray, is making such a request?" I replied arrogantly.

"Madame," said the mustachioed man, dropping his voice reverently. "It is of course...*Her.* The *Woman.*"

I flickered a glance toward the stage where Irene Adler, who Uncle Sherlock had dubbed *the* Woman (emphasis on the article, rather than the noun), still sang unconcernedly. I had a feeling Mr. Gillies was not referring to Uncle Sherlock's woman, but to...well, someone else.

The Woman...who could only be the proprietress and architect of The Carnelian Crow.

This was what I had been waiting for.

The game was about to begin.

Miss Stoker

~ A Far More Satisfactory Tete-a-Tete ~

WHEN PIX AND I AT LAST BROKE APART—I'M NOT QUITE certain who pulled away first—I was lightheaded and out of breath, and very, very warm. I probably shouldn't admit it, but my knees were trembling too.

Pix was still gripping my arms. I looked up at him, seeing past misshapen ears and a false nose (which had gone slightly askew during the very thorough kissing) to the emotion blazing in his eyes.

"Evaline," was all he said.

"I'm getting married," I blurted out—for I had just remembered that unpleasant fact. My stomach lurched at the thought.

"Not when ye kiss me like that," he responded. But then he stepped away, putting far too much space between us. His face slid into shadows.

"What are you doing here?" I asked, then wished I hadn't. That was the sort of thing Mina always rolled her eyes at— obvious questions or statements. But my brain was a little fuddled.

Pix was fixing his nose, pressing it back into place. "Tryin' to keep England from falling. Though why the devil I should care about this bloody country is a good question."

"England? From falling? What the blooming Pete are you talking about?" The last bit of delicious, shivery heat disappeared from my insides.

There was still a lot of emotion swimming in his dark eyes. His mouth, which was a little puffy from our kisses, twisted a little. When he spoke, I realized he'd almost completely given up his Cockney accent. "I'd have thought you and Mina would have figured it out by now. Especially since ye were witness to the first public move on Saturday night."

"The Ankh. And the wires. And Lord Cosgrove-Pitt." I fumbled around for an explanation, but couldn't seem to put the jumbled facts together. One thing I knew for certain: "There are a lot of vampires here."

Pix almost smiled. "Aye. There are. They're part of the entertainment—haven't ye been trained yet by Gillies?"

"I haven't seen him for a while. He's probably looking for me—I'm probably going to get sacked." I gave a little laugh, then sobered. "What do you mean they're part of the entertainment?" But I thought I already knew the answer.

"Some people take it like opium—they enjoy the sensation of a vampire drinking their blood. Some even get addicted to it. But much as ye might like to brandish your stake about, luv, and dust them into ash, the UnDead and the clients here who enjoy them are the least of our worries."

Luv. My heart flipped a little, drat it. There was something about the way he said it that reminded me of all the things we'd been through together.

And why the blooming Pete was I acting like this was the end of us?

Oh, right. My insides plummeted like a cannonball. I had to get married. To Ned Oligary. I felt sick again.

"Well," I said crossly, "if it's not the vampires, what is it?"

He took my hand. "Come on. I'll show ye."

Pix obviously knew his way around the back rooms and tunnels of The Carnelian Crow and its environs much better than me. Several times we had to duck into a doorway or hide behind a curtain when someone approached—and Pix seemed to know every hiding place. Not a surprise.

I heard the distant sound of voices and activity, and once again the strains of piano music. Apparently the club was open for business. I wondered how long it would be until Gillies and Matilda began to wonder where I was.

Had Mina and Grayling arrived? Were they sitting at a table, waiting to be served?

I told Pix of our half-formed plan in a low voice as we made our way to wherever he was taking me. "I'm supposed to serve Mina and Grayling," I finished. "And report on anything I learn."

He muttered something, but otherwise made no response.

Finally, after dodging and slipping about like a couple of sneaky mice, we came to a metal door that reminded me of a bank safe. Its front was a maze of cogs, bolts, and gears.

"In 'ere. I've been trying to break in for days," he said. "I keep getting interrupted. An' it's a complicated lock system."

I thought about the three rows of locks on the door to his hideaway and the numbers he'd chosen. I felt a little pang of pain, and thrust it away. "Do you know what's inside?"

He nodded, then pulled out a slender leather wrap that clinked softly. Crouching at the door, he unrolled the packet on the floor next to him. Inside was an array of tools—lock picks, skeleton keys, slender magnifyers, and even something that looked like a doctor's stethoscope.

And then he went to work with those slim, quick fingers and sharp eyes. He had to remove one of the false ears so he could insert the listening device.

It might have been an amusing sight, Pix with one ear on and one ear off, his bulbous nose askew once more, and the stethoscope cord trailing from where it was positioned in the one ear. But I found no humor in the situation at all. Instead, I stared down at the forlorn piece of false ear, swamped with a confused mix of emotions.

Things were never going to be the same.

Although the back of my neck had been chilled and prickly since I arrived, the sensation hadn't changed...until now. All at once, it became sharper and eerier.

I reached stealthily beneath my skirt, sliding the stake from its moorings. Pix glanced at me in acknowledgment, but continued his work without pause. For some reason, that gave me a little pop of warmth: unlike Mina, he trusted I would handle the threat.

I slipped away, intending to greet the vampire before he came close enough to see Pix and possibly sound an alarm.

Too late, I realized there were three of them. (My mistake.

I'd expected one, or two at the most.) I saw their shadows spilling onto the floor from around the corner.

I paused. Three against one meant that it wouldn't be a quick and quiet altercation. Which meant there was the chance of raising an alarm.

So I did the first thing I could think of that would distract them.

I pulled up my sleeve and sliced the sharp end of my stake down the outside of my arm. The cut stung, but blood immediately burst free.

Then, hiding the stake behind my skirt, I hurried around the corner.

"*Oh!*" I feigned surprise as I purposely nearly ran into them. "Hello. I…" I took on a confused expression.

"Are you lost there, my sweet morsel?" asked one, his eyes gleaming with interest. He looked hungry—and so did his companions.

I took care not to look any of them directly in the eyes, and didn't try to avoid it when one of them lunged for me. I let him take my arm, pretending to become faint as he plunged his fangs into my wrist.

As I sagged, a second UnDead caught me in his arms from behind. Falling against him, I tipped my head to the side in obvious invitation, keeping my eyes slit in order to avoid the alluring gazes of my attackers. I wasn't going to make that mistake again.

As my blood flowed freely from three different places, the strength began to seep from my limbs. I had to act soon. But with one UnDead taking blood from my wrist, and the other drawing it from the top of my shoulder from where he'd grabbed me behind, that meant my stake hand was free.

Fortunately, the last vampire was foolish enough to reach for that remaining arm, which hung seemingly helplessly toward the ground. As he made his move, tilting toward me to grab at it, my hand flew upward, stake-point first, and slammed into his heart.

He exploded into dust, and before either of my other

attackers realized what had happened, I swung the same hand over my torso in a powerful arc, shoving the stake into the back of the man feasting on my wrist. He never even knew what hit him.

Panting and a little lightheaded, I staggered, my knees buckling. The vampire who'd been dragging blood from my throat pulled away in shock. Maybe he'd smelled the ash; maybe he just noticed through the haze of bloodsucking pleasure that his two companions were no longer pulling his meal away from him.

But that was all I needed. Blood dripping from my wrist, I reached up and dragged the silver cross necklace from beneath my uniform bodice, then tossed the large pendant over my shoulder. It swung on its chain, slamming into the vampire's face.

He cried out in shock, and immediately I heard a sizzle as the silver connected with his flesh. The vampire released me completely as he staggered back. I stumbled into a pivot, bumping into the wall and nearly vaulting onto my face due to weak knees and a sudden lightheadedness from lack of blood, but on the way down, my stake rammed into his shoulder.

The man cursed, but the silver cross was still repelling him, so he didn't have the strength to lash out or to fight back very hard. This gave me the opportunity to try again, and this time, using the wall as leverage, I arced up. My stake plunged directly into his heart.

He froze, his eyes wide with pain and surprise. Then, in an instant, he was gone in a puff of smelly, UnDead ash.

Panting, I leaned against the wall. I was dripping blood everywhere—belatedly I realized that was likely to attract even more UnDead. (If Mina were here, she'd have a few things to say about my lack of forethought.) And the scent of musty ash would as well. But there was no help for it.

I returned to where I'd left Pix. He was still working on the door. He cursed under his breath when he saw me, and began to rise, but I held out a hand to stop him.

"I've got salted holy water," I said as I dug for where Pepper had sewn it into the hem of my uniform.

"How bad?" he asked, looking at me with those intense eyes even as his nimble fingers worked at their task.

"I've been worse," I replied, wincing as I poured the salted holy water over the bite on my wrist.

"I've almost— Ah," he said with great satisfaction. "No almost about it." He smiled a little and turned something on one of the large cogs. I heard a quiet clunk followed by an entire symphony of whirrs, clicks, and soft thunks.

And then, with a sort of sigh, the door shuddered in its hinges then exhaled as it came free.

Pix bundled up his tools, still studying me and my injuries. "What happened?" he asked, his attention bouncing between the bloodstains in various places on my clothing. He peeled off his nose (which was coming unattached) and stuffed it into his pocket.

I shook my head. Unlike Mina, I had no need to revisit every minute detail of my encounter. Besides, I wanted to see what was behind the door.

I didn't resist when Pix took my hand. In fact, I felt a wave of pure awareness when those talented fingers closed over mine: warm, strong, familiar. I swallowed past the burning in my throat, and we walked into the room.

When I saw what was in there, it took me a minute—but then the pieces began to fall into place. Maybe not as quickly and easily as for Mina Holmes, but when I saw what was inside the chamber and how it was arranged, I began to understand.

I looked at Pix. "Now what?"

"That," said someone behind us, "is a very good question."

Miss Holmes

~ Revelations, Requests, and Realizations ~

As Grayling and I followed Mr. Gillies, we were
flanked by the two guards. I couldn't quite subdue a spear of
nerves.

I wasn't concerned about my safety. I was more
concerned about…other things.

At last we arrived at a silken barrier of blood-red fabric. It
shivered as if in anticipation of what was about to occur.

A third guard stood blocking the way.

"Madam," said Mr. Gillies with a sweeping bow and a
gesture for me to proceed. But when Grayling took my elbow,
our host held out an arm. "No." The guards moved, blocking
my companion from following. "Not you."

My heart pounded wildly. I glanced at Grayling, saw that
he was about to protest, and shook my head sharply. *No.*

I needed to do this. To follow through whatever this was.
Behind the mustache and beard, Grayling's expression was a
mask of fury and fear. But it was a testament of his trust in
me, and perhaps even admiration, that he made no argument
other than with his eyes.

I had no trepidation as I turned from my simmering
companion to face the silken curtain that separated me
from…*her.*

My palms prickled. A great, billowing emotion that was a
combination of excitement and fear—and more than a
twinge of hope—accompanied me as the guard swept the
carnelian curtain aside.

The moment I stepped over the threshold, the swath of
silken tapestry flowed back into place, separating me from
Grayling and the guard. But instead of greeting my hostess, I
faced another barrier: this one of silvery white silk. A large
crow had been stitched upon it—a black crow with red details
glinting from the edges of its wings and piercing blue eyes.

The Carnelian Crow. The luminous cloth shivered from the air moving around it, and I discerned a faint glow of light burning through the fabric's translucence.

I swept aside the curtain and once again stepped forward.

She sat at a small table in the center of the spare, compact room. Its windowless walls were draped in wide swaths of black and red silk that rippled from some unseen shift in the air. Candles glowed everywhere, and seemed to be suspended in midair as their flames darted and sent dancing shadows along the walls and floor. A fire roared in a massive alcove on one wall. Other than the lighting and wall coverings, the chamber held nothing but the round table and two chairs—one for me, and one for her. On the table was a slender red carafe and two elegant glasses.

My heart thudded madly as I tried to make out her features, her face—but she was veiled beneath the black top hat she wore. I had no choice but to move closer as she made a spare, elegant gesture with a gloved hand. I was to join her at the table.

Hope pounded within me—a hope I had dared not name or even acknowledge. I felt certain I would recognize her, even from this distance, if it were—

But I refused to even entertain that possibility. I refused to even put a name to what I wished for.

The disappointment, were I to be wrong, would be…catastrophic.

"Sit." The voice was too low and nebulous for me to identify.

My feet seemed to float as I hesitated. My head felt strangely weighted down, my hands clumsy and swollen.

It took every bit of control I owned, every scrap of consciousness, to keep my eyes steady and cool on her veiled, seated figure—as if this moment wasn't a great, unsettling turning point. I gathered my courage, stiffened my spine, and leveled my eyes—then *swept* across the room and into the proffered seat as if I were the Queen.

"At last," I said in a strong voice, meeting what I believed was her eyes through the glaze of her veil. Then I mustered a hint of disdain. "Surely you no longer need to hide behind that."

Her laugh rolled through the charged air, and I felt a wave of disappointment, a shattering of that fragile piece of hope I'd nurtured…and then acceptance.

No. It wasn't my mother who sat across from me.

It was Isabella Cosgrove-Pitt.

She removed the hat and veil, and just as quickly as my flash of hope had come and gone, so were the two of us—two mere mortals, two strong and intelligent women—facing each other.

Alone. Unmasked. And fully cognizant of the other.

She was a handsome woman, perhaps in her early or middle thirties, with medium brown hair and gray eyes. The colorlessness of her irises had certainly contributed to her agility in disguising herself, as well as the unremarkable shade of hair and the angularity of her features. I'd seen evidence of how she adjusted the shape of her eyes and mouth—likely by using a dab of spirit gum at the corners to stretch or constrict the skin—as well as more subtle changes, like altering the arch and thickness of her eyebrows and the fullness of her cheeks and jaw.

The art of disguise was, Uncle Sherlock had impressed upon me, a subtle science. And Lady Isabella had demonstrated herself to be a master at it.

She assessed me as closely as I was doing to her. "The blond wig…it doesn't quite suit you as well as your natural coloring, Miss Holmes. I'm certain your handsome companion would agree."

I merely returned her gaze. Though it isn't a weapon I normally choose to employ, silence can be quite powerful. But her acknowledgment of Grayling's presence caused a bite of concern. Had she recognized him?

When, after a prolonged silence, she was the one to speak, I felt as if I'd won at least an initial skirmish. "You've proven yourself quite a commendable adversary."

I inclined my head in acknowledgment. I was curious as to why she wanted to see me. Was I now a captive of some sort? Did she merely wish to gloat over her recent triumph? Or did she have some other purpose?

"I never expected to be as challenged as I've been with you and Miss Stoker. The two of you make a formidable team." Her eyes—today in their natural almond shape, so far as I could ascertain—gleamed, and the dancing candle flames were reflected therein. "Though I suppose I shouldn't be surprised, knowing from whence you spring."

"The Holmes mental acuity and deductive abilities are, indeed, formidable," I said.

To my surprise, she laughed, and made a dismissive gesture. "Holmes? Forget what the men have told you, Mina. I was speaking of your mother."

I froze. It took me a moment to find the wherewithal to speak. "You know my mother?"

"Oh, yes indeed." Her brows lifted in a single, elegant arch. "I know all about Desirée Holmes—also known as Siri. A trainer of vampire-hunters."

I moistened my lips, trying to dig my thoughts out from the deep, dark, murky pit into which I'd been flung. "How— When did you know her?"

In retrospect, I realized Lady Isabella could have pressed her advantage now that I was completely off guard. Had that been her intention, she could easily have annihilated me in some way: either mentally or physically. I was that thrown off my game.

"In Paris, of course. More than twenty years ago, it was. We were young and adventurous. And the three of us were very nearly inseparable."

"Three of you?"

"Desirée, myself, and Irene." Her eyes narrowed craftily. "Did you not know this? Has your precious mentor not shared this bit of information with you? How negligent of her."

Miss Adler? Miss Adler knew my mother?

I believe I managed to keep the evidence of my shock to a minimum, but my adversary's eyes were sharp and unrelenting as I faced her across the table. I suspected she saw far more than I intended.

"Was that when you became involved in *La société de la perdition?*" I asked as some of the pieces began to fall into place. "When you became fascinated with the UnDead and vampirism?" I knew that Miss Adler had, at one time, an unhealthy fondness for being fed upon by vampires—just like, apparently, many of the women here. I subdued a shudder. Miss Adler had nearly died because of that old tendency—even, perhaps, addiction—during the charade surrounding Willa Ashton's spiritglass.

Perhaps that was how she'd come to be here, performing at The Carnelian Crow—which was obviously a haven for the UnDead. I wondered whether Lady Isabella knew Miss Adler was here. Had she recognized her beneath the disguise through which even I had barely discerned my mentor's real identity? Or, like most society women, did Lady Isabella give hardly any notice to her servants—treating them as if they were invisible?

My hostess made a moue. "*I* had no love for the vampires. Messy, violent, rapacious creatures they are. It was the concept of immortality to which I was attracted—but surely that's no surprise to you, considering our past interactions."

"Not at all. It was obvious you were—and presumably still are—seeking the power to live forever. It began with the Society of Sekhmet—no, it probably started long before that, didn't it? I only became aware of you and your...criminal tendencies...during that affair. When you killed Della Exington and Maryellen Hodgeworth."

"It was Irene and Desirée who found the UnDead fascinating, and who fell into the lure of that world."

"But Desirée—my mother—she *trains* people how to kill vampires..."

Lady Isabella laughed. "That was the delicious irony of

the situation. She unintentionally introduced us—Irene and me—to that world, to that way of life because of her involvement with the vampires...and the three of us had loads of fun. Surely you can imagine it: three young, beautiful, intelligent women, set loose in Paris—the city of beauty and hedonism. Three young women who answered to no man, who lived a life of freedom, and had their own resources. We were the belles of Paris, and for a time, the darlings of *La société*. Desirée wanted to infiltrate the secret society, and she couldn't keep Irene and me out of it. It was too delicious! One doesn't have to enjoy—or even allow—oneself to be fed upon by the UnDead in order to be a member, you know. There are other benefits: wealth, power, and pleasure."

I stared at her. My head, my brain—which could handle enormous amounts of data and observations—was spinning. It was with great effort that I reined in the maelstrom of thoughts, questions, and demands, and managed to focus on one—one meant to offer some reprieve from this onslaught.

"Of course I'm wondering why you sought me out tonight," I said, ruthlessly taking control of the conversation. "Surely it's not simply because I found my way into your secret club—which appears to be your own den of iniquity, a hearkening back to the days in Paris, no? I suspect you mean to gloat over the incident at Cosgrove Terrace. The apparent suicide of your husband—which was no suicide at all. Nor was it an accident."

"You are, as usual, quite correct." Her mirthful features sharpened as she looked at me. "As it happens, I've changed my mind about you, Miss Holmes. At first, when you interfered with me during my attempt to reincarnate as Sekhmet, I wanted to destroy you. You were a fly in my ointment. You and Evaline Stoker—and Irene, of course. She's always been...difficult. We were once great friends—but that changed long ago, and now, I want nothing more to see her destroyed. But I've since changed my mind about you. After having met you adversarially in several ways, I've come to the realization that to destroy you would be a detriment to us."

"Us?"

She spread her hands. "Our gender, of course. The so-called weaker sex." Now she leaned forward, her eyes sparkling. "Think what the two of us could accomplish. *Think.* We could change the world, Mina! We could, together, alter the way we've been controlled—the way our race has been repressed and *de*pressed. The way we've been forced to be broodmares and workhorses and delicate trophies to be brought out and glamorized and petted…then put back safely away in our gilded cages.

"We could work together to change the way we're perceived, treated. We'd have everything we ever wanted—the freedom to act and dress as we choose—trousers every day if we like!—the ability to possess and manage our own money, property, businesses… To marry whomever we wish—or not at all. I suspect your partner Evaline would be particularly interested in that part of it, wouldn't she?

"We could even govern a *nation*, unlike our own, which is managed by a cadre of *men*—most of whom are too rich and soft to have any concept of what it's like to lack for anything, let alone to be a female." She scoffed, flapping her hand at the absent Parliament. "These men make laws for and about us women without our consent or opinion—many of which keep us placed even more deeply under their control.

"And don't patronize me with the reminder that our current queen has reigned longer than any other. Victoria Regina is a mere figurehead, and you're intelligent enough to know it. The last time we had a queen who actually *reigned*, it was Elizabeth. And she was *magnificent*—yet even she had her limitations."

To say I was stunned would be an incredible understatement. The Ankh wanted me to *join* her? To become part of her murderous plot to…do what?

I managed to find my voice even as my heart thudded wildly in my ears. "What is it *we* would do? Together. If I…joined you."

"We would begin by wresting—gently, of course, for we females are, if nothing else, elegant and deliberate," she said with a sharp, tight laugh that might have bordered on maniacal. And yet I saw no hint of mania in her eyes. They were calm and lucid and very, very serious.

"We will wrest control of Parliament—beginning with the House of Lords. Oh, I have it all worked out, Mina. I've been planning this for *years*. You—along with many others— witnessed the first step in my plan last Saturday, at the tragic death of my husband." She gave a patently false swoon of grief, then smiled at me with sparkling eyes. "Of course you are aware I engineered that. And it was a demonstration to the other wives of parliamentarians, to other women shackled to their men, of what I am capable of doing...and what I would give them the power to do as well."

I was nodding. I'd suspected something of that nature, but I confess, I hadn't anticipated such a broad plan. Lady Isabella didn't only mean to rid herself of her husband. She meant to help other women do the same. But then what?

"I see you're beginning to understand." Her lips curved in a soft smile. "Good. But you have questions, of course."

"You used one of those small battery devices with the wires to...to somehow control Lord Cosgrove-Pitt. You also use it to control the vampires."

"Yes, yes, indeed. When you invaded my underground workshop weeks ago, you interrupted the final stages of my experimentation. I was forced to move the laboratory to a different location—namely, here, in a different wing of The Carnelian Crow. It's much securer here, as you have seen. Now the experimentation is complete, and I offered evidence of that on Saturday. Belmont did precisely what he'd been— if you will—rehearsed to do. He was impeccable in his role, do you not agree?"

I couldn't bring myself to verbally do so, yet I didn't deny that his actions had been quite convincing. "And now what?"

"Now that I've demonstrated the technique, I will be implementing the next stage of my plan: to take over Parliament by controlling the men in it—with the help of their wives."

"But…why would you not keep Lord Cosgrove-Pitt alive, and control Parliament through him?" I asked—quite reasonably, I thought. "Why kill him?"

"Because I detested him. Detested being married to him. Being controlled by him. *And* because—well, you'll see. My plan is to bring down the English government completely. Soon, there will be no Parliament—no Home Office." Her eyes glittered. "Your father will be one of the casualties, you know. Wouldn't you like that, Mina? Wouldn't you like to show him how you feel about having been ignored and shunted off by him for *years*?"

She was mad…and yet there was more lucidity and forethought in her plans than in those of many a sane man. Or woman, for that matter.

Lady Isabella leaned forward and covered one of my hands with hers. "The question is, Mina Holmes…would you like to join me?"

Miss Stoker

~ Wherein Miss Stoker's Acting Ability is Exercised ~

PIX FROZE NEXT TO ME, AND I TURNED AT THE FAMILIAR voice.

"Princess Lurelia," I said by way of greeting.

I wasn't completely surprised it was the Betrovian princess standing there. After all, the last time I saw her, she had been with the Ankh, publicly stealing the chess queen from us in the Tower of London.

(Obviously, not the real Ankh, as Mina had explained to me.)

Either way, both Mina and I had speculated on whether Lurelia had run off to get married to someone of her choice, or whether she'd gone into hiding and remained in contact— or cahoots—with the Ankh.

Our questions were now answered.

"Why don't you step inside?" she said, and I saw that she held some sort of wicked-looking weapon similar to Mina's Steam-Stream gun. Lurelia was pointing it at me, not at Pix, for which I was grateful. Whatever it was would do less damage to me than to him. "Since you were so eager to see what we have in here, perhaps you'd like a closer look."

My companion tried to position himself between me and the gun, but I elbowed him out of the way. Even with my blood loss and injuries, I was stronger, faster, and healed more quickly than he did.

He was mere mortal—as his previous death had proven.

Pix shot me a dark look as he recognized my manipulation, and I gave him one right back as we followed Lurelia's suggestion. This gave me a better look at the setup of the chamber that had been so securely locked.

There were chairs lined up along two walls in the room. In the center of the space was a large table that contained perhaps two dozen of the small, battery-like devices Pix had been buying and selling on the underground market. I knew he'd never intended for them to be used in the way the Ankh had done—in an attempt to control vampires.

Or to kill, which was what the Ankh had done to Pix in her underground lair.

"You—take a seat." Lurelia nodded at Pix, but kept the weapon trained on me.

I realized the blood was still trickling from my neck and wrist, despite the fact that I'd sprinkled salted holy water on the wounds. I realized I could use that to my advantage, especially since I didn't believe Lurelia knew the details about my vampire-hunting heritage.

As Pix sat in one of the ominous-looking chairs, I made myself stagger a little. I clapped a hand to the bite mark at my neck and tried to appear weak and confused without overdoing it.

Lurelia pretended not to notice, but I saw a light of satisfaction flicker in her eyes. Still training the gun on me, she moved behind the chair and appeared to be turning some dials or other controls.

There was a soft hum and restraints appeared from the back of the chair, fitting around his chest.

"Hands on the armrests," Lurelia ordered.

Pix's face was a little pale as he complied, and I guessed he was remembering the last time he'd been under the control of the Ankh. If it hadn't been for Dylan Eckhert, he'd still be dead.

But even as he complied with her orders, he looked at me, holding my eyes with intent, from across the room. I wasn't certain what he was trying to tell me, but I got the impression he had a plan.

Well, that made two of us.

By now Pix's wrists were affixed to the arms by a second set of restraints.

"Comfortable?" Lurelia asked as she came around from

the front of the chair. "Excellent. Now, let's see…what shall we do with *you*?" She eyed me.

I was pretending to surreptitiously lean against the wall, and made it appear like I was straightening up when she looked over.

"What are all those for?" I asked so she'd think I was trying to buy time.

"Those," Lurelia said when she saw I was referring to the battery devices, "are about to be sold to the wives of more than half the members of Parliament. As well as some other well-placed men in government."

"For what?" I swayed a little, and made a show of trying to hide the fact that I was clamping a hand over the bite on my wrist.

"You don't *know*?" Lurelia laughed. "Well, allow me to demonstrate. This is the training room, where all of the wives will learn just how to use those cunning little devices to control their husbands. Your friend here will be an excellent demonstration."

She smiled, and I was struck by the fact that she no longer looked like the bland, colorless princess I'd met almost three months ago. There was not only a spark to her eyes that hadn't been there before, along with a layer of determination, but her entire being was more…well, hardened. More experienced and confident.

"I was going to wait for *her*," said Lurelia as she picked up one of the devices, "but there's really no need." Two wicked-looking wires protruded from one end, and I shivered because I knew what she was going to do with them.

Still doing my best to appear weak and lightheaded, I sagged noticeably against the wall. "What are you going to do?" I asked, as I supposed most heroines in those novels Mina was always complaining about would do.

"Watch, my dearest Evaline." Still holding the gun pointed in my direction, Lurelia made her way back to Pix's chair. She wasn't taking any chances, but the gun wavered a bit as she had to work one-handed to set up the device.

I saw the way Pix's face tensed when Lurelia inserted first one, then the other, wire into the back of his shoulders and neck. He didn't struggle, but nor did he look at me.

I was afraid to make my move too soon—for she could just as easily aim her weapon at Pix as she could at me, and she was much closer to him. And then there were the electro-fying wires to be concerned with.

But my heart was beating like wild, and I knew I didn't have much time—but I also couldn't make a mistake. If I moved too quickly or too late, Pix would be fried or he'd be shot.

"There we are. Comfortable, now?" Lurelia asked Pix. She shot a sharp look at me as if to ensure I hadn't moved—I hadn't—and then, with a flourish, she turned on the device.

I heard the soft hum, and saw Pix's eyes widen and his mouth tighten as if in pain.

Oh, gad. I had to move.

"Don't worry, it takes a minute or two to warm up," Lurelia told me with a smile. She had that gun pointed straight at me as she walked over to where the wall was holding me upright. "We can watch together."

She trailed the barrel of the gun along the edge of my jaw as she leaned close and murmured, "You should know I have a particular fondness for you, Evaline. I—"

But I'd moved, surging up and knocking the gun from her hand. It went flying through the air, spinning over the floor— but I didn't go after it.

There was a sharp pain at my neck as I dove across the room and, without hesitation, yanked the wires from the back of Pix's neck. Something sizzled and burned my fingers, but they came free. In that instant, our eyes met and I saw relief, gratitude—and fury.

He was unhurt. I'd managed it in time. Thank Providence.

I turned back to face Lurelia, who, to my surprise, hadn't

gone after the gun either. Instead, she'd moved to what appeared to be a control panel in the wall. I noticed she had a large silver cross dangling from a broken chain in her hand. Mine. That had been the sharp pain when I pulled away.

"I'm not very happy with you now, Evaline," she said. "You're just going to make it worse—for him and for yourself."

With a great flourish, she slammed her hand down on one of the buttons inside the panel, then pulled a lever. "*She'll* be here any moment now. I wonder whether you'll still be able to greet her."

I looked over at the sound of a quiet rumble and saw a door scrolling open at the other end of the room.

All at once, the back of my neck turned to ice…and then the UnDead came in.

Miss Holmes
~ *An Exceedingly Satisfactory Tete-a-Tete* ~

As I considered Lady Isabella's offer, I thought of all the criticism I'd borne over the years—of being too intelligent, too unladylike, too loud and opinionated. Too emotional. I thought of the way people stared and whispered askance when I wore trousers, split skirts, or other Street Fashion ensembles with over-corsets.

I thought of the man who'd stood, haranguing me as I examined poor Belmont Cosgrove-Pitt's body as the blood oozed from his nose and ears, and the crowd that had snickered behind its hands and gasped in shock and ridicule when I chased after a pickpocket at New Vauxhall Gardens. I remembered Evaline's drawn, hopeless expression as she spoke of her predicament: to marry when she did not care to do so, because it was required of her.

And I remembered what Dylan had told me about the future. About how things were different there. About how women were treated differently then. Perhaps not completely equally, but they were, at least, allowed to wear trousers and curse and drink ale and smoke *and* not to marry. They could be doctors, lawyers, scientists—even members of government. They could *vote*.

But there were other ways to accomplish those improvements.

I pulled my hand back. "I think not, Lady Isabella."

Her face fell. "And in so doing, you will return to a world of repression and control by the male species. You resign yourself to such a restrictive life. You disappoint me, Mina."

"Then we are in agreement," I replied. "For you disappoint me. Instead of harnessing all of your brilliance—and you are brilliant, Lady Isabella; nearly as brilliant as a Holmes—and using it to improve the stature of women, you're using it to repress and control, and to even *murder* men. You mean to inflict upon them the precise antithesis of what you want for yourself: freedom to live as you wish."

"They deserve it. They *all* deserve it." Her expression became angry. "Very well, then, Miss Holmes. Consider my offer of partnership rescinded, and—"

A sound—a dull tolling noise like that of a bell—drew her up short. She muttered something most definitely unladylike and rose. Clearly, something had alarmed her.

"Our conversation is over, Miss Holmes. You may see yourself out." She snatched up her veiled hat and started toward the opposite end of the chamber from whence I'd come.

I stared after her. That was it? She made me an offer, I refused, and she was simply going to allow me to leave?

As if reading my mind, Lady Isabella paused at what appeared to be another doorway. "Oh, I could kill you, of course. But that would be too simple, and far too boring. I believe I'll find it more stimulating to continue to match wits with you—and to enjoy you watching, helpless to stop me, from my plans. After all, who would believe it of me?" Carefully replacing her hat, adjusting the veil into place, she smiled...then slipped past the open door. It closed behind her, and I heard the distinct sound of a lock clicking.

I wavered—wanting to follow her before she disappeared, and also wanting to retrieve Grayling, for Lady Isabella was correct. No one would believe me if I told them the truth, but if Scotland Yard Inspector Ambrose Grayling saw that the villainess was the wife of Belmont Cosgrove-Pitt—and his distant relative—then everyone would have to believe. Especially him.

My decision made, I spun and started back toward the silky curtain barrier, but I stumbled and caught the edge of the table. The force (and I) sent it tumbling to the ground with a great crashing sound.

I heard someone roar my name, and all at once, there was Grayling, flinging aside the curtains. His false mustache was dangling, and the beard was gone, and accompanying him was the unmistakable smell of UnDead ash. A large silver cross bounced on his chest as he fairly leaped across the room to me.

"Are you hurt?" he asked, but before I was able to respond in the affirmative, he pulled me to him in a rough embrace. His arms went around me, squeezing me tightly, and I discovered I rather liked the feeling of his warmth and the solidness of his figure, and of course I inhaled a great breath of vampire dust—along with his particular minty, lemony Grayling scent.

He spoke into my hair. "It took me far longer than I'd anticipated, there being two of them left to guard the door. I didn't want you to go in here alone, Mina. Did she hurt you?"

"No, no, of course not," I said, stunned by the show of— was it affection, or merely high emotion that I hadn't myself become the dead body I had the tendency to attract?

Grayling seemed to recover himself, for he released me and stepped back a bit, looking at me warily.

The mustache dangled from his upper lip, and without thinking, I reached for it, yanking it free. This seemed to be some sort of catalyst, for the next thing I knew, I was back in his arms and *he was kissing me.*

I forgot all about the Ankh and where we were, and the fact that I was a Holmes. I wasn't even certain I knew what my name was at the moment. Or for several moments afterward.

At last, when I realized I had forgotten how to breathe— and that I hadn't seemed to be required to—we pulled apart. I stared up at him and he looked down at me.

"Well, then," I managed to say, running a shaky hand over my blond wig—which had come loose from its moorings during the recent interlude. "I—"

"Miss Holmes," he said with great formality. He seemed a trifle out of breath as well. "I—er—I hope I didn't overstep my—"

"Perhaps if you removed that wig," I said, "it wouldn't be quite so odd."

"Right." He yanked it off as I did the same. A smile twitched his lips, which were more full than usual. "Is that better?"

"Yes, indeed. Now, where were— Oh, *blast!*" I suddenly remembered myself. "She went that way. Come *on!*"

He followed me without question. To my mild surprise, the door through which Lady Isabella had disappeared had a flimsy latch. Grayling made short work of it with a small device he withdrew from the depths of his pockets; we didn't have time for me to examine it closely, but it appeared to be a small metal claw that fit inside any keyhole and acted as a master.

As we burst through the door, I heard the sounds of altercation. It wasn't necessary for me to mention it to Grayling, for he'd already snatched up my hand and was towing me after him. Though his legs were longer, I was able to keep up fairly well, and his steadying hand helped keep me from the inevitability of me tripping over my own two feet.

We followed the sounds down a deserted hall to a massive, vaultlike door, which was slightly ajar. Instead of barging in as my counterpart Evaline would have done, I peered around the edge (along with Grayling, of course).

But once we saw the nature of the altercation in the chamber, there was no need to pause.

There were at least a dozen UnDead in the chamber, and Evaline was doing her best to battle them back on her own. I noticed a man in one of the chairs in the chamber—Pix?— and that there were two women on the other side of the fray, watching.

One of them was the Ankh—her features obscured by that dratted veil—and the other was Lurelia of Betrovia.

But that was all the time in which I was able to spare, for Evaline was clearly overmatched and Pix was no help. Grayling hadn't paused even as long as I had, jumping into the melee with his silver cross swinging and a stake in one hand.

Of course I'd come prepared, but it took me a moment to scrabble beneath my skirts and dig the stake out of my boot. By the time I did that, I was barely able to lunge upright in time to see a vampire coming toward me.

I stifled a shriek of surprise and somehow fumbled the stake into position. To my shock, it found its mark and the UnDead exploded into dust. Before I launched into the fray, I dug the silver cross from beneath my bodice and retrieved two vials of salted holy water from their moorings at my corset.

Flipping the top of one bottle open with my thumb, I charged toward a vampire who was about to attack Evaline from behind. I poked him with my stake, missing the heart, but getting his attention nevertheless.

He turned, and I shot the contents of the vial at him. He screamed, his hands going up to his face, and I pounced. The stake drilled into his chest and then he was gone.

I staggered back, shocked that I'd managed to destroy two vampires in rapid order, and was grabbed from behind. The next thing I knew, my attacker spun me around and yanked me by the hair, baring my neck.

I kicked at him, missed, and felt the sharp, hot pain as fangs plunged into my neck. I probably screamed; I don't remember, but I did manage, somehow, to maintain the wherewithal to open the second vial of holy water. When I spilled it onto my attacker, he screamed and released me. I staggered a bit, but before I was able to recover and go after him myself, he disappeared in a great, dusty cloud.

I looked over to see Grayling, who didn't even pause before pivoting in a swirl of his long coat to meet a new threat.

Weak, out of breath, and still spilling blood, I decided I'd see if I could release Pix so he could join the battle. But by the time I stumbled over to him, he was just pulling loose of his final restraint.

It was a good thing, for he grabbed the stake from my hand and used it to stop an attacker right behind me.

I'd hardly had the chance to recover when Pix shoved the

stake back at me, ducked, and pulled another from his boot, all in one smooth movement as he vaulted toward a vampire who had pinned Evaline against the wall by the throat.

As I turned to catch my breath, I saw that the Ankh and Lurelia were no longer standing at the far end of the room.

"They're getting away!" I shouted, though I doubted anyone heard me. I tore across the chamber to where I'd last seen them, but there didn't seem to be an exit there.

Just as I whirled in the other direction, I saw the vaultlike door behind me begin to swing closed.

I charged toward it, pulling out my Steam-Stream gun as I did so. The door was nearly closed as I tripped. I fell, flying across the floor, tumbling and sliding painfully toward the door with my stake and the gun's barrel aimed toward the slowly narrowing opening.

I slammed into the wall, but my gun barrel made it into the opening just in time to keep it from closing all the way.

Head spinning, and aching and throbbing everywhere else, I wedged my stake into the space between the bottom of the door and the floor, just to make sure.

And then I realized everything was quiet.

I turned my head, and through a cloud of UnDead ash, I saw Evaline, Grayling, and Pix standing around, breaths heaving, blood dripping, clothes torn, disguises askew or simply gone, and the chamber in shambles. In the midst of the mess was a pile of the battery devices that appeared to have been knocked to the floor during the fight.

"She's getting…away," I managed, pulling myself to my feet. Grayling moved toward me as if preparing to assist, but I managed it on my own.

Pix was gathering up the devices. "We have to…take these," he said, still breathing heavily. "If she doesn't have them, she can't…do…it."

Evaline and Grayling helped him put them into a box one of them retrieved as I pushed the door open. I wasn't going to wait for them. The Ankh was getting away, and I *needed* Grayling to see her.

"I'm going…after her," I called.

I suspected that was why she'd left. The Ankh had seen that we were winning the battle with the UnDead, and surely she'd recognized Grayling during the altercation. Lady Isabella would not want him to see and identify her, and so she'd fled before she lost the chance—or her veil.

But she wasn't going to get away this time. I was aching and sore, but I forced myself to run. I didn't know where the villainess had gone, but I couldn't just let her escape.

There was no sign of her anywhere, and by the time I reached the club room—where the musicians were still going about their entertainment as if nothing had happened, and the smell of blood had eased—I could hear my companions coming along in my wake.

I didn't wait, however. I hurried into the club room, bursting onto the scene where couples still sat at their tables.

Grayling was on my heels, and as he came into the room, he said, "Scotland Yard! No one move!"

There was another type of melee at that, but it took only a moment for us to ascertain that none of the people in the room were the fugitives, and whatever UnDead might have been there providing "entertainment" had gone. Perhaps they'd smelled the ash from their executed kin, or perhaps Lurelia had somehow called them back as part of the attack on Evaline and Pix.

Either way, that didn't matter.

What mattered was that the Ankh had gotten away.

Again.

The music had stopped, and I looked toward the stage. Miss Adler had quite a bit of explaining to do, and I was steaming over toward her and her accompanist to accost her when I got a good look at the piano player for the first time.

I froze. Everything froze. Even my throbbing injuries stopped hurting. "*Dylan?*"

Miss Holmes
~ Far Too Many Questions Than Answers ~

"DYLAN?" I SAID, LOUDER. I MIGHT HAVE ACTUALLY shrieked it, in fact.

"Mina!" He turned toward me, shock and pleasure on his face. The next thing I knew, he was embracing me in a strange sort of way, swinging me a little from side to side as my toes brushed the floor. "Oh, Mina, I'm so glad to see you again!"

"What—what are you doing here?" I was numb. Shocked, numb, completely blindsided. My brain simply couldn't comprehend it.

"I came back. I was helping Miss Adler," he said, looking down at me with those bright blue eyes and handsome smile. Then it faded. "I returned to my time, 2016 and—and things were really, *really* different. I felt as if I were living in an alternate reality."

"I…"

He was still talking, in a sort of confused tone. "I thought maybe me being here and doing things had somehow changed the future. So I thought I'd try to come back using the statue of Sekhmet like before and…well, I wanted to see if I could fix things. By coming back. And then Miss Adler… well, she and I had been in touch twice through the cell phone—you know, that telephone thing I left here? She helped me figure out how to get back. And then she asked me to help her go undercover here for a while."

I looked over and saw the others watching us.

I lowered my voice. "But…you didn't… Why didn't you… But I didn't know. Why didn't you tell me you were back, Dylan?"

"I was going to," he said with a crooked smile. "I just— Well, I was helping Miss Adler here and didn't want to take the chance that I'd blow our cover. Did you like the music? I thought it would be interesting to bring some of the stuff from my time here, just to see how it would go over."

"Right," I said. I was very, very confused. I was happy Dylan was back, but I had a lot of questions. Some of them were more painful than others.

But before I could begin to pick through them and try to ask—and receive—some answers, I heard the distinct sound of someone clearing their throat.

I looked over to see Evaline making some of those weird facial expressions I can never understand. She always seemed to be having a twitch.

When I looked at her blankly, she rolled her eyes.

"Well," I said, suddenly blinking back tears. My head felt a little woozy too. I absently touched the bite mark at my neck. "Well."

I looked around and noticed that the club's customers all seemed to have melted away—run off, most likely. It was just the group of us remaining.

I blinked and focused on Miss Adler. "Did you send me the carnelian crow pin?"

"No," she replied. I was glad she appeared at least a little abashed; I somehow felt that she'd betrayed me, but I couldn't put my finger on why or how. "It wasn't me. I...well, I didn't think The Carnelian Crow was a place for a young lady—even for you. However," she added quickly when I began to bristle, "clearly I was wrong. You and Evaline acquitted yourselves handsomely."

I was slightly mollified by her compliment, but I still felt an underlying burble of anger.

"And what about Lady Thistle?" I asked in a brittle voice. "It was Magpie who killed her, right? Did the Ankh have her do the deed in order to keep me from finding the entrance to this place?"

"That was Magpie," replied Miss Adler. "Acting on her own." When I looked at her in question, she explained, "I might not have gotten as far as you did, but that doesn't mean I didn't learn *anything* during my stint here as the evening's entertainment. Magpie acted on her own, believing the Ankh would have wanted her to do so. She killed Lady Thistle, and then made sure the entrance to The Carnelian Crow was destroyed."

I nodded. I had many, many more questions for Miss Adler—about my mother and Lady Isabella—but I was far too weary. And heartsick. And confused. They could wait.

"I suppose we're done here. At least for now, then," I said —since I seemed to be the only one interested or able to form words. "The Ankh has once again gotten away. But we've stopped her plot—at least for the time being." I gestured to the box of batteries they'd gathered up. She wouldn't be controlling Parliament anytime in the near future. "There's nothing more to be done. Tonight, anyway." Perhaps even for longer. Surely it would take Lady Isabella time to regroup and reform her plan. And get more batteries...

I suddenly felt very weary. I just wanted to go home.

Perhaps I could share a hackney back with Grayling, and we could discuss the next steps. And...other things. I brightened a little at the thought. I felt my cheeks warm at the memory of our intimate interlude. I couldn't tell him about the Ankh's identity—not yet—but perhaps I could begin to lay the groundwork for the painful revelation.

"Not quite," said the man in question. "There is one more thing to which I must attend."

I turned to Grayling. He wasn't looking at me, however. There was a set expression on his face—quite different from the one he'd had only a short time earlier, when we were sitting at that private table in this very room.

"What do you mean?" I asked. But he still didn't look at me.

Instead, he turned to Pix. "Mr. Edison Smith, I am placing you under arrest for the murder of Hiram Bartholomew."

"No!" exclaimed Evaline. "*No.*" She whirled between Pix and Grayling, her eyes flashing.

Pix gave the inspector a measured look. "When did you figure it out?"

"I'd thought for a time you looked familiar," replied the inspector. "But wasn't certain until I saw you again—more clearly, and without your ever-present disguises—tonight."

Pix gave a brief nod, then turned to Evaline. "Now you can be free to marry Ned Oligary." He stood there stoically as the restraints were fixed around his wrists with dull, final clinks.

Evaline and I watched in taut silence as Grayling took Pix away.

Neither of them gave us a backward glance.

~

Stoker & Holmes continues

Stay tuned for the fifth and final book in the Stoker & Holmes series, coming in 2018!

Don't miss the announcement, cover reveal, and title:
Sign up for the Stoker & Holmes newsletter
http://cgbks.com/StokerHolmesNews

~

ABOUT THE AUTHOR

Colleen Gleason is an award-winning, New York Times and USA Today best-selling author. She's written more than forty novels in a variety of genres—something for everyone!

She loves to hear from readers, so feel free to find her online.

Subscribe to Colleen's non-spam newsletter for updates, news, and special offers!
http://cgbks.com/news

Connect with Colleen online:

www.colleengleason.com
books@colleengleason.com

The Cards of Life and Death

The Gems of Vice and Greed

~

Stoker & Holmes Books

(for ages 12-adult)

The Clockwork Scarab

The Spiritglass Charade

The Chess Queen Enigma

The Carnelian Crow (July 2017)

~

The Marina Alexander Adventure Novels

(writing as C. M. Gleason)

Siberian Treasure

Amazon Roulette

Sanskrit Cipher (forthcoming)

~

Writing as Alex Mandon

The Belle-Époque Mystery series

Murder on the Champs-Élysées